This wasn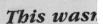

Get a grip, Carla told herself. She closed her eyes, counted to three, then angled around so she could see him.

"Oh," she said aloud, as several things struck her at the same moment.

One: Not only had she never been in this room before, but she was naked—and she never slept naked.

Two: The man next to her in the bed was the drop-dead gorgeous incredible lover from the dream she'd been having. Which meant…

Three: It hadn't been a dream!

Dear Reader,

It's month two of our special fifteenth anniversary celebration, and that means more great reading for you. Just look what's in store.

Amnesia! It's one of the most popular plot twists around, and well it should be. All of us have probably wished, just for a minute, that we could start over again, be somebody else...fall in love all over again as if it were the first time. For three of our heroines this month, whether they want it or not, the chance is theirs. Start with Sharon Sala's *Roman's Heart,* the latest in her fabulous trilogy, THE JUSTICE WAY. Then check out *The Mercenary and the Marriage Vow* by Doreen Roberts. This book carries our new TRY TO REMEMBER flash—just so you won't forget about it! And then, sporting our MEN IN BLUE flash (because the hero's the kind of cop we could all fall in love with), there's *While She Was Sleeping* by Diane Pershing.

Of course, we have three other great books this month, too. Be sure to pick up Beverly Barton's *Emily and the Stranger,* and don't worry. Though this book isn't one of them, Beverly's extremely popular heroes, THE PROTECTORS, will be coming your way again soon. Kylie Brant is back with *Friday's Child,* a FAMILIES ARE FOREVER title. Not only will the hero and heroine win your heart, wait 'til you meet little Chloe. Finally, welcome new author Sharon Mignerey, who makes her debut with *Cassidy's Courtship.*

And, of course, don't forget to come back next month for more of the best and most excitingly romantic reading around, right here in Silhouette Intimate Moments.

Leslie Wainger

Leslie Wainger
Senior Editor and Editorial Coordinator

Please address questions and book requests to:
Silhouette Reader Service
U.S.: 3010 Walden Ave., P.O. Box 1325, Buffalo, NY 14269
Canadian: P.O. Box 609, Fort Erie, Ont. L2A 5X3

WHILE SHE WAS SLEEPING

DIANE PERSHING

Silhouette®
INTIMATE™ MOMENTS®

Published by Silhouette Books

America's Publisher of Contemporary Romance

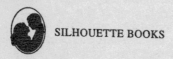

SILHOUETTE BOOKS

ISBN 0-373-07863-3

WHILE SHE WAS SLEEPING

Copyright © 1998 by Diane Pershing

Printed in U.S.A.

DIANE PERSHING

cannot remember a time when she didn't have her nose buried in a book. As a child she would cheat the bedtime curfew by snuggling under the covers with her teddy bear, a flashlight and a forbidden (read "grown-up") novel. Her mother warned her that she would ruin her eyes, but so far, they still work. Diane has had many careers—singer, actress, film critic, disc jockey, TV writer, to name a few. Currently she divides her time between writing romances and doing voice-overs (you can hear her as Poison Ivy on the "Batman" cartoon). She lives in Los Angeles, and promises she is only slightly affected. Her two children, Morgan Rose and Ben, have just completed college, and Diane looks forward to writing and acting until she expires, or people stop hiring her, whichever comes first. She loves to hear from readers, so please write to her at P.O. Box 67424, Los Angeles, CA 90067.

To the Monday group—the other Diane P., Jamie, both Karens and Shannon. They made me do it.
And to Captain John Wehner, Manhattan Beach Police Department (Retired). One of the good guys.

Chapter 1

Sunday Morning

The sound of gulls crying and the smell of the ocean registered before she was fully awake. Daylight and its glare awaited her behind her closed eyes. No, she thought, she didn't want to deal with it. Not yet.

Not after a night of fabulous dreams like the ones she'd had. Hot, thoroughly *wanton* dreams in which she'd been made love to by a gorgeous, muscular, thoroughly sexy, *perfect* lover. And not just once or twice, but several times and in several sensational ways. Her body thrummed as she mentally went over each and every time.

Especially the last time. The best time. She sighed aloud, keeping her eyes shut so she could replay it without any distractions.

It had been slower, much, much slower. And far more personal. After the intense, acrobatic, brain-burning first few times, after their bodies had strained and sweated with seemingly insatiable hunger, that final time had been surprisingly gentle. Tender, even. For what felt like an eternity, he'd played and licked and stroked her till she'd nearly risen off the bed at her body's intense reaction.

How had her dream lover found the strength? she wondered, smiling to herself. Surely even a superhero couldn't have stamina like that, could he? She sighed again. No, he couldn't. Which was why that kind of lovemaking could only have happened in a dream, could only have been an invention of her imagination. Ah, well.

But she wasn't really disappointed. After all, how lucky could one ordinary working girl get? To take part in a once-in-a-lifetime nocturnal fantasy, in which her mind was being granted all the sensations of reality without any of the responsibilities.

The entire encounter had been...life-altering. His hands had played over her and molded her as though they'd created her out of clay, as though nothing and no one else existed. In his arms, she'd been the most important woman in the world, the original Earth Woman. The fate of mankind hinged on their coupling....

She smiled once more. Okay, now she was getting a bit carried away, but still it had been sheer, unadulterated pleasure. She could die now, she knew, and not feel cheated of life experience.

Nearby, a bird squawked loudly, and another joined in. Reality awaited just outside the window. She turned onto her side—maybe she could put off getting up for a few moments more. If she concentrated hard enough, she could go back to sleep...and dream again.

A small twinge of guilt momentarily spoiled her train of thought. Richard. That look he used to get on his face that was part disapproving grown-up and part hurt puppy, the one that always made her want to shake him and say, "Cut it out," which always led to her feeling ungenerous and insensitive.

Richard.... Why was he, that awful man, intruding on her

dream? How dare he? Mentally swiping him away, she ordered her mind to restart the dream.

But it was too late. The night had slipped away and now it was morning. Time to open her eyes and start her day. She tried to raise her lids, but they felt as though during the night, someone had coated them with shellac. She grinned; should she use that as an excuse to turn over onto her stomach? Yes. Hugging the pillow, she tried to bury her head more deeply in the deliciously soft goose feathers and down stuffing.

Hold it... Her pillows weren't the goose-feathers type because Richard was allergic to feathers. Oh, that's right, she reminded herself, curling onto her side again. She was no longer married to Richard, so she could have an entire goose and several goslings in bed with her and he couldn't do a thing about it.

The image made her laugh softly, which was odd. She was not one of those women who woke up with a chuckle. She hated mornings, hated the fuzzy, foul taste in her mouth and the fact that neither her muscles nor her brain functioned too well for a while. But on this morning, smiling, even chuckling, was what was happening.

It was the dream, she thought, rubbing at the stickiness around her lids and opening her eyes. What a way to start the day. Sighing happily, she reached over to the bed table for her glasses.

There was no bed table.

She squinted—her nearsightedness made her dependent on her glasses, but sometimes, by squeezing her eye muscles, she was able to sharpen the focus.

It didn't help. Next to the bed there were no glasses and no night table, only a blank wall. Her gaze darted around the broad expanse of a room, on its far wall what appeared to be the outline of a floor-to-ceiling window, with daylight streaming around the edges of some kind of window covering.

But not her window. Her window was high and narrow, above the bed. She didn't have a window on the opposite wall.

Her heartbeat accelerated as the first ripple of fear sliced through her. Her breathing quickened, her hands turned to ice; as always, her first reaction to being thrown off balance was to give in to panic.

She'd tried to change that pattern, especially in this last difficult year, when she'd tried to change so much else about herself. There'd been no miracles, but there had been some progress. All right, then, she told herself, it was time to utilize the tools she'd learned.

Closing her eyes, she forced herself to inhale and exhale slowly, several times. There was a reasonable explanation for this…this strange room, she assured herself. There had to be. Her mind scurried around for that explanation. She was always a little slow on the uptake in the morning, so even if she thought she was awake, maybe this was the end of her dream, that moment between sleep and waking when imaginary occurrences still seemed real. Yes. That made sense.

After another deep breath, she opened her eyes again.

Same room.

She was not dreaming. She was not in her cozy bedroom in her cozy one-bedroom apartment. She was in a much larger room, one with an enormous window and no bed table. She was in a strange bed with strange pillows. She was…where?

The mattress groaned slightly as something—someone?—behind her shifted. All the panic symptoms returned full force. Her hand flew to her mouth to cover the sound of the scream that threatened to come out. With her heart thumping loudly in her ears, she tried to draw air into her lungs. Paralyzed with fear, that's what she was. Paralyzed.

A sleepy clearing of the throat, a *male* throat, sounded in her ear, followed by the sensation of warm breath on the side of her neck.

"Oh, God," she whispered, instinctively trying not to draw attention to herself so she could avoid trouble. *Move,* she told herself. *Do something.* But even as she gave her body instructions, her terror kept her frozen, glued to the bedsheets. Blue-and white-striped bedsheets. Definitely not her bedsheets.

A long, well-muscled forearm slung itself over her waist; the hand at the end of the forearm slowly moved up on the sheet to cup one of her breasts possessively. The man's skin tone was olive and the fingers long, both sturdy and artistic at the same time. As though in a trance, she watched the hand's movement, the gentle, slow massaging of her breast. Her nipple tightened with fear. Then a sudden surge of moisture between her legs informed her that fear was not the only reaction she was having to this intimate touch.

The owner of the hand made a low grunt of satisfaction in the back of his throat, then she heard the deep, even breathing of a man sleeping contentedly, felt again the warm breath on the side of her neck.

Something was familiar about his embrace, about the touch of those long fingers. Her own breathing slowed momentarily, as though some signal of trustworthiness had passed itself from him to her. Yes, familiar. And the association wasn't negative, somehow. Thank God for small blessings.

But…who was he? As her brain whirled with all these new sensations and questions, she squeezed her eyes shut, wishing it all away.

Get a grip, she told herself. *Stare the truth in the face this time, instead of giving your imagination all the power.* Another careful lesson of the past year took hold. Clenching her hands tightly, she counted to three, opened her eyes, then angled her head around so she could see him.

"Oh," she said aloud as several things struck her at the same moment: One—Not only had she never been in this room before, but she was naked, and she never slept naked.

Two—The man next to her in the bed was the drop-dead gorgeous incredible lover from the dream she'd been having. Which meant…

Three—It hadn't been a dream.

Now, she moved.

As though shot from a cannon, she scrambled out from under the man's embrace and tumbled off the side of the bed and onto a wooden floor. She barely noticed the resulting pain in her rump because her heartbeat was again escalating furiously. *Thump. Thump. Thump.* As adrenaline whipped through her bloodstream, she stared up at him. Without her glasses, his outline was fuzzy, but she knew his face and body by heart. He was the kind of guy who in real life had never given her the time of day—tall, rugged, with jet-black hair and a tanned muscular body with a couple of intriguing scars.

More of her "dream" came back to her in quick flashes. Something about a bar and noise and music and feeling cold. About glittering green eyes staring at her with suspicion. Walking near boats and water and smells of the ocean. More clearly now—images of her kneeling on the floor, watching the man sleep and wanting to touch him, of *needing* him frantically. Throwing herself at him, practically begging him to make love to her, something she'd never done in her life.

Oh, yes, it was coming back to her now, all too well. The poor man, he hadn't even wanted to. He'd tried to turn her down, tried to push her away, but she'd persisted.

Shame at such aggressiveness made her want to die. It *had* to have been a dream, she told herself desperately. This was totally out of character for her. She wouldn't, couldn't— No, she'd never been in a situation like this.

As though he sensed her staring at him, the man opened his eyes, stretched his arms over his head, smiled lazily and said, "Good morning, Amanda."

Amanda?

She bit down on her lip, but still a sound somewhere between a moan and a scream escaped. Then she scrambled to her feet, grabbed the folded blanket at the foot of the bed, wrapped it around herself and took off, scurrying through the first door she saw. Finding herself in a bathroom, she slammed the door shut and locked it. She sank onto the tile floor, her back against the door, her bare skin protected by the soft material of the blanket.

Her head was a whirl of sensations and thoughts and fears, pounding with a kind of foggy pain; her mouth felt as dry as the floor of a sawdust factory, and she knew her heart couldn't keep going for a record number of beats per minute without serious results.

Hugging herself, she rocked back and forth while all kinds of questions popped in and out of her brain. Where had she been? How had she wound up in that man's bed? Who was he? What in God's name had happened to her?

Help, she said silently. *Please, help.*

"Hey, Amanda? Are you okay?"

She felt the pressure of the man's knocking on the wooden door at her back; her immediate reaction was to escape, so she scooted around to the far wall to sit under a towel rack. A navy blue bath sheet draped over her eyes. She grabbed it by the edge and buried her face in it. It smelled faintly of bleach and she inhaled it gratefully. Clean, familiar bleach. Clean clothes and linens. Civilization, at least.

He knocked some more, impatiently this time.

"Amanda? Let me in." His voice was low with morning huskiness. "Are you all right?"

She couldn't answer; she had no words. The panic, like bile, clogged her throat and rendered her speechless. She didn't think she could stop shaking long enough to get words out. Dear God, what was happening?

Think, she told herself. *You have a brain, use it.*

But her mind was too busy sorting and discarding images like a videotape on fast forward. The pictures were too vague to bring into focus, and her quivering body wasn't helping her concentration.

"Hey, it's a little late for modesty," she heard him say with amused sarcasm, "don't you agree? I mean, after last night?"

Last night, she repeated silently. The dream. No, not a

dream. Reality. Hot bodies, out of control. *Her* body out of control, brazenly fired with desire.

She had actually done all that.

"Oh, God," she groaned out loud.

"Amanda? Come on now. I'll make some coffee. Okay?"

And why did he keep calling her Amanda?

"That's not my name." It came out in a weak croak.

"What? I didn't hear you."

She clenched her hands around the towel and made herself speak up. "My name is not Amanda. It's Carly."

She sensed him pausing to consider this. What was he thinking? Probably that she was crazy. Not that she could blame him. She probably *was* crazy. Only, she was usually pretty rational, so her descent into insanity had to be a very recent development.

"Well, whatever your name is," he said finally, "I'm about to make coffee. How do you take it? Black or with cream? That is, if I have any." This last part was said from a slight distance, as though he was walking away from the door.

"Wait, don't go!"

"Huh?"

"I…I'm sorry." She wished she could cry. But lessons had been learned early on, so she rarely did. "I don't know what's going on. I mean, I don't remember anything." Did she have a brain tumor? "What time is it?"

"About noon, I think."

"I mean, what day is it? And where am I?"

"Sunday," he said, less amused now for sure. "And you're at my place. Listen, could you open the door? I'm not going to hurt you or anything. I mean, after last night…"

Why did he keep referring to last night? Surely he should have better manners than that. Manners? Where had that come from? Some book on morning-after etiquette?

"I don't know what you'd do," she admitted. "I mean, I've never seen you before in my life. I don't know you. I mean, I didn't know you, until…" Now thoroughly flustered—on top of the panic—she allowed the sentence to trail off and leaned back against the wall, willing herself to be whisked away to another planet.

After another pause, he expelled a loud, irritated breath. "Look, come out, don't come out, whatever. I need coffee."

Then she sensed his presence no more. He was gone, off to perform a normal, mundane morning ritual like making coffee. His universe, of course, was totally in order. Lucky him.

She began to rock back and forth again, as she used to do as a child, when all the angry chaos in her home had made her anxious.

She was no longer a child, but Carla Anne Terry had never felt so alone or lost in her life.

Nick slammed the carafe into place, then dumped ground coffee into the filter and punched the start button. Muttering an oath, he shook his head. Just his luck—you meet a woman, engage in astonishing, mind-bending sex, and the next morning she does a number on you. "What? I did what? Oh, no, not me." "What time is it? What day is it?" "I'm not Amanda."

Yeah, that was the best one of them all—someone *else* did all those nasty dirty things with you, not me. Man oh man, he'd thought modern women had thrown that kind of thing out with girdles.

What a shame, he mused as he watched the heated water drip into the pot, willing it to move along—he really needed his morning coffee. A damn shame. A woman who gave herself in bed like that, who'd lapped up everything he'd offered as if she was starving, to feel so guilty the next morning she had to make up a story rather than face who she was. Guilt was an emotion he tried not to indulge in himself, although he wasn't always successful. It could do all sorts of things to your brain.

Nick shook his head again. Man, was he p.o.'d.

Not just upset. He felt...let down. Disappointed. There had

been a few moments there, that last time, when he'd sensed a strange kind of connection to her. There, at the end, the sex had been different than before—not so much mindless sensation. Something had stirred him that had nothing to do with what was happening to his body, a kind of a…heart thing. Like it was no longer about sex, but something more important than that.

Ridiculous, he told himself, uncomfortable with the direction of his thoughts. A wish left over from when he still had hopes. Hormones, that was all it had been. Good old-fashioned primal urges and needs, nothing more. He was a man with a healthy appetite who'd been without a woman for a while, and he'd done his damnedest to make up for lost time.

So, he thought, propping a hip against the tile counter, that was him. But what was her story? Why the reversal? Maybe she was some kind of wacko. She'd sure changed personalities a lot the night before. Hell, maybe he was dealing with a schizophrenic and he'd better watch it. In the movies, this was the moment when the crazed woman came after you with a knife and began to slash away.

Uneasy, Nick glanced over his shoulder, but the kitchen doorway was empty. Come off it, he told himself with a chuckle. He needed to put a hold on his imagination. Don't spend any more energy on it, he advised himself, because whatever was going on with this Amanda—or Carly…hell, whatever her name was—wouldn't take away from what had happened between the two of them last night.

It was a memory he'd keep locked in his mind forever.…

He'd been at his temporary place of employment, Morgan R's on the marina—two nice-size, wood-paneled rooms with ocean views, one a restaurant, the other a bar. Officially, he wasn't supposed to be working, as he was on medical leave from the Manhattan Beach Police Department; unofficially, he was acting manager for his buddy Kyle Morgan while he was on vacation. What that meant was showing up on Saturday nights when the bar filled up and the crowd often got raucous. It was policy to let them know the boss was around.

Last night, the early hours, at least, had been like the others. The sound of jazz poured out of the loudspeakers, a couple of guys argued sports teams, some others laughed loudly over tasteless jokes. There were couples and singles, people looking for company and others who wanted to be alone in the midst of company.

It was around midnight when she walked in. Slipped in, really, through the side entrance near the end of the long wooden bar. He'd happened to be looking that way, or he'd have missed her. If she'd come in through the main entrance just off the boardwalk, no one would have, or could have, missed her.

Not with those long bare legs and that little slip of a dress that just hit the top of her thighs. It was made of some shimmering, cream-colored stuff; thin straps held up a low-cut bodice that revealed a juicy amount of cleavage. Generous breasts, high and firm. The appreciative male in him checked her out head to toe, while the manager part of him made note that a young, attractive woman, unescorted and dressed as this one was, was potential trouble.

She had lots of wavy yellow-blond hair that fell past her shoulders, slender arms, a long neck and heavily made-up eyes with half circles of smeared mascara under the lower lids. Could have been anywhere from twenty to thirty. He watched as she slid onto the end bar stool, a couple of empty stools over from where he sat. Her feet were bare, but he didn't go up to her and say something about the "no shoes, no service" policy, because, for the moment, he liked watching her. She settled herself, crossed those long legs one over the other, then brushed back several strands of pale hair that had fallen over one eye. Elbows balanced on the bar, she rubbed her hands up and down her bare arms, seeming to huddle into herself.

Joey, the bartender, finished wiping a glass and spoke to her. With the noise level, even sitting as close to her as he

was, Nick couldn't hear their conversation. He could, however, see Joey shake his head once, then again, before Nick
signaled him to come over.

"What's she want?" he asked the bartender.

"She can't seem to decide."

"Loaded?"

"Maybe. She's slurring her words."

Nick glanced at the woman again. "Give her water or juice,
on the house, then tell her to take a hike. Nicely."

"Will do."

He watched as Joey related his message to the woman,
pointing toward Nick as he did. The woman turned her head
and looked at him, surprise and something else—fear?—on
her face. The proverbial doe caught in the headlights. She
squinted as though she had trouble focusing, then closed her
eyes and rubbed the lids, smearing her mascara even more.
Joey brought her the juice, then went to wait on a customer
at the other end of the bar.

Nick watched her sip her drink, then gulp it more thirstily.
Was she drunk or high? he wondered. From all his years on
the force, especially working Vice, he was pretty good at spot-
ting the hard-core dopers and boozers, but she didn't seem
hard-core anything. There was an innocent, almost angelic
quality to her, in spite of the dress and the hair and the
makeup.

A customer he'd never seen before, a big guy with a full
beard and a fuller gut, plopped himself down on the stool next
to her, effectively blocking Nick's view. "Hi, sweetheart," he
bellowed in a voice loud enough to cut through a bomb det-
onation. "Can I buy you a drink?"

Nick couldn't see her reaction. He glanced at the long mir-
rored wall behind the bar, but several tall bottles covered his
view. However, he had no trouble hearing the man's next offering.

"What's the matter, can't you talk, sweetheart? My name's
Lenny. What do they call you?"

Nick sighed. He was going to have to step in. He told himself it was in his official capacity as management, to prevent a scene in the bar, but he wasn't fooling himself. He had some kind of radar for people who couldn't take care of themselves and was repeatedly drawn toward helping them out. He'd gotten kicked in the teeth for it a few times, but he probably wouldn't change.

He got up from his stool, felt the familiar twinge in his knee, winced, shook it out, then moved over to stand behind the thickset man.

"Please, no," the woman was saying very carefully and slowly. She was looking down at her lap where her hands clutched each other tightly.

"No, what?" Lenny said. "No time to lose?" He laughed loudly, then emitted a cigarette smoker's cough.

Nick tapped the man's shoulder twice. "Hey," he said. "It'd be best if you left the lady alone."

Lenny turned on his stool and glared at him from under bushy eyebrows. "Who the hell asked you, friend? She's alone, ain't she?"

Nick's hackles rose automatically at the challenge in the other man's tone, but long experience had taught him to keep his temper in check at moments like these. He sighed patiently. "Lenny, I'm the manager here and I'm not looking for trouble, promise. Just do me a favor this time, okay? Let me buy you a drink and leave her alone. She's a friend and she's not feeling well."

"What's the matter with her?"

He waited a beat, then, making his tone ominous, said, "You don't want to know."

"Jeez." Lenny jumped off his stool and backed away from both his former quarry and Nick. "Forget it. I'm out of here."

The woman's head jerked up in surprise and she watched Lenny's retreat into the crowd, squinting again as she did. Nearsighted, Nick thought, and too vain to wear glasses. He'd

known other women like that. Stupid hang-up. You could miss
a lot of pretty terrific views that way.

She shifted her gaze to him, studied him almost solemnly
for a moment, frowned, then ran her tongue over her lips as
though they were dry. Whatever the intention of that little
gesture, it had the effect on Nick of making his groin tighten
momentarily. His reaction took him by surprise, but he
shrugged it off. It was like that sometimes, he told himself.
One look and instant hard-on.

"Thank you," she said, her voice husky and low-pitched,
her words again slow and deliberate.

"No problem." He took Lenny's place on the stool next to
her. A faint whiff of something very expensive wafted into his
nostrils—but there was no booze smell. "Look, you probably
ought to go home."

"Home?" She tested the word on her tongue as though it
were a new one. She seemed distracted, even slightly disoriented. Up close, he saw a sweet, pretty face, round and
smooth. Dainty. A small nose, unexpectedly full lips with a
beautiful, sensual bow to the upper one.

Her large eyes, encircled with dark smudges that were not
just smeared mascara, were the color of warm golden brandy.
No dilated pupils, he noted, crossing off several substances
immediately. Hers was such an unmarked face, he thought,
not at all hard or lived-in. It didn't go with the provocative
outfit, the deep V of the neckline and the way her pebbled
nipples were outlined by the thin fabric.

Another bolt of desire hit his groin with a suddenness that
threw him. He stifled a groan. It hadn't happened like this in
years, not since he'd been a randy teenager. Down, boy, he
told himself.

"Yeah, home." He shifted a little on the stool for comfort.
"You know, where you have things like a kitchen and warm
clothes and shoes."

"Shoes?" she repeated, then looked down at her feet as

though realizing for the first time that they were bare. "Shoes."

"Hey, are you all right? Joey," he called to the bartender, "bring over a couple of black coffees, will you?" He turned back to the woman. "Are you feeling okay? Sick?"

She shook her head. "No."

"All right. What did you take, then?"

"Take?" She looked off somewhere over his shoulder, her eyes becoming unfocused. "I don't understand."

"Come on. Blow? Ludes? Meth? You're high on something."

Again she frowned, shaking her head slowly, then brought her gaze to meet his. "No. I don't...do that. Ever."

There was so much sincerity behind the words, he half believed her, even though the cop in him was pretty sure she was getting a buzz, and it was not a natural high. "Look...what's your name?"

She had to think about it for a moment. Her eyebrows knit, then she said, "Amanda?"

"Okay, Amanda, I'm Nick. I'm the manager here."

"Pleased to meet you."

"Thanks, Joey," he said as the coffee cups were set down in front of them. "Amanda, what I think is that you ought to drink this coffee and get home. Where's your car?"

"I'm not sure." She yawned, then covered her mouth with her hand, as though she'd been brought up to be a lady at all times. "Sorry."

"You probably shouldn't be driving anyway. Where's your purse? Do you have money for a cab?"

Holding up both her hands, she gazed first at one palm, then the other. "No purse."

She looked at him in amazement, then smiled—a wide, enchanting smile that brought a sparkle to her eyes. "No shoes and no purse," she said, then bit her bottom lip with her front teeth, like a guilty child. "Isn't that the silliest thing?"

He drew in a ragged breath as the zipper area of his jeans

got tighter. Man, that combination of innocence and worldliness, it was a major turn-on. "Yeah, real silly."

"I'm not sure what to do." Another huge yawn escaped. Again, Amanda covered her mouth daintily with her hand. "I'd like to sleep, though. Would it be all right if I put my head down?" She proceeded to make a pillow with her crossed arms on the bar and began to lower her head.

Nick grabbed her elbow. "Didn't anyone ever tell you you can't sleep on a bar? Come on." He helped her off the stool. Standing, she was about five-three, he figured; as he was a couple of inches over six feet, she seemed tiny.

"Where are we going, Nick?" She shivered, and he realized her skin beneath his palms was cold and clammy.

He retrieved his windbreaker from a nearby hook and put it around her shoulders. "This isn't real heavy, but put it on."

"Oh. Okay."

She seemed so pliable, so docile. So lost. It brought out all his protective instincts, in spades.

He'd always been that way. As a kid he used to bring home stray dogs and kittens, eggs from birds' nests. He'd tried to balance that caretaking instinct with constant reality checks all twelve years on the job. He'd learned to mind his own business and watch his back, but every so often that need to take in hurt puppies popped up again.

Amanda was not a puppy, he reminded himself. Not even close. "Where do you live?" he asked her.

Huge doe's eyes, a little sad and bewildered, gazed up at him. "I...don't know." Her forehead cleared. "Yes I do. Hull."

"Hull?"

"Yes."

"Never heard of it. Where's Hull?"

"Across the bay."

"Across what bay?"

Her forehead wrinkled again. "I'm not sure." As he took her by the shoulders, she gazed up at him, startled.

"Look, here's the deal. You're spaced on something, and what I should do is take you to a hospital—"

"No," she said quickly. "I don't like hospitals." He felt her sag a little. "All I want to do is sleep."

He emitted a sigh. She really didn't seem sick, just disoriented. Probably needed a good night's sleep.

Which he was about to offer. Hell, he'd probably lost any battle for self-protection the minute she'd walked in the door, but he'd tried to put up a fight. Sucker, he called himself silently.

"Then come over to my place," he said. "My couch, I mean. I'm no danger to you, you can ask Joey if you'd like. I won't jump your bones."

"Jump my bones?" She seemed puzzled.

"You know what I mean. I won't try anything. Not that I'd turn down an invitation, but there are rules, as they say. You're not yourself."

"I'm Amanda." She yawned again. Her complete disinterest in any sexual danger he might pose, he had to admit, bruised his male ego just a little.

"Joey, I'm taking off," Nick called out. "Call me at home if there's trouble. Come on, Amanda."

"Okay."

He wondered if she went home this easily with men all the time. The thought disturbed him. What a dumb thing to do, with all the hopped-up lunatics around.

They walked along the docks toward his condo. It was a warm October night, and the marina was busy. Aside from a couple of private parties on larger boats, noise and music poured out from all the dockside watering holes. A patrol car sped by with sirens blaring; Nick stifled his automatic curiosity.

It took five minutes to get to his building, one of three large complexes in the area. He'd bought the condo four years ago, after his divorce, something temporary, he'd told himself, until he set up a real home. Somehow, with all the years on the job, all the time-and-gut commitment, he'd never come any closer to making the place a real home than the stark white walls, small balcony with a view, one-bedroom, one-bath condominium. Clean, efficient, impersonal.

Amanda seemed half-asleep by the time they came through the front door. When she padded into his bedroom and fell facedown on the bed, her dress crept up to uncover pale cream silk bikini underpants and nothing more. The smooth, pearl-colored flesh of her buttocks and thighs made his loins tighten again.

He wished momentarily he were the kind of man who didn't have a conscience. However, he believed in rules of behavior, as well as the legal kind; it was why he'd joined the force. Not that he was some kind of straight-arrow Dudley Do Right—he approved of anything between mutually consenting adults. But the mutually consenting part didn't happen when one adult was unconscious.

Tugging her dress down, he resisted the temptation to touch the pad of one finger to that smooth skin. Instead, he pulled the covers up to her neck. She put her arms around his pillow and hugged it to her. Several golden strands of hair draped across one cheek and he eased them off her face, tucking them behind an ear.

He stood a moment more and stared at her sleeping, innocent, angel's face. Her eye makeup would get all over his sheets, he thought distractedly, but it wouldn't be the first time a woman had left her mark on his bed; besides, that was what soap was for.

Feeling a strange emptiness, Nick made up the couch in the living room, watched a little TV and dropped off to sleep.

Sometime later—it could have been fifteen minutes, could have been three hours—he awoke with a start. Sensing a presence near him, he reached for his gun then remembered it was in the closet.

He was about to sit up when he realized the presence he'd felt was Amanda. She was close, very close, her face and his only inches apart. Visible by the outside porch light that shone through his living-room curtains, she was on her knees, her arms folded on the cushion next to his pillow, her chin on her arms. She stared at him with huge eyes, but said nothing.

Sitting up, he scrubbed a hand across his face. "You scared the crap out of me."

"Sorry." In that low, hoarse voice.

"What do you want?"

Still on her knees, she straightened her torso, her hands braced on the edge of the cushion. That's when he saw what he hadn't quite noticed a moment earlier. She had no clothes on.

Her breasts—smaller than they'd appeared in the dress, but still high and firm—stood out in the pale yellow light. Her waist was nicely indented, but her hips were surprisingly round and womanly on one so thin. Her stomach, too, was slightly rounded, enticingly so, but his angle didn't allow him to see below that. And man, did he want to.

"What do you want?" he said again, but this time it came out harshly.

"You," she said. "I want you."

She leaned to one side and stretched out along the floor. It was a pose out of a girlie magazine, but seemed somehow not to go with this woman. The way the dress hadn't really gone with her. She offered temptation, but not with self-assurance. There was—what?—a shyness, a modesty about her. He found that more attractive than any blatant come-on. Even if Amanda wasn't about to win Cover Girl of the Year for her nude-modeling skills, she got to him, all over.

Now he could see the junction of her thighs, just make out the wedge of pale pubic hair that disappeared into the V and the womanly mysteries there. She followed his gaze, looked down at herself, then back up at him. She bit her lip; he could have sworn she was blushing, although it was hard to tell in this light.

Most of the breath whooshed out of his body. "Uh, I don't think—"

"Hold me." She sat up and raised her arms toward him. "Make love to me. Please."

He stayed right where he was, trying not to stare at the rosy, temptingly puckered nipples on her creamy breasts. "Look, you don't really mean that."

"Yes, I do."

He might have been asleep thirty seconds earlier, but his body was now fully awake and raging with desire for Amanda. Hot blood coursed all through him, crowding his brain and rendering coherent thought almost impossible.

He made one last attempt to be a good guy. "I'm not sure you know what you're doing...."

She moved closer, placed one hand on his chest and ran it slowly down his torso. Her touch was light, tentative, but effective. "If I don't know what I'm doing, you'll help me, won't you?"

When her hand arrived at his already throbbing phallus and she cupped its base in her palm, it was all over.

With a groan, he went to her, only too glad to oblige. First on the living-room floor, then on the couch, then in his bed.

He didn't have to help her much, after all.

Nick poured himself a cup of black coffee and took a sip. Shaking his head, he thought again what a damn shame it was, all that good loving, and this morning the "ruined-virgin" bit.

"I'm sorry to bother you..."

Her voice startled him out of his reverie. She stood in the kitchen doorway wrapped in his blue terry-cloth robe. She'd washed her face; without all that eye makeup on, she was definitely less glamorous. Almost, but not quite plain. And still angelic—except for those frightened, dark gold eyes and that great mouth. Her arms were crossed over her chest and she seemed to be both self-conscious and determined not to show it.

"Good morning," he said easily, leaning back against the counter. "You're not bothering me, promise. Coffee?"

"In a minute. Um, Nick, is it?"

"Yup."

"Can I ask you something?"

"Fire away."

"The ocean outside the window. Is it the Atlantic?"

"Nope. Pacific."

"So, I'm in...?" She let her sentence trail off, but her large eyes begged for an answer.

"Marina del Rey, California."

Closing her eyes for a moment, Amanda/Carly took a shaky breath, then opened them again. With a brave but trembling smile, she said, "How interesting. I've always wanted to see California. I just...have no idea how I got here."

Chapter 2

"You what?" His eyes narrowed with suspicion.

Carly said it again. "I don't know how I wound up here. In your apartment."

"Bull."

Carly took a step back. His epithet not only stung but took her by surprise. "Excuse me?"

"I said bull. You know exactly how you wound up here. We met in a bar last night. You came home with me." The harsh planes of his face seemed sculpted out of marble. His eyes were unfriendly, untrusting.

Flustered, she dug her hands deep into the pockets of his robe, which she'd found hanging on the back of the bathroom door. "Well, yes, of course. I'm sorry, I'm talking about how I got to the West Coast, to California."

"Plane? Car? Hitchhiking?" The low rumble of his voice dripped with sarcasm.

"I'm sorry, but why are you so angry?"

An eyebrow lifted and he studied her. Then he leaned against the door frame and draped his well-muscled arms across his broad chest. "Okay," he said slowly. "Just tell me one thing—do you remember what happened after you *did* get here? To my place? I mean, when exactly did this memory loss come over you?"

She had no idea how to answer him. Removing her hands from the robe's pockets, she rubbed up and down her arms nervously as she glanced around the kitchen. It was small, bright and clean, and totally lacking in personality. No plants, no refrigerator magnets. Either he was a housecleaning fanatic or this room wasn't used much. She got the feeling it was the latter.

"May I sit down?" she said.

He vaulted away from the doorway. "Where are my manners?" he said sardonically. "Of course. Grab a chair. I'll even get you some coffee. It's all part of the service."

He pulled a chair out for her and she sat. Then she looked at him. Up at him, actually; he was quite tall. His expression seemed mocking now. Wordlessly, she studied his face while her mind ran up and down the corridors of its confused maze.

Dear heavens, he was good-looking, a part of her brain was able to register. Rumpled, sexy, his nearly black hair not yet combed, his face not yet shaved. Tanned skin, penetrating green eyes, the color of old jade. A strong, slightly crooked nose and a wide unsmiling mouth.

And he was so big. Too big. Maybe a foot taller than she. He had put on sweatpants to make the coffee, but his upper torso was bare. Black curly chest hair, a Saint Christopher's medal on a silver chain. Well-muscled shoulders and biceps, but not overly developed. His wasn't the physique of a narcissistic bodybuilder, just a perfect example of how men were constructed a lot differently than women.

Another wave of trembling swept over her, making her shudder again. This reaction to him was unsettling. Yes, it was part fear of his anger, but also a large part raw, sexual attraction, heightened by memories of the dream....

No, not a dream, she corrected herself. The night before, she'd given in to that raw sexual reaction fully and thoroughly.

Carly felt her skin heating with the blush she knew was taking it over. Ripping her gaze away from his, she concentrated on the bare tabletop. "Thank you. Coffee sounds good. I'm sorry to bother you, but do you have any cream?"

"I'm out."

"Then black will be fine."

He went to the bare white tile counter and removed a cup from a hook. His back was broadly powerful; the sweatpants fit snugly over tight buttocks before they draped casually to his ankles. His feet were bare; as were hers. At least, she thought distractedly, the floor was cool without being cold.

Weary, she rubbed her temples. "I'm sorry. I hope you don't mind me wearing your robe, but I didn't know what else to put on."

"Do you always apologize for everything?" he asked abruptly, glancing over his shoulder and startling her.

Her hands fell to her lap while she swallowed the urge to apologize for apologizing. What a wimp she could be sometimes. This morning she could take the prize for low self-esteem. "No. I don't always apologize for everything," she managed to say with some spirit. "Or I mean, I used to, but I don't anymore. Except now, of course."

She took a deep breath and exhaled it. "I'm completely at a loss here. I mean, I've never been in a situation like this. It's, well, it's insane."

He turned to concentrate on pouring the coffee. "Keep talking."

Staring at his broad, intimidating back, she shrugged helplessly. "I...don't know what to say. I seem to have some sort of blackout about how I got here."

He turned around, coffeepot in one hand, her steaming cup in the other. "So you keep saying. Do you remember me being in you, and you being in me, with several variations, for most of last night?"

Carly recoiled from the cool, almost brutal directness of his question. But she answered him. "Of course I do. I remember it all...." Letting the sentence trail off as mortification overtook her, she looked down at her hands. Anything to avoid looking at him. "Oh, Lord."

After a moment he said, "So, that's not the part you've blacked out."

She shook her head, but couldn't look up at him.

His voice gentled slightly. "It's okay, you know."

"No, it isn't," Carly murmured, shaking her head even more vigorously. "It is most definitely not okay. I...don't do that."

"Don't do what?"

Nervously rubbing her thumb, wishing she could close her eyes and disappear, she said softly, "Go to bed with people I don't know." Even as her skin continued to heat again with embarrassment, she made herself raise her head to meet his gaze. "This has to be the most awkward morning of my life."

She kept her eyes focused on him; she *had* to stop coming across as some flustered ninny, had to stop trying to run away from dealing with this, with him, with the raw truth about what they'd done together.

He stared at her a moment longer, then nodded, a small smile quirking at one side of his mouth. It was the first remotely pleasant expression she'd seen since they'd been in the kitchen talking. As the atmosphere of deep suspicion lifted slightly, Carly actually felt her own inner tension let down somewhat.

He returned the coffeepot to its holder. Then, crossing to the table, he set her cup in front of her. "Here. Yeah, you don't seem the type to hop into bed with strangers."

He retrieved his own mug from a nearby counter, put it on the table and pulled out the other chair. With a fluid movement, he turned it around, straddled the seat and crossed his arms on the top. "Okay. Let's talk about it. Do you remember coming into the bar?"

Closing her eyes, she rubbed the lids as she concentrated. "Yes, I think so. Laughter…men's voices… It was cold. Green eyes. Bits and pieces, is all. Most of it's a blur."

"Where were you before that?"

She shook her head. "I have no idea."

"Drink your coffee," he said. "Maybe the caffeine will help."

Her eyes snapped open. His tone was peremptory, but she ignored it. Wrapping her fingers around the cup, she took a sip, then another, grateful for the warmth spreading through her system. "Oh, this is good."

"It's about the only thing to eat or drink in the house. I haven't shopped for food in weeks. I can't even offer you any orange juice."

Her stomach turned over at the thought of food. "This is all I want for now. Thanks."

"Okay then, start talking again."

"Was that an order? I mean, should I salute and say 'Yes, sir!'?" It popped out of her before she had a chance to censor it, but she really hated being ordered around.

"My turn to say sorry," he said ruefully. "Ignore me. I was in the marines."

Nick rubbed a hand over his face, then raked his fingers through his hair. He hadn't meant to bark at her; it was just something he did when he was off-kilter. "I'm not sure what to make of all this," he confessed.

Stretching both arms over his head, he took a couple of deep breaths, then rotated his shoulders to get the stiffness out. He was tired. And he was sore, that was the truth. Last night's little amorous workout had taken quite a toll on him, he had to admit. Even though he hated to.

Back to the business at hand, he thought. She was claiming she'd had a blackout. At least she wasn't denying she'd been with him. Hell, maybe there was even some truth to her story; she sure didn't seem to be an accomplished liar by nature. He was curious, and he was a cop—he loved a good mystery.

"Okay," he said, willing to give her the benefit of the doubt. "Let's start from the beginning. What's the last thing you remember, I mean, from before?"

She closed her eyes again, as though trying to recall a picture. Brown lashes fanned the faint blue shadows underneath. "Richard's face," she said after a moment. "Friday night. Yes, that's right. I was having dinner with Richard."

"Richard?" Even as he stiffened inwardly, Nick tried to keep his voice impersonal. It shouldn't have surprised him that she mentioned a man's name. He knew nothing at all about her, including if she belonged to someone else.

"My husband. No, ex-husband, sorry." She gazed at him with a small smile of apology. "I'm a little foggy. We've been divorced for a year."

Divorced. He relaxed somewhat, wondering momentarily why that brief burst of tension had felt like jealousy. Not possible, he thought. Not even reasonable. Jealousy implied possessiveness—he never went down that road. Not to mention the fact he'd just met the woman.

"Go on." Gulping down the last of his coffee, he rose and refilled both their cups. "Tell me about dinner with Richard," he said as he took his seat again.

Wrapping her fingers around the cup once more, she stared into the brown liquid, her eyebrows furrowed with concentration. While he gave her time to think, he studied her. Her face was shiny and clean, her amber eyes were slightly bloodshot. Still, except for that incongruously pouty mouth, she could have been cast in a movie as the girl next door, the one who was good for you, the one your mother encouraged you to ask to the senior prom. Even though you had your eye on the class wild woman.

Nick nearly smiled at the direction of his thoughts. Corny images like that were from movies and books he'd read, not from firsthand experience. He'd had nothing like a normal high-school experience. Motherly advice? Not so's he could

remember. Prom? No way. Too busy working nights. Too
busy keeping the old man away from the booze.

"What else?" he encouraged her. "Anything."

"We were at a restaurant, the Greenery in Old Town. That's
in Boston. He wore a suit. We talked about…everyday stuff,
I think." She frowned, chewed on her lower lip. Then, as
though a new thought had crossed her mind, her head jerked
up and she stared at him. "This is Sunday?"

"Yes."

Her hand flew to her mouth. "My God, I've lost almost two
days. How could I have lost two days?" As panic hit her eyes
again, the other hand fisted on the tabletop.

The lady was thoroughly spooked. Reaching across the table, he grabbed her hand and squeezed, hard. "Amanda—"

"That's not my name." Even her lips were quivering.

"That's right, sorry."

"And I don't know why you think it is," she cried out.

He kept his voice even. "Because you told me your name
was Amanda. At the bar. Listen…Carly, right?"

She nodded, that bottom lip of hers getting a good workout
with small, white teeth. He could see her struggling to catch
her breath, fighting for some kind of calm.

"Carly what?" he said.

"Carla Anne Terry. Carly is what they call me."

Releasing her hand, he offered his as though inviting her to
shake it. "Nicholas Constantine Holmes. Nick." His mouth
quirked up as he added, "Pleased to meet you."

Thoroughly disoriented, Carly stared at his hand. What in
the world was going on? A brief moment ago she'd been trembling enough to dislodge her brains; now she felt ready to
burst into nervous laughter. He had just introduced himself.
But, wasn't that backward? Shouldn't she have known his full
name before…before…

Before experiencing the most exciting, most sensual night
she'd ever had or would have in her life.

"Oh, Lord," she said. "What have I gotten myself into?"

"Beats me," Nick said easily. "But, at the risk of upsetting you even more, I want you to know that I found our night together, every moment of it, thoroughly satisfying, in every way."

When her mouth dropped open with shock, Nick congratulated himself. He'd said that to jolt her. Hell, something needed to be done to lighten the mood; experience told him the woman was on the verge of hysteria.

She continued to stare at him, her eyes huge and tawny, her mouth agape, but gradually, her trembling diminished.

He let another few moments pass in silence before adding, "And I'm pretty sure you enjoyed it, too. But if talking about last night makes you uncomfortable..."

He let the sentence trail off. Carly seemed to realize how she looked then, and she closed her mouth with a snap. Then she started to work on that lower lip again, but now her features took on a determined aspect.

"No. It happened." He could see her throat constrict as she swallowed. "And I'm glad you said it out loud."

Atta girl, he thought. It was pretty obvious Carly was not basically assertive by nature, but she was trying to face facts as bravely as possible.

"I'm not a child," she went on, her chin jutting forward slightly. "I mean, I'm not, well, a prude or some sort of, you know, totally inexperienced person." Her eyes opened wide with a sudden thought. "Did I seem like an inexperienced person?" A pained expression crossed her face. "I can't believe I asked you that."

Even though she looked thoroughly miserable, he couldn't help grinning. "No, ma'am, I'm here to tell you that after a bit, it was like...something wild had been let out of a cage and needed to celebrate its freedom."

"That bad, huh?"

"Uh-uh. That good."

Her color rose, but a tentative little upswing of her mouth

told him she was okay. "You're trying to embarrass me, aren't you?"

"Just a little. How'm I doing?"

"Great."

"I figure it's better than watching you fall apart from shaking."

"Well, it's working."

They smiled at each other, hers sheepish but more relaxed. Nick felt his own body unclench. He hadn't realized how tense he'd been; it was as if he'd picked up on her distress and made it his.

He took a long swig of hot coffee. "So, how long did you say you've been divorced?"

His change of subject seemed to startle her but didn't keep her from answering. "Over a year. Twelve months and fourteen, no, sixteen days."

"But who's counting?" he said sardonically.

"I am."

"Not a shining example of marital bliss, huh."

"It wasn't the best time of my life, no," she agreed, then heaved a sigh and drank from her cup. Her hands, her whole body, had stopped trembling. Dr. Nick to the rescue, he thought wryly.

"Yeah, I had one of those," he said. "Hell while it lasted and nothing but relief when it was over. Was that your only marriage?"

"Absolutely."

"Same here. One marriage, one divorce. Enough to last a lifetime."

Leaning an elbow on the table, Carly rubbed her forehead distractedly, then seemed to notice that the movement had made a gap in the robe. She quickly drew the lapels together and smoothed down the fabric. Not much of a temptress this morning, Nick observed silently. More like a well brought-up young woman of good quality. He could picture her with white gloves, her legs crossed at the ankles.

What a change from last night to today, he thought, not for the first time. But...which one was she? Temptress or good girl? He would just have to find out.

Interrogation was one of his strong suits; the guys at the station always said he had "the feel." When to come on strong, when to wait. When to play good cop, when to play the bad guy. He'd always been adept at sizing people up and, even though Carly had presented two totally different personalities, he instinctively knew she would respond to patience, that if she felt rushed or threatened she would shut down.

But she was a puzzle, no doubt about it. He had no idea what kind of setup he was dealing with here. And—he reminded himself—even with her girl-next-door looks and his gut reaction to trust her, she could still be the most accomplished actress he'd ever come in contact with.

"Where do you live, Carly? Do you mind me asking you a couple of questions?"

"No, not at all. Hull, Massachusetts. It's a small town across the bay from Boston."

"Where do you work? Do you work?"

"Oh, yes, I work. At Aces Insurance Company near Cambridge. As a bookkeeper." Her face lit up with pleasure. "See? I remember all that. Mr. Caudhill is my immediate boss. My best friend is Margie Gillis. I like movies and books and love to browse in hardware stores and thrift shops." She frowned again, and he was sorry to see the sunshine leave her face. "How did I lose two days?"

He shrugged. "A blow to the head will do it. Maybe you need to see a doctor."

"I don't think so. I mean—" her fingers tentatively explored her head "—there's no bump or anything. Although I do have a headache."

"Want some aspirin?"

"I already took some. In your bathroom. I hope that was okay," she added anxiously, as though asking permission.

"I think I can spare a couple of aspirin. More coffee?"

When she shook her head, he got up and refilled his own cup. "I have four or five cups every morning, to get me going. Tell me, is there any history of mental illness in your family?"

When she didn't reply, he turned to face her.

"You think I'm off my rocker, don't you?" Her face registered hurt mixed in with a little indignation.

He raised his shoulders in an easy, no-big-deal shrug. "Hey, it's an explanation, isn't it?"

Carly told herself not to feel insulted by Nick's question. It was perfectly reasonable. But she needed to set the record straight. "Listen, Mr.— I mean, Nick. I know how it looks. But truly, I am considered pleasant, efficient, a nice person. Good old dependable Carly. Thoroughly sane. Never even close to nuts, I swear. I mean I always wished I could be a little *less* sensible. You know, break loose, live it up." She emitted a short hiccup of laughter. "Sensible sounds absolutely terrific right now."

"Then we're left with drugs." Nick returned to the table, restored his chair to its normal position and sat down again.

"But I don't take drugs."

"Then someone gave them to you. If your last memory is in a restaurant with Richard, it probably happened there."

"Richard gave me drugs?" It was hard to imagine.

"Or someone else."

"But why?"

He shrugged. "You can probably answer that better than I can."

"No, I can't. I don't know why he would do that, why anyone would do that, honestly."

Nick rested an ankle on the opposite knee. He seemed too big for the spindly chair. "Anger? Revenge? A joke? It happens."

"But not to me—I'm not the kind of person people get angry at, or play jokes on, or even feel that strongly about. Oh, Lord." She chewed on her bottom lip as a whole new world of terror opened at her feet. "This is awful. To be given drugs, to be…vulnerable. Just now, you could have put something in my coffee and I would never know it.''

"Carly," he said firmly, "stop. There's nothing in your cup except what's supposed to be there. Don't start falling apart on me again or we'll never find out what happened to you."

What he said made sense. With an extreme effort at self-control, she reined in her rampaging fantasies. Nick was trying to help her. "You're right, of course. Thanks. Okay, what do we do now? Do you know anything about this kind of thing? What kind of drugs make you lose your memory?"

"Several. And there are more and more being whipped up in labs all over the world every day. Better living through chemicals."

"Drugs," she mused, still trying to come to grips with the concept. "I tried marijuana once and coughed so hard I practically had to be given CPR. One glass of wine and I'm asleep." It was her turn to shrug. "But you're right. I must have been given some sort of drug. Even though I don't take drugs. And I don't go home with strangers."

She grabbed a lock of hair. "And my hair is lighter and yellower than it used to be. And longer." She pulled and several strands came off in her hand. "Someone put in hair attachments—do you know how much work that is? It takes hours. When did that happen?"

He pushed his chair back so it was balanced on the rear legs only. "Good question. Also, who changed your hair color and why?"

Her heartbeat accelerated again, but she made a major effort to stay in control. "I have no memory of it at all. But how could my hair have been dyed, and done up like this, without me remembering?"

Nick had just about made up his mind. He bought it, her whole story. This was too good to be an act. And why would she act? If, as he'd thought originally, the amnesia story had been invented so she could pretend the night before hadn't happened, well, she'd already admitted that it had. So that theory was shot.

He clasped his hands behind his head and rocked back and forth on his chair while he gazed at her. Yeah, he believed her. He admired the way she kept control of herself, even though he could sense the effort behind it.

Finally, he sat forward and leaned in, smiling. "Listen. This is your lucky day. If you had to go home with a stranger, you picked the right one." He nodded reassuringly. "I'm a cop, employed by the Manhattan Beach Police Department. Actually, I'm on medical leave right now—bum knee—but that's my background and training. And I'm good at my job. So I'm pretty sure I can help you find out just what did happen to those two days. Okay?" Having given her the good news, he smiled, expecting to see her tight facial features relax with relief.

Nick's revelation hit Carly like a bolt from hell. A policeman? This man sitting across from her was, of all things, a gun-toting, power-hungry, bullying cop?

Just like her father had been?

It made sense, now she could see. He liked to give orders, liked to be in charge. A quick temper seethed under that cool, self-possessed attitude. He'd even just interrogated her, for heaven's sake.

Nick was a cop.

She shuddered as old, unpleasant memories washed over her. Her family had suffered mightily under the rule of one bullying cop. How much more of this nightmare would she have to endure?

"Carly?"

"I'm all right," she said, scurrying around someplace inside her mind in search of safety.

"Sure?"

"You just surprised me."

"Leave it to me, okay? What we need to do now is find out where you were before you came into the bar."

Nick wasn't her father, she told herself, but he might be a lot like him. She really didn't know him, did she? Except…as a lover.

At any rate, she would be on guard now. He'd gotten beneath her defenses pretty easily, but she knew how to act from now on. She would accept his help—heaven knew she needed help from someone!—but would be less forthcoming. And definitely less trusting.

"I barely remember the bar," she said evenly, "so how can I remember what came before?"

Nick seemed to study her for a moment, then he rose from his chair and offered his hand. "Let's go out on the terrace. You're pale. You need some fresh air."

"Terrace?"

He chuckled. "More of a small balcony. But it does have an ocean view. Maybe your head will clear a little. Coming?"

She stared at his hand, then got up without taking it, fussing with the robe to cover her reluctance to have physical contact with him. If he noticed her hesitation, he didn't show it. Instead, he walked to the glass-paned door next to the refrigerator, opened it, then stepped aside.

Walking through it, she found herself on a small concrete balcony, about fifteen feet wide, just enough room to hold a small ice-cream table, two wrought-iron chairs and a padded recliner.

The day was warm without being hot and there was a nice, gentle breeze that felt more like spring than autumn. From somewhere nearby came the smell of frying onions. She could hear the deep bass sound of hip-hop from a far-off radio. And, indeed, there did seem to be a view of the ocean. It was all fuzzy, of course, as she didn't have her glasses. But she was able to see a broad expanse of pale blue sky, with soft clouds scudding by, and white dots in the distance that might have been sails.

"Want to stretch out?" Nick indicated the lounge chair.

"No, thank you." Carly perched on the edge of one of the ice-cream chairs. "I'll be more comfortable here."

She thought he'd sit down too, across the table from her as he had before, interrogation-style. Instead, he leaned his back against the balcony railing, his arms crossed over his chest, and faced her. She was in the shade, but he was in full sunlight. The tanned olive tones of his shirtless upper torso seemed to soak up light, turning him into a bronze-gold god even as shadows outlined the harsh contours of his face.

Power. That's what he represented. Both professionally and personally. The ability to punish. The physical and mental strength to crush her. She shivered as quick memories of their night together flashed in her mind. Slick, naked bodies thrashing wildly on the bed, his biceps bulging as he supported himself on his hands, his mouth all over her, no part of her body left unmarked by his touch. She shivered again, not quite sure exactly why. With Nick, there seemed to be such a fine line between menace and sensuality, between fear and sexual attraction.

A cop, she thought once again. Of all things. She stiffened her spine, telling herself that she was a grown woman and could get through whatever she needed to get through.

"Let's do it this way," Nick said. "We'll start at the bar. I'll tell you what I remember, and you tell me if you remember it, too. You came in around midnight. You sat down on a bar stool. A guy hit on you, some creep with a beer belly and a beard—"

"—and sweaty hands." Carly shivered. "I remember. He was awful. I felt like I was being sized up for white slavery."

"And that's when I came to the rescue," he said mockingly.

Peering up at him, she studied his face as objectively as possible. "Yes. I remember your face, coming out of a blur, getting closer."

He uncrossed his arms and spread his hands on the balcony rail. "You're nearsighted, aren't you?"

"Uh-huh. I can see you, but behind you, everything starts to get blurry."

"Why don't you wear glasses?"

"I do. I don't know where they are."

"I see. So it's not because you're vain. Did you have them on at dinner with Richard?"

"Yes. I always wear my glasses. And," she protested, "I'm not in the least bit vain."

His mouth quirked up. "All right then. We talked at the bar. You wanted to go to sleep."

"Yes, I was so tired." Carly rubbed her eyelids. "Would you mind moving out of the sunlight? It's too bright."

"Oh. Sorry." He sank onto the edge of the lounge chair, elbows on knees, his hands clasped loosely between his legs. "So then I offered my place for the night."

"Really? And I went? I mean, that's a pretty stupid thing to do, isn't it?"

"Yeah. But you seemed not to be bothered by my offer. Also, I promised to keep my hands off you."

"And I actually believed you?"

He grinned. "Hey, I meant it."

"If you say so," she said doubtfully. "Then what?"

"And then we walked over here."

Closing her eyes, which seemed to help her concentration, she tried to put herself in the picture Nick was describing. Amazingly enough, some of it did come back to her. "On some sort of boardwalk." She nodded as more bits of memory took shape. "People rushing by. Someone laughing, a woman. A strong ocean smell—fishy. Sirens, I think."

"Yes. A patrol car passed us heading north. Probably some ruckus at one of the restaurants. You're doing great, see?"

"It's still in bits and pieces. So, we're walking. What happened next?"

"We got here and you passed out on my bed."

She tried to picture it but couldn't. "That part's fuzzy. But I think…later, I remember a couch."

"That was much later, when you showed up in the living room and said I should make love to you."

Her eyes snapped open, then she winced at the all-too-vivid memory. "I guess I was...naked?"

"Yes, ma'am." He grinned.

"And...pretty insistent?"

"Yes, ma'am."

Sighing loudly, Carly shook her head. "I'm so sorry."

"I'm the furthest thing from sorry you can imagine."

Nick shifted a little on the lounge chair, bringing his knees closer together to hide what was happening to his body. Damned if Carly wasn't getting to him again, and he was responding in the usual, age-old manner—again—the way men's bodies always did. Amazing. After the exhausting workout of the previous night, he wanted her again. Right now, right here on his terrace under the blue California sky. Back off, he told himself. The woman is half out of her mind with her own troubles and doesn't need any more hassles. Still...what a shame.

Anyhow, he believed her.

Of course, he reminded himself, his gut had let him down before. Especially where women were concerned. They had a habit of running out on him. His mother, when he was six. And Lenore. His ex-wife had had the face of a Girl Scout and the soul of a con; she'd wrapped him around her finger, then taken off with all their savings. No, when it came to his gut instinct about women, Nick had learned to ignore it.

Carly's hands were steepled in front of her mouth and she seemed to be thinking about something. Finally, she let her hands drop to her lap and smiled shyly at him. "I suppose I should thank you. For rescuing me. I *do* thank you, really."

The sweetness of her expression tugged at him, but he waved away her apology with his hand. "Don't. It had less to do with me being a noble guy than with the way you looked when you walked into the bar."

"How did I look?"

"Sexy as hell. The dress was a knockout. It had half the guys in the place drooling."

"What dress?"

"You don't remember?"

"No." Her expression said she expected bad news. "Am I going to hate this?"

"Could be." He got up, strode into the bedroom and managed to find the dress among the rumpled bedclothes. When he returned to the balcony, Carly was sitting there as though she hadn't moved, that same almost comical look of dread on her face. Tossing her the garment, he resettled himself on the lounge and watched her.

Slowly, she picked up the dress and held it in front of her. Her mouth dropped open, then she snapped it shut. "Oh, my." She turned to gaze at him with a look of pure wonder. "I was wearing this?"

"Absolutely."

"But, this isn't a dress. It's more like a…oh, what do they call them? A slip-dress, with a built-in push-up bra. Like in the *Victoria's Secret* catalog. But…I would never buy a dress like this. I'd be too uncomfortable. I mean—"

"I know what you mean. But that's what you were wearing. What did you have on when you met Richard for dinner?"

Clutching the dress to her chest, she thought for a moment. "My blue silk suit. A white blouse. A blue and green scarf." She looked around her. "Where's my purse?"

"You didn't have one last night. This—" he reached over and fingered the hem of the dress "—this was all there was. I take that back. There was one other piece of clothing, a pair of silk, uh, panties, very tiny. But I don't see them right now. Probably mixed in with the blankets somewhere."

Setting the dress on the ice-cream table, Carly got up, turning her back on Nick while she faced the view off the balcony rather than look at him. Embarrassment warred with an odd sense of unreality. It was all too fantastic, too strange. Surely, soon, someone would snap their fingers and she would awaken from this nightmare.

She gazed sightlessly on what she assumed was the harbor, with its blurry outlines of boats and people. "So," she said carefully, "I have no purse, which means no credit cards, no money, no ID, no glasses. And a dress I wouldn't be caught dead in. What do I do now? Pray?"

"Go to the police, of course. It's the smart thing to do. I'll—"

"No!" She whipped around to face him; then, to cover her too-strong reaction, she tried a halfhearted smile. "I mean, why go to all that trouble? Let's see what I—what we—can find out…" It hit her suddenly. Richard! She'd hate to think he had anything to do with this, but he might know something. It was a start. "Nick, may I use your phone?"

"Sure."

"It's long distance, but I'll pay you back."

He smiled, as though amused by her good manners. "Whatever."

Apparently, Nick found her entertaining. At the moment, Carly didn't care. Fired with purpose, she went through the door into the kitchen, snatched up the portable phone lying on the counter and punched in the numbers. Richard's phone rang, then his machine picked up, announcing that he was unavailable and to leave a message.

"Richard. It's Carly. I need to talk to you, and it's really important. I'm in California. I'm at— May I give him this number?" she called out to Nick.

He ambled into the kitchen, holding the flimsy dress in his hand. "Sure."

After reading the numbers off the phone, she pressed the off button, then stood there, thinking about what to do next. As though he could divine her thoughts, Nick said, "Anyone else you can call? Parents?"

She shook her head, still trying to come up with her next

move. "Dead. One elderly aunt who would have a heart attack if I told her a story like this."

"Friends?" He propped a hip against the counter and crossed his arms.

He seemed so large again, and she felt so small, so intimidated, standing next to him. Some of her sense of purpose faded in his presence, so she moved away, still carrying the portable phone. "I guess I could call Margie, my friend. Oh, that's right, she's in Europe. But she's due back today. I was going to go with her, but I couldn't afford it. Boy, do I wish I had." She nodded, feeling more confident now, again determined to take action. "I'll leave word for her, and maybe she'll know something, although I don't know what." She sighed. "I wish I could just close my eyes and have the whole thing gone."

"All of it?"

She could tell by the deliberate way he used the phrase that he was recalling the previous night, which made her recall the previous night, too. Despite her best efforts to resist him, she met his green-eyed stare. It seemed to penetrate to her very core and sent a delicious warmth spreading all through her. It was distracting. She had to fight him, had to resist the sudden feeling of sensual helplessness this man aroused in her.

"No, not all of it," she said candidly, then hugged the phone to her chest for protection. "But I'd be really grateful if we could switch the subject for now. It confuses me."

He didn't respond immediately; instead, he kept his gaze on her. It was powerful, hypnotic. She thought he was going to ignore her request by taking the two steps that would put him right in front of her, that would make him close enough to put his arms around her, to kiss her.

And the crazy thing was, she wanted him to. Or, her body did. Her mind wanted no such thing.

"Nick," she said weakly, but as the word came out of her mouth, he put his hand up to stop her.

"You're right." He nodded. "First things first. Look, I'll

hop in the shower while you call your friend. I'll leave an old pair of sweats on the bed for you to wear." One side of his mouth quirked up again. "Unless you'd rather wear the dress."

She shuddered. "Definitely not. But then what?"

He pushed himself away from the counter and headed for the door to the living room. "We'll go down to the station, get the wheels in motion."

"I'd rather not." It came out sounding too emphatic, and she knew it.

He stopped in his tracks and turned to face her, one black eyebrow cocked. "Hey, are you wanted for something, Carly? Do you have a record?"

"Of course not," she said indignantly.

"Then what's the problem?"

Jail cells. Bars. Locked doors. No way of getting out. Endless terror.

She fumbled for a reply. "I just meant my memory seems to be coming back in little bits and pieces. Maybe I'll remember everything soon. You know, maybe there's a perfectly innocent explanation—" She cut herself off before finishing the sentence. How silly, how utterly lame she sounded. Innocent? In that dress? With "tiny" panties the only undergarment? With masses of bombshell-blond hair?

She gripped the edge of the counter with one hand as the panic threatened to overtake her again. What had happened to her in those two days? Where in God's name had she been?

Nick strode over to her and placed his hands on her shoulders. His grip was gentle but firm. "Carly, the reason we're going to the station is because they have computers there. We can find out if anyone's reported you missing, or if your purse has turned up. Nothing major, I promise. Then we should probably go to the hospital, get you a blood test, find out just what kind of drug you were given and if there's anything to worry about. It's the smartest thing to do, trust me."

Carly stared up at him. Trust him? Trust a cop?

Still, she had to admit, he had a point. When something like this happened, the logical move was to report it to the police. That's what most people would do. Short of asking for a miracle, in which her memory would return in one swift instant—and dreading what she might find out if it did—it didn't seem as though she had a lot of choice.

"All right," she agreed reluctantly.

"Good." He squeezed her shoulders, then dropped his hands and headed off again. "Give me ten minutes to shower and shave."

Dispiritedly, Carly lifted the phone and punched in Margie's number. Her machine answered, so Carly left word for her, too, to call her back at Nick's. Then she walked slowly into the bedroom.

On the bed was a pair of bright purple sweats, with the logo Beavis Butts Heads written in white across the chest. She had to smile—how totally absurd. But then, this whole morning had been absurd, hadn't it? She picked up the clothes. They were clean and well-worn. Without thinking, she buried her face in the shirt, breathing deeply. It smelled of Nick. If she allowed herself, she could get lost again in the memory of the night before with him. But she couldn't, not now.

When she put on the outfit, the sweatshirt came down to mid-thigh, and she was able to roll up the bottoms above her ankles. Not too terrible, she thought, squinting into the mirror over his bureau. If you favored lost-looking waifs with questionable clothes sense.

No shoes, of course. She would have to do something about that. And she sure wished she had her glasses. She was okay for one-on-one talking to people, but beyond five or six feet, objects got increasingly hazy.

Sitting on the edge of the bed, she glanced around the bedroom for the first time in daylight—with all that had happened, she hadn't really seen it. The walls were white and almost bare, the few pieces of furniture were plain dark wood. Like the kitchen, there wasn't a lot of personality to the decorating.

But the bed was huge, taking up half the space. A brass headboard offered the only brightness in the room. It looked as though Nick had bought it all from a catalog or a showroom. Functional, without any homey touches.

Carly thought of her modest apartment back home. Its walls were packed with colorful prints and nature photographs. Each piece of furniture had been handpicked at secondhand stores and refinished by her on her days off. Chairs and couches were overstuffed, there were flowers everywhere, both on the fabrics and in vases. She was a homebody, and she'd made the place into a kind of nest, the first safe, real home she'd ever had. The sudden yearning to be there, and not here, rose in her chest and practically overwhelmed her.

"Stop it!" she said aloud. No. She would not give in to self-pity.

She heard the sound of the shower being turned on. Nick was in the bathroom, about to step into the tub. She started to picture his hand pulling aside the curtain, his tall, muscular, tan, *naked* body, lifting his leg—

Uh-uh, she told herself. Stop that. Out of the bedroom. Now.

She wandered into the living room and noticed a tied and folded newspaper on the coffee table. Yes, she thought. Get your mind off your troubles. Read about the world and *its* troubles. Much bigger troubles than hers.

Dropping onto the couch, she unfolded the thick Sunday *Los Angeles Times* to the front page. Her gaze roamed the headlines: an earthquake aftershock, a political scandal, a lottery winner. In the far right-hand column, under the title Late Breaking News, she read, Drug King Found Dead, then,

Peter "Pete" Skouras Demeter, reputed head of a worldwide drug syndicate, was found dead on his yacht in Marina del Rey shortly after midnight Sunday morning. He had been shot three times in the head...

Demeter? The name rang a bell.

The article went on, but Carly found her eyes drifting lower on the page to a picture of the dead man. It was a studio portrait of a male with swarthy skin and thinning dark hair. The smile on his face seemed more sinister than joyous.

As Carly stared at the picture, she felt suddenly dizzy; with her head swirling, she closed her eyes. An image came to her.

The same man is lying on a wooden floor. Half his head is blown away, while blood pools all around him.

Chapter 3

The panic started up all over again. She could feel it rising through her bloodstream, making her want to scream, to tear at her hair, anything to loosen the tight knot of nerve endings that seemed to define her very being.

A dead man. She'd seen a dead man.

Or had she? Had she made it all up? Maybe she was hallucinating as a result of whatever drug she'd been given. That was a reasonable explanation—wasn't it? Her mind sought refuge in the concept, but her senses told her no. The picture in her head, with all the details, was all too real. Somehow, sometime, she'd seen this man, this Peter Demeter, dead, in a pool of blood.

But when? Carly closed her eyes again, trying to summon more details, such as what had gone before the picture, or after, or anything. But the sound of her own blood pounding in her ears was too strong. It drowned out all other noises, all other pictures.

She splayed her hand over her chest, as though its touch could actually calm her rapidly beating heart. *Think,* she told herself. If this image was of a real event, if she'd actually seen this man dead, then she had to have been there, either when he was killed or shortly after. She grabbed the newspaper and read the rest of the article. They'd found him on his yacht just after midnight; the neighboring boat owner had heard shots and summoned the police.

Nick had told her she'd come into the bar around midnight. So, Carly must have been on this yacht, must have been at the scene of a murder minutes before wandering into the bar. How and why, she had no idea. Her brain wouldn't release any more pictures, no matter how hard she tried. Richard and dinner Friday night, then nothing until the image of a murdered man late Saturday night.

After which she had slept with a total stranger.

She almost laughed out loud, but held it back. *And I used to wish for something interesting to happen to me,* she thought. She'd been granted her wish. In spades.

She looked at the article again, but there were no other details. If she'd been on the boat, there must be traces of her still there. Would they find her fingerprints? Her purse? Her glasses? Maybe even her clothes, the suit she had worn to dinner with Richard?

Richard. Where was he? He hadn't called back yet. Had he had a part in this? He'd always made such a mess of his life. What in God's name had he involved her in now?

Murder, it seemed.

Who had killed Peter Demeter? Not Carly, she knew that. But…how did she know?

Her mind, her basic nature, rebelled at the thought of shooting anyone. She balked at killing moths, for heaven's sake. But then, she'd thought herself incapable of going to bed with a stranger, hadn't she?

What she needed was more information.… She snapped her fingers. Of course. The television. There was one on the opposite wall. She'd find a news station.

Just as she was about to get up to turn it on, she heard the shower in the bathroom stop. Reality hit her with the cold clarity of an ice pack. Nick. She was in Nick's apartment. Nick, who had said he would help her, get all this cleared up.

Nick...who was a cop.

Nick, who was about to come out of the bathroom all dressed and ready to accompany her to the police station. If she told him what she'd just remembered, she was done for. His impression of her would change from amnesiac bed partner to a woman who was involved—somehow—in a murder. Nick had said he'd help her, but that was before. If she told him any of this, he'd turn her in. He'd have to, it would be his duty.

Run, she told herself. *Move.* Now!

As though being chased by demons, Carly vaulted up from the couch and dashed to the front door, but stopped before she got there. Money. She'd have to have some money. Running into the bedroom, she glanced at the top of the dresser, then at the table on Nick's side of the bed. Men always dumped out the contents of their pockets before they took off their pants.

Sure enough, there they were—wallet, keys, money. She grabbed some bills and change, dumped them into a rumpled cocktail napkin lying next to the lamp, debated quickly with herself, then opened Nick's wallet and took one of his credit cards. After stuffing everything in the pocket of her sweats, she reached for a nearby notepad. "Nick," she scribbled, "I'm sorry. Will return everything." Then, still barefoot, she dashed out the door of Nick's condo, into the bright California sunshine.

After using his towel to rub a circle in the steam-drenched mirror, Nick took a moment to check his appearance. His face was clean-shaven, his hair still tousled from towel-drying it. He noticed a few scratches on his shoulders and back, souvenirs of the night before. He smiled. The scratches didn't hurt. Hell, they weren't even very deep. Even in the depths of passion, Carly hadn't actually caused him any pain. Now, having spent time with her this morning, he knew why.

She was one of those basically gentle types, innocent about the dark side of human nature, or, at least, the dark side of her own nature. It had been that innocence he'd picked up on the night before, that had drawn him to her in a protective fashion.

The smile left his face as he felt anger building toward the scum who had set her up. Because that's what had happened, he was sure of it now. She'd been the victim of some kind of vicious stunt. Probably initiated by that ex of hers.

Just what had happened, Nick had no way of knowing, not yet. Had she been raped? There hadn't been any bruises on her pale skin, no redness or signs of violence on her thighs or between her legs. In fact, when he'd entered her that first time, she'd been real tight. Like it had been a while since anyone had been in the vicinity.

As though it were on automatic pilot, his body responded to the memory of that first time. He shook his head ruefully. Innocent or not, Carly sure got his blood up. But he had to use the organ between his ears right now, instead of the one below his waist. She needed him.

All right, he thought, pulling up his briefs. Not raped—he hoped—but kidnapped and dressed up as a sex toy. Had she been involved in a cheap party trick? A trophy in some sort of game? Or had Richard sought revenge, a cruel payback for divorcing him?

Nick knew nothing about the guy except his first name. Was her last name—Terry, she'd said—his, or had she gone back to her maiden name? There was a hell of a lot about the lady he didn't know.

But he sure didn't like anyone taking advantage of innocence. His jaw clenched as he pictured what he'd do to whoever was responsible for this. Quietly. In an alley. Good thing he was temporarily out of uniform, because if he was still on active duty he'd have to be more careful about how he taught the guy a lesson. But a lesson he would learn, one he'd never forget.

Nodding with satisfaction, Nick whistled as he pulled on his jeans. He'd brought his clothes into the bathroom with him so as not to embarrass Carly by parading nude in front of her. He found himself chuckling at the thought. Modesty *after* the fact. Great, no-holds-barred sex, then behaving with politeness, as though it hadn't happened. But it was something he was glad to do for her. He liked her, believed her, too.

And that strong chemistry between them was still there. He knew it and she knew it. Even with her freshly scrubbed face and the rest of her covered up totally by that robe of his, she'd turned him on. A couple of times this morning their eyes had locked; he was pretty sure he could have taken her right back to bed.

Lots of time, he told himself. They'd get this memory-loss thing behind them, then he'd convince her to take a week's vacation so the two of them could play. Good plan, he told the mirror. One of his better ones.

After pulling his polo shirt over his head, Nick opened the bathroom door. "Carly?" he called out, then looked around. She wasn't in the bedroom, so he strode into the living room. "Carly? Where are you?"

Probably out on the balcony, he thought. It was a great day—lots of sun, no smog. After he took her down to the station and they filed a report, maybe they'd go for a drive. He could show her the coastline with its harbors and sailboats and water-skiers. The dolphins might be playing close to shore today; she'd like that. Maybe they'd stop off somewhere later for a drink and dinner. He had the day off from the bar, and Kyle, the owner, was due back tomorrow, so his temp job was over. Nick was free for a while. Free to be with Carly.

Whistling, he walked out onto the balcony.

She wasn't there. He frowned. Not on the balcony, not in the kitchen or the living room or the bedroom. Was she lying somewhere, behind the couch or on the other side of the bed where he couldn't see her? Had she fainted? She'd been under a lot of strain.

Worried, he tore through his small condo, but no Carly, anywhere. Something was wrong. He glanced at his wrist to check the time, but didn't have his watch on. He grabbed it from the bedside table. As he was buckling the leather strap, his eye fell on the note. He picked it up then read it.

"Son of a bitch."

Carly had taken off, with his money and wearing his clothes. She was sorry. She would return everything.

Right.

And pigs flew.

The first thing she did was to find a drugstore and get a pair of cheap rubber thongs—$5.99, plus tax. She glanced around nervously as she paid the cashier. It would be nice if she could see clearly; since leaving Nick's place, she'd had this creepy feeling, like someone was watching her. But, with her poor eyesight, how would she know?

She considered trying to find one of those one-hour eyeglass places, but she didn't have her prescription, and they would have to get it from her eye doctor in Hull and it was Sunday. Besides, she didn't have enough money, and Nick's credit card was for a true emergency only. So, she'd just have to make do with squinting. She could see far enough in front of her to avoid tripping or running into anyone, she assured herself, and with all the other things in her life to worry about at that moment, not seeing clearly was something she'd just have to live with.

When she came out of the drugstore, she looked up and down the street, but no one who resembled Nick was anywhere in sight. Still, she couldn't shake an inner voice warning her to be on guard. Maybe some of this was the aftereffects of whatever drug she'd been given, but when a man brushed past her, she almost jumped out of her skin as he muttered, "Sorry." Leaning against a display window, her hand over her racing heart, she told herself she simply had to stop this panicked reaction to every sudden movement. She *had* to.

She started walking. She always thought better on the move; it was as if her brain got more oxygen. Think, she ordered her mind, as it seemed she'd been ordering it to do all morning. What should her next move be?

Instead of an answer, all she got were more questions about the night before. How had she wound up on the yacht? And had she run away from the bloody scene? If so, the bar must have been nearby, because without shoes she wouldn't have gone far. And Nick's condo was a short distance from there. Should she go back to the bar? Try to jog her memory by finding out where Demeter's yacht was?

Not a smart move, for heaven's sake. She had to avoid being anywhere near the murder scene. What she needed to do was get as far away from Marina del Rey as possible, so Nick wouldn't find her.

A kid on in-line skates passed her and called out, "Great shirt!"

"Thanks," Carly said automatically, then stopped and stood in place for a moment. There it was again, that feeling of being followed. She whipped around suddenly, but the skater was already down the block, and all she could see was a blur of faces, many of them, strolling, hurrying, jogging. If someone was following her, and was keeping more than ten feet back from her, she had no way of knowing.

She had no way of knowing a lot of things; she had blacked out several important hours in her life. What she felt was helplessness. Utter helplessness. And alone, so alone.

Stay on the main streets, she told herself. Keep moving. If someone was after her—and who knew, she might be so paranoid at the moment, she could be imagining the whole thing— she was safe in crowds. Wasn't she?

A bus drove by and pulled up half a block away. She ran toward it. She would ride it to wherever it led, until she felt safe. From Nick, anyway. She wouldn't actually feel safe, she was sure, for a long, long time.

The only other person to get on the bus with her was a blowsy-looking woman wearing an L.A. Dodgers cap. Carly breathed a sigh of relief and settled herself into a seat by the window.

The bus route took her through winding streets and onto a main thoroughfare. Carly tried to concentrate on the blurred view from the window, past shops and palm trees, people in shorts and summer clothes strolling and laughing. Back home it was autumn and an early frost had hit. It had been snowing for the past week, the skies gray, the daylight dim. Here, it was all bright sun; here, it seemed to be perpetual summer.

Half his face shot off. Pool of blood.

The image kept coming back to her, like some kind of visual tune you couldn't get out of your head. But nothing else, no associated memories. Just the picture, as if she'd taken a snapshot and kept bringing it out from some photo album in her mind. She tried to shut it out, tried to focus as best she could on the scenery. After a while, the bus pulled up to a stop right next to a sign that read, in giant letters, "TELEVISIONS!!!!" and another underneath, "HUGE SALE!!!"

That's right, she'd been about to turn on the TV at Nick's place, to get more information about Pete Demeter's murder. A murder like this would be on all the local stations, she was sure. They always latched on to anything sensational in their own backyards. She hopped off the bus and went into the store.

It was a small space, with twenty or so television sets in the whole place, all of them tuned to football games. The store was poorly lit, and it seemed to Carly the whole thing could use vacuuming and dusting.

The only other person there was a portly man in a white short-sleeved shirt who stood in front of one of the sets, intent on the game.

Carly approached him. "Excuse me?"

"Yeah?" he said without looking at her. "Offside, you jerk!" he yelled at the picture tube. "The ref's blind!"

"Um, pardon me—"

The man wheeled around with such a look of angry impatience, she leaped backward automatically. "What?" he said sharply.

"Are you the salesman?" She hated how timid she sounded, but she had never done well with being yelled at.

"No, he's on a break. I'm just watching the store." He returned to his game. "Come back in ten minutes."

"Well, then, do you mind if I switch the channel on one of the sets?"

"Lady, I don't care what you do."

She walked to the TV farthest from the man and punched both the up and down buttons, trying to find some news. All she got was football, ice hockey, figure skating, a program about fish hatcheries, but no news.

"Excuse me?" she called out.

"What?"

"Where is the news? CNN? Anything like that?"

He dragged his attention away from the game and came over to her. "Listen, you want cable you gotta pay for it. You buying a set or planning on living here?"

"No, I-I'm sorry," she stammered. "I just want to see the news."

"Go buy a paper then. Got it?"

Weren't the people in California supposed to be nicer than this? she wondered, walking toward the front of the store. Then she stopped. If she was being followed, she needed to take precautions. Edging around the perimeter of the store, hoping the rude man was wrapped up in his game, she headed toward the back, through a storeroom, and out into an alleyway.

A deserted alleyway, from what she could tell, filled with garbage cans and empty cartons. And the smell of rotting food. She glanced both ways, trying to decide her direction, then arbitrarily chose right. Not pleased to be alone in an alley, even in broad daylight, she picked up speed as she walked, then broke into a full run.

Suddenly, she stumbled over something and slammed into a garbage pail, managing to right herself before falling. Looking around for what had caused her to trip, she let out a scream. A filthy man in tattered clothes, obviously napping between the garbage cans, sat up. He gave off a powerful unwashed odor. The man smiled at her; his teeth were cracked and rotten. She'd tripped on his feet.

"Sorry," Carly said, backing away in the opposite direction. "So sorry," she said again. Then she started running, and she kept on running for as long as she could.

Nick drained the last of his beer and set the bottle on the bar. "Eileen? Same way."

The day bartender, a happily married mother of five who could have passed for twenty-six, grinned at him as she brought out another cold one and pushed it down the length of the counter toward him. "Feeling the heat, are you, Nick?"

"You could say that. Damn," he cursed, his eyes glued on the overhead TV in the corner. "Shoulda gone for the field goal. Damn rookies, always hotdogging it."

"I don't know," came a voice from the bar stool next to him. "Looked like a judgment call to me."

Nick wheeled around, ready to give the guy a lesson in strategy, but grinned instead. "Dominic!" He clapped his friend on the back. "Hey. Where you been?"

"Glad I found you here. I took a chance."

"What are you drinking?"

"Same as you. And—" Dom indicated the young man on the stool behind him "—another one for Miguel here."

"Eileen, two more," Nick called out, then pivoted his stool to face Dominic D'Annunzio.

Dom, who was a little shorter and stockier than Nick, with the black hair and brown eyes of his southern Italian ancestry, worked for the L.A. County Sheriff's Department. He and Nick had struck up a friendship a few years back, when the Manhattan Beach P.D. had called in L.A.S.D. for help on a homicide. The two men had found they had a lot in common, including the fact that they were the same age, shared a passion for beach volleyball and being cops, and were annoyed by strict adherence to proper police procedures.

"Nick, meet Miguel," Dom said, his Brooklyn roots strong in his accent. He leaned back so the two men could shake hands. "I've told you about Miguel, Nick. I'm the kid's Big Brother, you know, for like ten years."

"Oh, yeah. Hi, Miguel." The young man was twenty or so, slender and olive-skinned, but his grip was strong.

"And," Dom went on, "he has this dumb idea of being a cop. I keep telling him it's hero worship and he'll get over it. But he tells me I'm wrong. So, I need you to talk him out of it. You're better with explaining things than I am." He angled his head to grin wickedly at Miguel. "Nick's my hero. Strange dude, but okay. And he knows how things work."

"Stuff it," Nick said good-naturedly.

"Yeah, ol' Nick's like a teacher, makes you want to listen. So, tell Miguel, Nick, about being a cop."

"You mean about how most of us have a death wish, and about the alcohol stats and the divorce rate?"

Dom grinned. "Yeah. And how it ain't for anyone who goes to museums, like Miguel here likes to do."

"Hey, Dom, knock it off," Miguel said with a sheepish face.

Nick joined in Dom's laughter. But what Nick had said about police work was true, and the two older men knew it. Men and women who were too "sensitive" rarely made the cut at the academy. If things got under your skin too easily, you couldn't tolerate the violence and cruelty that went with a cop's life. Violence and cruelty were ninety percent of what they saw on the job.

Nick was glad to sit here at Morgan R's, glad to shoot the

breeze with Dom and Miguel, answer a couple of questions for the kid, give him some pointers. Back when he was on the job, he'd always liked working with rookies. It was probably his rescue thing again—the new ones were so cocky, but so damned innocent—but he was often assigned to help them along.

Yeah, Nick was glad to sit here and drink beer and watch the games. Glad to talk about the Demeter murder, which was all over the news. It had probably been a mob hit, and Dom and he tossed around some names of possible wise-guy shooters.

Nick was glad to do anything except think or talk about Carly. If Dom, or any of the other guys on the force knew he'd been two-elevened by a lady he'd spent the night with, he'd never live it down.

So, he wasn't going to think about Carly and last night and how, once again, a woman had turned his head inside out and told him pretty lies, then had ripped off his money and walked away. If he thought about that, he'd get really p.o.'d, and there was no telling what he'd do then. He gulped down half the bottle of beer. Nah. She wasn't worth thinking about. He would consider the twenty or thirty bucks payment for services rendered and forget about her.

"Come on," he told Dom and Miguel. "Let's get us a table and do some serious drinking."

Carly sat at the phone booth and gazed dispiritedly out the glass windows as people came and went at the hotel's circular auto entrance. She'd been trying to reach both Margie and Richard all afternoon, without success. She'd found some news at a Sports Deli, but learned nothing more about the murder. She'd also bought a candy bar, had taken another bus and was now at a hotel on Ocean Avenue in Santa Monica. It was five o'clock in the afternoon and she was so tired her brain wasn't functioning—except to realize that she had seventeen dollars left and absolutely no idea what to do next.

On an impulse, she picked up the phone and punched in Nick's number, managing to remember it from this morning. His phone rang, but there was no answer. When his machine came on, she replaced the receiver. A feeling of emptiness washed over her.

Nick. He'd been with her, on the edges of her mind, all day. She remembered everything about him—his hard exterior, that occasional glimpse of compassion in his eyes, the way he made her feel as a woman.

He must be furious with her, might even have reported her to the police for stealing his money and credit card. What a fool she was.

She glanced down at the change spread out on the phone table and at the cocktail napkin she'd grabbed from Nick's bedside table. Morgan R's, it said on one corner in bright red letters. Restaurant and Bar, Marina del Rey, California. Was that the bar she'd met Nick in last night? She picked up the napkin and stared at the name again. A phone number was printed there. Without giving herself time to think, she lifted the receiver, dropped two dimes in the slot and punched in the number of Morgan R's.

Nick, now at a table with Dom and Miguel, on which was littered several empty bottles of Sam Adams and vacant peanut shells, was explaining to the kid how his knee had gotten smashed to bits by a crook's bullet. "And the docs keep telling me it'll never heal all the way. But they don't know who they're talking to. I'm going to prove the docs wrong. Hey, Dom," Nick said with a grin, "you keep eating those peanuts, you're going to turn into an elephant."

Dom broke open another shell. "Can't help it. I really miss my cigarettes."

"Let that be another lesson to you, Miguel," Nick said, aware he was slurring his words, but not giving a damn. "Don't start, then you don't have to stop."

"Screw yourself," Dom said good-naturedly.

"Hey, Nick," Eileen called out. "Phone for you."

He glanced up at the bartender. "Who is it?"

"One of your lady friends."

Nick sent the two men a smirk and rose unsteadily to his feet. His knee gave out and, wincing, he held on to the chair until he could regain his balance. Damn. After three operations, and with all the exercises and physical therapy, couldn't the stupid thing work right yet? Cursing softly and weaving slightly—how many beers had he had? Five? Six? More?—he went around to the other side of the bar and grabbed the receiver.

"Yeah?" he said, not in the mood to be nice to anyone at this moment. Damn knee. It was screwing up his life and he wasn't happy about it.

"Nick?"

He knew her voice right away and he went still.

"Nick? It's Carly."

"Carly who?" he said deliberately.

There was a long pause. "I...I know you must be angry at me," she said finally.

"Now, why would I be angry at you?"

"Did you read the note? I said I'd pay you back. And I will, Nick, I promise. I'll need to get your address, of course. I don't know why I took the credit card—"

"Credit card?" Frowning, Nick fished around in his pocket for his wallet. When he opened it, he saw the empty slot where his Visa usually was.

"Oh, God," she was saying. "You mean you didn't know? I'm sorry. I won't use it, but I just thought, you know, in case—"

"You stole my credit card, too?"

That was it. The last straw. Now he was out for blood. "It wasn't enough that you told me a cock-and-bull story. 'Trust me, Nick'—" he parodied a high-pitched woman's voice "—'I don't know how I got here,' and 'I'm lost, I can't remember anything.' No, then you run out with my money and my credit card and you're sorry?''

He was shouting now, and several customers looked up from their drinks and conversations to stare at him. He turned his back to the crowd and continued more quietly, but just as intensely. "Look, idiot that I am, I didn't report the money, but if you stole my credit card, too—''

"So, you haven't reported it?'' Carly interrupted. She'd been wincing under the barrage of Nick's angry words, but now she leaned back in the seat with relief. One load off her mind—no one was hunting for her. For theft, anyway. "Oh, thank you, thank you, Nick. As soon as I can, I'll mail back the card and the money and everything. You have my word.''

"I have your *what?''* His tone dripped sarcasm. "Your word, you said? What do you think I am? A moron?''

She flinched again at the hostility in his voice, but she knew she owed him an explanation. "Nick, I...I'm in trouble. There are things going on, things I can't talk about—''

"What things?'' he barked.

Through the glass window, Carly watched as a van pulled up to the auto entrance. On its side, painted with large enough letters for her to read was written AIRPORT SHUTTLE. Airport, she thought. She needed to get to the airport. Now. So she could go home. Home, where it was familiar. Safe. No palm trees, no yachts, no murders. No ambivalent attractions and messy emotions.

"Carly?'' Nick drew her attention back to the phone call.

"I have to go now,'' she said quickly. "I want you to know that I'll always be grateful. You saved my life. I'm...I wish... Goodbye.''

She hated to do that, hated to leave him like that, but really, she had no choice. She hung up and without allowing herself to think again, called an airline and used Nick's credit card to make a reservation on the next flight to Boston.

By the time she got outside, the shuttle had left, but a taxi driver said the ride to the airport would cost about twelve dollars, so she got into the cab. Rap music was playing softly on the radio. "Would you mind putting on the news station?" she asked him.

Without answering, the driver punched in a button. A traffic report came on, with all kinds of freeway numbers and names that were totally unfamiliar to her. Then, after a few minutes of listening to sports scores, she was rewarded.

"Authorities are still keeping mum about the murder of underworld figure Pete Demeter, late last night on his Marina del Rey yacht. So far, all police will say is that some articles of women's clothing were found on board, but further details were not released. What is known is that Demeter had, since the death of his wife, Amanda, become a near recluse on his boat."

Amanda.

"Police are asking anyone who might have information to call…"

Amanda. Nick had called her Amanda this morning. Carly stared at the back of the taxi driver's head. Somewhere in her mind, new images were forming, floating, waiting for her. "Amanda…Amanda" played like a melody inside her head, like some kind of audio flashback. When she closed her eyes, the picture followed right behind.

A sobbing man, kneeling on the floor in front of her, crying the name Amanda over and over again. Noise. Explosions. Carly is looking at her hand. In her hand is a gun. The man is lying down, half his face shot off, blood pooling all around him.

Just as abruptly as the image had come to her, it stopped right there again. She clasped her hands together, squeezing for dear life. She had been there, had been involved, had held the murder weapon in her hand, had…

No. She balked at the thought that she might have pulled the trigger. *No,* her mind screamed at her, even as she had to admit that, logically, it was all too possible that she was a murderer.

"Are we almost there?" she asked the driver, trying to keep her voice steady.

"Five more minutes."

She hardly dared breathe for the rest of the ride, paid him quickly when he pulled into the terminal and got out on the run. It was now five-thirty and her flight was at eight. Maybe there was an earlier one. She had to get away, get home, get safe.

There was a long line at the terminal ticket counter, but a sign indicated that people with reservations and without luggage could pick up their tickets at the gate. She couldn't make out her gate number on the overhead departures monitor, so had to ask someone to read it for her, then got directions from a skycap on which escalator to take to get there. Running through the crowded, bustling terminal and onto the moving ramps, she elbowed her way past everyone, up some stairs and reached her destination.

There was a line at the gate, too, but only three people. She got in place, willing those ahead of her to take care of their business quickly. She squinted up at the monitor again, trying to find an earlier flight, but without her glasses it was impossible, so she asked the man in front of her to read them to her. There was a six o'clock flight to Chicago.

Maybe she could get on that one and make a connection to Boston from there. Would that be the smart thing to do? She knew she wasn't thinking clearly, but was going on pure animal instinct to escape from danger. She *had* to get away from California.

She didn't hear him approach. He made no noise and no warning alarms went off in her head, until she felt something solid being rammed into her back and heard a whispered, "Not a word. I have a gun." She gasped, then stood very still while he went on. "Good. Now, quietly and quickly, I want you to turn to the right and walk away. Do not look around, just walk toward the escalator. Remember, I have a gun and I will use it."

Her thudding heart was in her throat. Almost afraid to breathe, she did as she was told, not looking back. She went down the escalator and stepped off at the bottom. The man was right behind her. Now he whispered, "Walk slowly on the floor between the moving ramps toward the exit. Try anything funny and I'll kill you."

Again, Carly did as she was told. She had no doubt he would do as he promised.

But her mind was working. Escape, she thought wildly. She had to escape. She shifted her glance from right to left, looking for something, anything, she could use to get free. Passengers moved in both directions on the ramp. By squinting, she could see that coming toward them was a small vehicle, either an airline maintenance vehicle or one of those carts that gave rides to passengers.

The man behind her nudged her to one side, to get them out of the vehicle's way. But Carly kept watching until she could make out the figures of two men in gray uniforms. She had to do this, and it had to be…now!

Surprising her captor—and herself—with her audacity, she stepped in the path of the vehicle, screamed and fell down to the ground, praying the man with the gun wouldn't be stupid enough to shoot her right there. The brakes squealed as the vehicle screeched to a halt. In moments, the walkway was filled with the sounds of the angry driver yelling at her and other pedestrians running up to help her.

She lay still for several heartbeats, but there was no gunshot. Allowing herself to be helped to her feet, and murmuring assurances that she was unhurt, Carly was just in time to see the back of a man as he pushed his way through the crowd. Her immediate impression was that he was short, no more than five-six, with brown hair. He wore a tan raincoat that seemed too long for him. He did turn once, and she might have imagined the waves of pure malevolence emanating from him, but she didn't think so. Then, like a scurrying rodent, he melted into the crowd.

Safe, she thought with a shudder. For the moment. And she'd had an admittedly nearsighted glimpse, more of an impression, of his face. Pale skin, high forehead.

As the people gathered around her asked if she was sure she was all right, Carly made a quick decision not to mention the man or the gun. That would involve the law, and she wasn't eager to deal with them.

She'd caught her rubber-soled thongs, she told the maintenance men, on something sticky. Again assuring everyone that she was fine, she thanked them all and headed back toward the gate. Now thoroughly out of breath, but with adrenaline roaring through her, she pushed past a small white-haired lady wearing a flowered dress. Murmuring apologies, Carly stood before the ticket attendant.

"I'm sorry, but I'm in a huge hurry. I have a reservation, under Holmes, but I need to change my flight."

The woman, all crisp efficiency in her uniform and short, no-nonsense hairdo, seemed annoyed. "I'm sorry, too. But you can't push ahead of someone else."

"It's all right," said the white-haired woman, raising her hand to indicate her acquiescence. "I have lots of time. You go on, dear."

Carly practically sobbed her thanks, then watched tensely while the pursed-mouthed attendant processed her ticket. "Did you check any luggage?" the woman asked.

"No. I don't have any."

"How are you paying?"

"Credit card." Carly placed it on the counter.

"ID, please."

"What?"

"I need to see a picture ID before I can process your ticket."

"Why?"

"It's the rule."

"Since when?"

The woman's eyes narrowed with suspicion. "It's been that way for a few years."

But Carly hated being enclosed in planes, and hadn't flown anywhere in eight years—not while she was conscious, anyway, she reminded herself bitterly. She sure hadn't expected this and was thrown by it.

"I'm afraid I lost my purse, so I don't have ID. I really need that ticket. Look at me." She tried to smile. "I'm not a criminal or anything. Please, give me the ticket." She was close to grabbing the woman by the uniform lapels. "Please."

A tall man in an official-looking blue jacket stepped up to the counter. "Problem?"

Picking up the phone, the attendant punched in some buttons. "This woman has no ID," she told the security guard. "I'm checking on the credit card to see if it's been reported stolen. It has a man's name on it."

"My husband's name," Carly lied weakly. The guard, an unsmiling, imposing man with a build like a bricklayer, stared back at her. "Please, I'm begging you." She gripped the edge of the counter. "I have to get to Boston."

"You're not going anywhere," the guard said, taking her arm just above the elbow.

"Uh-huh," the ticket attendant said into the receiver, then read the numbers on the card. "I'll do that," she said, then hung up, a look of triumph on her face. "This card was reported lost fifteen minutes ago. I'll have to confiscate it. And I'd advise you to go along with the guard now, quietly. Unless you'd rather be taken off in handcuffs."

Chapter 4

Sunday Night

"Nick? It's Carly. I hope you don't mind..."

It was 6:00 p.m. Nick was home, hungover and not happy. The last thing he wanted to hear right now was her voice. He almost slammed down the receiver, but couldn't quite bring himself to do that. "What do you want?" he growled.

"I need your help." Even through the sluggish pounding in his head, he could hear her tension, like a thin wire stretched to the breaking point.

He steeled himself against her. "Tough."

"Nick, please." Her voice broke on the last word. "I'm being detained by airport security for trying to use your credit card. I promise I can explain—"

"I'll just bet you can."

"—but not now. I wouldn't have called you, honestly, but you're the only one I know in California."

"Then I guess you need to make some new friends."

She didn't respond to his sarcasm for a moment. Then, she said brokenly, "They're about to turn me over to the police. I can't…" He heard her swallow. "I told them you lent me the card. They don't believe me, but they said I could call you."

He could hear her suck in ragged, desperate breaths. It got to him. Something about her had gotten to him from the first. Damn, he wished he didn't feel so plugged into her, wished he could ignore his own knight-to-the-rescue inclination where this woman was concerned.

He made a last attempt to fight it by reminding himself that he had some pride left and was angry at her. But the day had been spent with too much anger, too much wounded pride. Also too much beer, too much trying to ignore his injured knee, too much trying to forget the night before.

Carly was at the end of her rope, he could hear it in her voice, feel it in his gut. She sounded lost and frightened.

She needed him.

He clenched his jaw, then said, "Put the head of security on the phone."

She whispered her thanks and, after a minute, a male voice came on. "This is Evan Williams, LAX Security."

"This is Nick Holmes. It's my credit card you're holding. What's going on there?"

"Well, sir, this woman said she was your wife, then she changed her mind and said you were friends, that she borrowed the card and you'd say it was all right. She has no identification and frankly, her story sounds fishy."

Nick rubbed his eyes. He couldn't believe he was doing this. His body was screaming at him to fall into bed, most definitely alone, and sleep off the beer. He told himself Carly had gotten herself into this situation, so she could damn well get herself out of it.

Instead, he said, "Yeah, she's right. She's a friend. She can use it."

"Then why did you report it lost?" The guard's voice was filled with suspicion.

"Because I didn't know she had it."

"So, it *was* stolen."

"No." He sighed. He'd phoned the credit card company after hearing from Carly an hour ago. Now he wished the whole thing would go away. "Look, the lady and I are friends. Really good friends. Okay? It was a screwup."

"Well, the card's no good till they issue you a new number. Ms. Terry wants to buy a one-way ticket to Boston but she doesn't even have ID."

Oh? Did she? Good, he told himself. If she were gone, she'd be out of his hair. Out of his life, probably. She would disappear.

He frowned. She would disappear, again. With no explanation. And he wanted to know what the hell was going on. "Look," he told the security guy, "I'll be right down."

"Wait just a minute. I—"

"I'm a copper. Just hold on to her till I get there."

Carly sat perched on the edge of the bench in the small, windowless security office. Nick was coming, the guard had said, and she was to wait. But why was he coming? she asked herself, rubbing her hands together nervously. She hadn't asked him to come, didn't want to see him. He'd been so angry on the phone—what would his mood be when he got here?

Should she try to look on the bright side? she wondered wildly. Maybe it would turn out all right; maybe he was worried about her, would offer his help, with no strings attached. Right. Tell me another one.

She was doing something she'd done all her life, she realized, engaging in magic thinking—the wish of a child who hoped her fairy godmother would arrive to save the day.

Not that Nick fit that description—Carly almost laughed out loud at the thought—but she sure did need some rescuing.

Except… No, Nick was a cop. She had to avoid the police. She might be a murderer.

She had no idea how much time had passed when the door banged open and he stepped into the room. He stood still, hands fisted at his sides, a fierce look on his face. She offered up a tentative smile and started to rise from her chair.

But he didn't smile back, didn't open his arms to her, just stood there glaring at her. He seemed tired, but even so he radiated power and strength and an unmistakable maleness. He wore jeans and a long-sleeved green shirt over a black turtleneck; his eyes matched the shirt and his mood matched the turtleneck.

He was still angry. Even more so than he'd been on the phone.

A shudder rippled all through her body, and she sank back onto the bench. Nick wasn't going to save her, wasn't going to make everything all right. The shaking began in earnest then, and she didn't seem able to make it stop. It was as if she'd been plugged into a mixing machine. She hugged herself, but a sob rose in her throat. She made an effort to cut it off, but this time she could do nothing to keep the pain from coming up.

By sheer strength of will, Carly had been holding herself together for hours, but she had no more strength left. For the first time since she'd woken up that morning in a strange, terrifying world, she felt herself coming apart, and even though, years before, she'd been trained by a master not to cry, tears pooled from some secret river behind her eyes. She covered her face with her hands and, turning toward the wall, began to sob uncontrollably.

It was too much. It had all been too much. There was nowhere safe for her. Nowhere in the world.

Carly's despair sliced through Nick with the impact of a bullet, and his righteous anger evaporated quickly. Crossing to her, he grabbed her elbows to pull her out of her seat. The action dragged her hands away from her face, revealing tears streaming down her cheeks. Her expression was one of such utter desolation and helplessness, he felt at a complete loss.

"Over here," he said gruffly, pulling her to him. Still sobbing, she tried to push him away, but he was stronger. Gathering her to him, he cradled her in his arms, caressing the back of her head. "It's okay, Carly," he soothed. "It's okay."

"Look here." The uniformed security officer had been observing the whole scene without Nick even registering his presence. "I don't know what's going on, but—"

"Are you Williams?" Nick asked. "The one I talked to on the phone?"

"Yes."

He sized him up; the tall, dark-skinned man with a military bearing seemed solid, a man just doing his job. Without releasing Carly, Nick reached into his back pocket and extracted his wallet. Offering it to Williams, he said, "Flip it open and check out my ID, okay?"

He continued to hold Carly, to stroke her hair. She felt so fragile in his arms he thought she might break into pieces.

"This woman is Carla Anne Terry," Nick went on crisply as his wallet was being examined. "She is a good friend. She has my credit card with my permission. I reported it lost, not stolen. Needless to say, I will not be pressing charges."

The officer eyed Nick's identification card, then him, then the card again. Finally, with obvious reluctance, he said, "Well, all right. I guess I don't have to push it. Though you have to admit it sure is strange, all her stories. I couldn't keep track of them. Yours are pretty changeable, too."

Nick shot him a small, comrade-in-arms smile. "Yeah, well, we've both been stressed-out lately. Just give us a couple more minutes."

While Carly wept on, Nick held her, glad to be able to offer what he could, but experiencing the sense of utter helplessness most men feel at women's tears. So, he stroked her hair and murmured soothing words until, eventually, the sobs diminished.

"I've been so scared," she hiccuped into his chest. "All day." She raised her head and met his gaze. "So s-s-s-scared."

Her skin was red, her eyes water-soaked. His heart did a strange flip-flop at the sight of so much misery. Reaching under her eyelids with his thumb, he wiped some tears away. "It's okay, you know. Really."

"I never cry." She sniffled.

He had to smile at the absurdity of her statement. "Coulda fooled me."

At first she seemed confused, but then she got it. Her answering smile was shaky, but at least she smiled. "Forget I said that."

"Come on, let's get you out of here." After thanking Williams, Nick wrapped one arm around Carly's shoulder and walked with her out of the office, through the terminal toward the exit door.

Outside, the night air was cool. As he hugged her close, he observed how snugly her body fit next to his. He'd missed touching her, he realized, missed being with her all day. Now he needed to get her someplace quiet where he could find out what the hell was going on.

Sunday-night travelers made the pick-up and drop-off traffic heavy. Too impatient to wait for the green light, Nick navigated them through the slowly moving vehicles to the parking lot across from the airline terminal. He guided them down the dimly lit aisle to where he'd parked his car in a No Parking zone.

Carly, still trembling in the aftermath of her emotional release, found herself all too willing, for the moment, to be led by Nick, to be sheltered by his protecting arm around her shoulders. After a day spent running, she was exhausted, ready to drop. Her numbness was of both mind and body. She'd been on emotional overload for too long. All she wanted to do was rest. Against Nick.

They had reached his car, a dark red Camaro that looked a

little the worse for wear, before she became aware of her surroundings. Nick opened the passenger door and started to help her in. "Come on," he said. "We're going to my place."

His place.

An alarm went off in her head and she stiffened. No, she thought. Nick's car, Nick's place wasn't where she needed to be. She'd just escaped from a gunman, then from airport security; Nick, with all his soothing words and strong arms, represented even more danger. He was still a cop.

Don't go with him, she told herself. As far as she knew, no one had yet connected her with Demeter's murder, but Nick was too closely associated with the people who might. She had to remember that. She might have flirted briefly with thinking him Sir Galahad, but no more. She could not allow herself to stay with him another minute. She couldn't take the chance.

Standing in the car's open doorway, she stared at the seat back. "Nick?"

"Uh-huh?"

"Thank you for coming down here."

"Sure. Get in."

She took a deep breath, then went for it. "I...have to ask you one more thing."

A beat went by before he responded. "What?"

Forcing herself to turn around so she could look him straight in the eye, she said, "Will you advance me the money so I can go home?"

Their faces were close, only inches apart. "So you can what?" He obviously hadn't expected that.

"I want to go home, Nick. To Boston. Tonight."

Nick felt as though he'd been slapped. He took a step back, his shoulder butting up against the open car door. Home, she'd said, she wanted to go home. Not home with him, but to Boston. That's why she'd been at the airport.

What was going on here? More to the point, what kind of stupid fantasy had he been playing out in his mind? That Carly had turned to him for help and he'd done the manly thing and taken over and now she was so grateful she was his? Like some sort of prize? He stared at her. In the shadows from the parking-lot lights, her expression was strained, her lids still puffy from her crying jag. But there was determination in her eyes.

"That doesn't make sense," he said evenly. "Unless your memory's come back. Has it?"

She shook her head. "No, but I just want to go home."

"Before you explain what went on in there? Before you find out where you've been, what happened to you?"

She averted her eyes, as though she knew he made sense but she didn't want to hear it. "I just want to."

Let her, he told himself. Let her go. He'd mopped up the mess she'd got herself in, so his job was done. She owed him nothing, and if she was in such an all-fired hurry to get away, tell her goodbye and be done with it.

But there was still a puzzle here, and he hated not knowing the answers. The woman changed moods with the speed of a magician. There'd been defeat, sorrow, softness, belligerence. Now she looked and sounded like a scared little kid. Studying her with a frown, he was barely aware when his mind-set underwent a subtle shift of gears. Within the short space of half a minute, the police officer took over from the man.

There was something more than mood swings going on here, Nick realized, and whatever it was, it was scaring the life out of her. He'd been so busy all day resenting her for walking out on him, then wrapped up in his rescue fantasy since, that he'd let it get by him. But that would stop. Right now.

"You want to go back home? Tell me why first."

She didn't reply, just chewed her bottom lip and kept her gaze averted.

"Carly, you're hiding something." He rested a hand on the car frame next to her head, subtly but effectively imprisoning her. "A lot of things, I think." When she didn't answer him, he went on more forcefully. "Why did you run away this morning? Why did you say you're in trouble? What kind of trouble?"

"I...can't."

"Sure you can." Grabbing her chin, he forced her to meet his gaze. "What are you keeping from me, Carly? I deserve answers. Tell me what's going on."

Carly felt trapped. Nick's expression was so stern, so unmoved. Her savior was history. Her situation was hopeless, she decided, utterly hopeless. Nick had as good as announced that he wouldn't lend her the money to leave and he wouldn't go away.

Not that she blamed him, of course. In his place, she would have the same reaction. But fair play was not—could not be—uppermost in her mind now. She urged her tired brain to function. Escape, it said. It was her tried-and-true reaction to most unpleasantness, to break away and hide.

But where? Even if she managed to get away from Nick, what would she do? Wander the streets the way she had all day? Go back to the airport? Sit up all night near a boarding gate? With nowhere to rest? With no money? With an armed man looking for her?

Even backed into a corner, she tried to weigh all her options. But, she realized, there really was no choice. Of all the alternatives, the man facing her represented the least threatening one—shelter and a reprieve from immediate danger. Temporarily, at least.

She lifted her chin out of his grip. "I know how I sound, Nick. Believe me, I do. The best thing for both of us would be for me to get out of your hair. But if you won't lend me the money to get back to Boston—"

"Not till I hear some answers," he snapped.

She ignored his retort. "—then, I have one more favor to ask of you." A bitter laugh seemed to come up from nowhere. "If you turn me down, I don't blame you."

He stiffened, but said nothing, waiting.

"Shelter," she said finally. "For one more night. I will go with you to your place. I'll sleep on the couch. Alone. Believe me, you don't want to get involved with me." She shrugged with defeat. "I have nowhere else to go. Tomorrow, I'll get through to my friend in Boston and she'll pay for my ticket, then I'll leave. You can forget you ever met me."

The muscle in his jaw twitched. "Not good enough. I want answers."

"I can't give them to you."

They locked gazes, two combatants facing a standoff. Carly half expected him to get into his car and drive away. She wouldn't have blamed him if he had.

Instead, he surprised her. "You'll come home with me now?"

"Yes."

"But let me get this straight. No sex."

"I wouldn't feel right."

Was that a fleeting expression of regret—no, hurt—she saw in his eyes? It must have been her tired imagination, because in the next second it was gone. Now Nick's gaze turned calculating, and she understood. One more night to work on her, he was thinking, to wear her down and discover her secrets. She prayed she could find the strength to resist another interrogation.

"Fine," he said. "Get in the car."

She slid into the seat. He closed the door after her, then went around to the driver's side. He shot one more speculative look at her as he put the key in the ignition, then took off.

She was not surprised that he drove fast and expertly once they got out of the terminal area. It went with the car, the profession, the man. They were on the freeway within minutes. The air between them was fraught with Nick's unspoken questions, but Carly told herself that all she had to do was get through a few more hours. Margie would surely be available by morning and would arrange her ticket home. She felt a tug of sorrow at the thought of saying that final goodbye to Nick.

If only they'd met under different circumstances. If only the timing had been better. But if only's were a luxury right now. The farther away she could get from this mess, the better off she'd be.

"All right, Carly." Nick surprised her out of her reverie. They were exiting the freeway now, and turning onto a main thoroughfare. "Something pretty heavy is going on," he continued, "but you don't want to tell me about it. Why, I don't know. Answer me this—is there *anything* about the whole situation you can let me in on that won't upset you?"

Guilt hit her. Yes, of course, he did deserve some answers. She'd done nothing but take and take from him; she had to give something back. She racked her tired brain. What could she say that didn't incriminate her and yet would be the truth?

She stared out at the passing cars, the overhead lights, before she came up with it. "A man, at the airport..." She stopped. Was it all right to tell Nick about this? A wave of sheer exhaustion washed over her.

"A man at the airport," Nick prompted.

Carly willed herself to continue. "He held a gun on me."

"He what?"

"I was going to buy my ticket and this man put a gun in my back and told me to go with him."

Nick glanced at her quickly, obviously not sure what to make of this latest revelation. Then he returned his attention to the road. "Who was he?"

"I don't know."

"What did he want?"

"I don't know that, either. But...please don't laugh at me, but I think he may have been following me all day. Although it could have been my imagination." She looked down at her lap and lifted her shoulders. "I don't know. He could even be following us now."

Nick pulled up at a red light. "He's not."

"How do you know?"

"I'm a cop—checking my rearview mirror is an automatic. Why would someone be following you?"

"I…I'm not sure. I mean, I don't know."

"Take a shot at it," he said. The edge of sarcasm in his tone made her glance at him again.

His expression was no longer speculative, and she had no trouble reading it. It was that look of suspicion, the same one she'd seen this morning—had it just been this morning?— when she'd said she had no idea how she'd wound up in California. He didn't believe her.

"I'm not lying," she said, knowing she sounded defensive. "I don't lie. Nick, I swear I don't."

He studied her, his eyes unyielding green steel. "Maybe you don't lie," he said slowly. "But you sure do leave things out, don't you?"

The light changed and he took off, passed a slow-moving pickup truck and changed lanes. "What happened after the man put a gun to your back?"

"I managed to escape. I, uh, caused a diversion. Threw myself in front of a maintenance vehicle."

"And then?"

She shrugged. "He ran off."

"I assume you reported the incident."

"No."

"Why not?"

"Because I didn't want to deal with the police!" The sentence was out before she could pull it back.

"Why? What's wrong with that?"

She scrambled for some way to cover her gaffe. "Well, I…didn't want all the fuss—I had no purse, no money, no identification. I was worried, you know." Weak, she told herself. Pitiful. Her mind struggled to find further, more reasonable-sounding answers for him. "Besides, he was already gone. There was nothing that anyone could do to catch him. And he didn't do anything to me. I mean, he didn't rob me or anything.'' She let out a shaky laugh. ''Not that I had any-thing for him to rob.''

''Did you see his face?''

''Sort of.''

''What do you mean, 'sort of'?''

''Without my glasses, I couldn't make out details. But he was about my height, and thin and pale with brown hair and a receding hairline, but I didn't get the impression that he was very old. He wore a long tan raincoat that looked too big on him, like it belonged to someone else.''

''And you're positive he had a gun.''

''It sure felt like it. I mean, what was I supposed to do?'' Again she laughed weakly. ''Say, 'Show me your gun or I'm not going with you'?''

He ignored her feeble attempt at humor. ''Yeah, well, it probably wasn't a gun, because it's real difficult to get one past the metal detector.''

''Oh.'' Of course, she thought. How stupid of her not to have realized that.

''Okay.'' Nick's fingers drummed restlessly on the steering wheel as he drove. ''Some scumbag points a gun at you, or you think he does. It happens in all big cities, in all airports. We can report it now, we'll turn around and I'll go with you. Security should know if there's some creep hanging around LAX who's a potential—''

''No, I can't,'' she blurted out.

''Why can't you?''

There it was again. The million-dollar question. How had she painted herself into this corner? Was it sheer exhaustion? Or had she, unconsciously, done this to herself because she wanted to unburden herself? To throw caution to the winds and just tell him all of it?

Plus, he was right. If other people were in danger from this man, she *should* report it.

But then she came up against the same barrier—to report it would mean involving the police. What if they were already looking for her in connection with Demeter's murder? What if someone had seen her on the yacht? Or what if they'd traced her fingerprints and knew her name? It was lunacy to go anywhere near the police.

But she'd called Nick for help and she owed him. Dear Lord, she'd managed to get herself between a rock and a hard place, hadn't she, and there was no relief in sight.

"Nick, please believe me when I say I would like to tell you all about it, but I can't."

"Dammit!" he shouted, slamming his hand on the steering wheel. "What is it with you?"

She shrank against the car door, covering her face with her hands. There it was again, the rage. Like her father, that sudden explosion of fury, the violent temper. It was as though she was back in her childhood, helpless against the words, the fists, the superior power of a man. She cowered against the side of the passenger door, trying to protect herself as best she could, trying to hide.

She felt the car swerve then pull to a stop. The engine was still running when Nick touched her shoulder. She flinched.

"Carly? What's the matter?"

She didn't answer.

"What happened? Open your eyes, look at me."

Slowly, she removed her hands from in front of her face.

They were in the parking lot of a convenience store. Several other cars were parked nearby, and people came and went through the glass doors into the brightly lit store. She was not back in her childhood, was she. Her father was not towering over her with that look of fury on his face.

She was in the present, and she was a grown-up woman who had come a long, long way.

She faced Nick and told him the truth. "I thought you were going to hit me."

He sucked in a breath. "I don't hit women."

"It was because you were so angry."

"Hell, do you blame me?" He shook his head with exasperation. "You have got to be the most frustrating person…"

He let the sentence trail off, then raked his fingers through his hair. He stared out through the windshield, obviously working on calming down. She had to agree with him, she was, must be, incredibly frustrating, especially for him. He had questions he wanted answered, and she was trying to save her life.

She studied him, his face lit by the neon reflection of the convenience store. She observed his strong profile, his resolute jaw with its dark bristles shading it, the way the ends of his hair curled against his collar. He was beautiful, she thought abstractedly, in a brutish kind of way. Tough, street-smart, untrusting. And his rough beauty affected her deeply. Beneath her breastbone, she felt a breathless, excited fluttering; yes, even on this, the worst day of her life, engaged with Nick in a silent struggle for her secrets, she was still attracted to him, still drawn to him at a deep gut level.

He turned off the ignition, then, leaning the back of his head against his door, angled his body so he was facing her. "Did someone beat you?" he asked quietly. "Your husband? Is that why you shrank from me?"

The question threw her momentarily, but she responded, "No, Richard never laid a hand on me."

"Then who was it?" There might have been a hint of compassion in his voice, but mostly he just sounded curious.

"My father. And he didn't beat me, well, not often, anyway. Five or six times. He reserved most of the punishment for my sister. He was terrifying when he was in one of his rages, and I guess I've never learned how to be in a room with an angry man. I'm…always expecting the worst."

Nick stared at her, the harsh planes of his face softening slightly as he did. "That must have been tough."

Her short laugh was without humor. "For Nina, my older sister, it was a lot tougher, believe me. She was the rebel. We were, are, I guess, so different. She was so, I don't know, aggressive. And flashy—she dyed her hair the first time when she was ten, started smoking at eleven, snuck out at night to see boys. I was the opposite of her—well-behaved, good grades. I always stayed in the background. I felt safer that way.''

"From your father."

"Yes." Uncertainty crept up on her, and she felt awkward. "I'm talking a lot. Are…are you sure you want to hear this?"

"I'm sure."

He seemed truly interested, so she went on. "The beatings only made Nina more rebellious. The house was always filled with yelling and crying, my mother sobbing for my father to stop, Nina challenging him and taunting him, my father roaring like a bull, all red in the face." Carly shook her head at the memory. What a sad, sorry excuse for a family they'd been.

"Where were you during all this?" Nick asked.

"Under the dining-room table." She stared out at the neon sign while the scene came back to her, in stark detail. "We had this huge oak table and my mother always kept a tablecloth on it, white, with silver candlesticks in the middle. I don't know why, no one ever came to dinner. The tablecloth came almost to the floor, and I used to get under there and put my fingers in my ears and close my eyes and pray that they would stop." She held one hand to her heart as another wave of sadness swept over her. "Once, I remember I came out from underneath and grabbed my father's arm, begging him to stop hitting Nina. But he just looked at me as though I were a pesky fly, shook me off and went back to beating her. She ran away several times, but he always brought her back. Except for the last time. I haven't seen her in over fifteen years."

Nick listened in silence, but all the while his heart was racing. Another son of a bitch he'd like to take care of in an alley. Another one who preyed on the innocent. The injustice of it got to him; it always had and it always would. Carly had

had a rotten father and, from what little Nick knew, a loser of a husband. No wonder she had a little trouble being open with men.

Listening to her made him want to do something physical like hit the steering wheel again, but he clenched his fist instead. She didn't need another display of temper; she'd had a lifetime of them.

"I hate men who hit women," he said darkly, "but even more, I hate anyone who beats up on kids."

She glanced over at him, then nodded wistfully. "I always had trouble understanding why he needed to do that. Nina was frustrating, sure, but his reaction seemed so…extreme." Her thoughts seemed to turn inward again for a moment, then she went on.

"This past year, since my divorce, I've been doing a little soul-searching and a lot of reading about dysfunctional families. We could have posed for the cover of one of those books." She counted off on her fingers. "A violent father, submissive mother, one rebellious daughter and one meek one. Me, of course. When I knew my marriage was over, and that I had chosen badly in the first place, out of fear, I wanted to understand, so I…"

Stopping herself, she covered her mouth with her hand, then lowered it again. She offered him another tentative, shy smile, as though she wasn't sure if she was appearing foolish. "I really am talking too much."

"If you start getting boring," he said with deliberate lightness, "I'll tell you."

Maybe he didn't have the facts he wanted from Carly, but he understood her so much better now. There'd been no one in her corner when she was a kid, and she'd had to invent whatever confidence she had as an adult. He fought the urge to cup her cheek, to smooth some strands of pale hair off her forehead.

Physical contact might be what he needed, but it was not

wanted by Carly. "Tell me what you found out," he told her, keeping his hands to himself. "I want to hear it, all of it."

She smiled her gratitude, then continued. "I needed to understand about anger. I found out that anger and fear are two sides of the same coin—did you know that? They're both reactions to chaos." Her expression was earnest now. "We—people, I mean—we need to control our universe because it's a scary place. And when we can't control it—when someone won't listen to us, or we feel victimized by other people's behavior, or someone lets us down—it's threatening. Do you see? I had no control over my father, so I became frightened. I guess my father had no control over Nina, so he lashed out at her. But both reactions—fear and anger—were about not having control."

Nick never went in much for soul-searching, but what she said struck a chord of recognition. It was true—his temper came out most when he was thrown by a situation. He'd blown up at Carly because he'd been frustrated by her nonanswers, another way of saying he had no control over her.

He nodded. "So, you woke up this morning in a strange bed. You had no control over it and no explanation for how you got there, so you panicked."

"Yes." She smiled, obviously pleased he understood.

But he wasn't done, not yet. "All right, I'll buy that. But later, after we talked and decided to take some steps to—okay, let's use your word—take some control of the universe, go after some answers…after that, why did you run away? Without saying a word to me? Can you tell me that?"

In an instant, Carly felt all the energy leech out of her body. They'd been having this nice, reasonable conversation. She and Nick had been talking like two grown-ups—friends, even. He'd listened to her story and he'd heard her. She'd even managed to forget, for the moment, that she had to keep her distance from Nick, that she'd had a blackout, that Pete Demeter had been murdered.

But Nick hadn't forgotten he was a cop. He'd steered the

conversation back to the questions, and if she felt manipulated, she also felt guilty. Again. Oh how she hated this subterfuge, hated her automatic reaction to anger, hated the miserable, god-awful mess she was in.

"I would tell you," she said, "honestly I would, if you were a lawyer, a doctor, a plumber, a used-car salesman, I would tell you. But you're a cop."

He frowned. "And that's why? Isn't that a little distorted? Didn't anyone ever tell you when you're in trouble you go to the police, not run from them?"

"Yes. Someone told me that," she said dully. "My father."

"And because he was a sick bastard, does that mean everything he told you is automatically wrong?"

When she didn't reply, his jaw tightened. He turned his head so that his profile was to her again; his hands gripped the steering wheel. "So, you're one of those cop haters. The kind that call us pigs and slap lawsuits on us every time we try to do our job, but when they get in trouble scream bloody murder when we don't get there fast enough. Is that it?"

She let that one sit there. She could have told him her father's profession, and he might have understood. But maybe it was better this way. Let him think the worst of her, she told herself wearily. Let him believe anything he wanted to, as long as he stopped asking questions.

"That's all I can say," she said. "That's all I'm going to say."

"Not good enough, Carly."

She shrugged. "It's the best I can do."

She sensed his temper flaring, saw him struggling with the urge to erupt at her again and steeled herself to face it. But this time he threw open his door, got out and slammed it shut.

They were back to square one.

Thoroughly miserable, Carly watched Nick through the window as he walked down the side of the building toward a chain-link fence that separated the convenience store from a house. Obviously frustrated, he kicked at something, then stumbled and caught himself on the side of the large rectangular trash container.

Like a shot, she was out of the car and rushing up to him. Nick was bent over double, wincing as though in pain. Resting a hand on his arm, she said, "Are you okay?"

Damn knee, Nick thought. Damn temper. Damn woman. Damn himself for being a one-hundred-percent sucker when it came to her. She sent his emotions, reactions ping-ponging all over the place—it had never been like this with any other woman he'd known.

Wrenching his arm away from her, he muttered, "I'm fine. Just fine."

He stood up straight, shook his leg a few times, winced, then gritted his teeth. He would not give in to it. He walked away from her and stared through the window of the store while the pain settled down. Two kids were playing a computer game; people were in line to pay for hot dogs, sodas; a mother wheeling a stroller was examining a box of diapers.

Here he was, he thought bitterly, staring at humanity. People came and went, spoke to each other and then went away. Every person who scurried in and out of the doors had a story, a history, people to love, axes to grind. Here he was, just one man, and his story was about a woman who opened up, but only to a point. A woman who begged him to let her go, but he couldn't. Because, even with all her evasions, she'd gotten under his skin, bad. He wasn't willing to say goodbye to her.

Talk about not having control. He was irritated with her, frustrated by her. Also attracted to her, dammit—the memory of last night hadn't left him all day. More ping-ponging. And worried about her. Her fear was real, he was sure of that. But she refused to tell him its source. In her way, Carly was as stubborn as he was.

"All right." He kept his back to her. "Get back in the car. I promised one more night and that's what you'll get. And I'll stop asking questions."

He heard her huge sigh behind him; it was filled with such

a relief, such a letting down of tension, that he almost whipped around to, one more time, ask her, *Why?*

But he didn't.

"Thank you," she said. "From the bottom of my heart."

So, he thought, he'd blown his chance to let her leave. Now they played it on her terms. No more questions, no more frenzied reactions. That, at least, ought to mean the upcoming night would be more peaceful.

But his gut told him he was wrong. It wasn't peace that was ahead; it was a gathering storm.

A light fog clouded the windshield as they rode through the night along Washington Boulevard. "When's the last time you ate?" Nick asked as they neared the turnoff to the marina.

"I don't remember."

He pulled into the parking lot of a coffee shop. "Let's do it, then."

She laid a hand on his arm. Her touch was tentative. "Let me cook dinner for you," she said. "It's one way I can pay you back. I'm a terrific cook, even if I do say so myself."

"Not necessary," he said gruffly.

"But I want to."

And he wanted answers, but he'd stopped asking for them. "I'm a meat-and-potatoes guy."

"Then meat and potatoes it will be."

They went to the neighborhood supermarket and bought the food. He noticed Carly glancing behind her from time to time. Had the incident at the airport really happened? he wondered. Did she really think someone had been following her all day? Or had she made that up, to keep him distracted? He wanted to believe her, but she sure made it difficult.

Nick continued to keep an eye out anyway, in case her story was for real, but no one approached them or even looked remotely suspicious. Back at his place, they unpacked the groceries—steaks, potatoes, salad fixings, wine. Then she told him to rest while she made dinner. He offered to make the salad but she shooed him out of the kitchen, assuring him she worked better alone. There were still shadows under her eyes, but at least she seemed more lively.

He almost smiled then, at the way she took charge when she was on her turf. There hadn't been much evidence of this side of her nature since they'd met. He liked it, a lot. "Well, if you're sure you don't need me?"

"I don't," she replied.

"Then I guess I'll check out the ball scores."

After Nick left the kitchen, Carly emitted an enormous sigh of relief. Without him there to distract her, to remind her, she might be able to park her troubles for a while. She would concentrate on the task in front of her—the creation of a meal. Maybe both she and Nick could unwind…just a little.

After searching through his cabinets and drawers, she found a corkscrew and opened the bottle of red wine they'd bought. As she pulled out the cork, the sound made her hand stop in midair. She stood very still.

Wine.

She stared at the cork. Something about the wine.

"More wine?" the waiter is saying to Richard.

Carly set down the bottle and clutched the edge of the kitchen counter; she was having another flashback.

Richard. Talking and talking, trying to be casual. But she can see through him to the anxiety right beneath the surface. "Carly, please, I'm begging you. All you have to do is spend one night with this guy—that's all, one night. No rough stuff, you have my word. I wouldn't ask you but I'm in deep trouble. They're going to kill me, Carly, I swear it, if you don't do this."

She can't believe what she's hearing. "You want me to go to bed with some…some stranger, to get you out of debt?"

"Yeah. One night, that's all. Hell, you can close your eyes, pretend it's Robert Redford, like the movie. Please, Carly, I'll never ask you to do anything else."

She stares at him a moment longer, then throws down her

napkin, grabs her purse and storms out of the restaurant. In the parking lot, he catches up with her, grabs her by the shoulders and whips her around so she's facing him.

"I'm sorry," he says, his fingers digging into her arm. "Really sorry."

"You're sorry? Why, you son of a—"

A wave of dizziness comes over her.

Then blackness.

Chapter 5

Nick was stretched out on the couch, alternating between dozing and watching ESPN, when he heard a small cry from the kitchen. Instantly alert, he leaped to his feet, his hand drawn to his nonexistent holster. He was in the doorway in the time it took to exhale one breath.

Carly, her stance rigid, was near the sink, staring at a cork she held in her hand. An open wine bottle stood on the counter next to her.

Registering the fact that she was physically unhurt, he halted in the doorway instead of going to her. So fierce was her concentration on the cork, he didn't want to shock her.

"What happened?" he asked.

Without looking up at him, she answered, "I remembered the dinner with Richard. I remember more details, I mean." Then she did shift her gaze to him. It wasn't fear he saw on her face, which was what he'd expected; no, it was indignation. Her eyes were filled with it.

"He, Richard, asked me to go to bed with someone," she said slowly, as if she was having a hard time believing it. "To pay off a gambling debt. Just like the movie, he said, the one with Demi Moore. He actually asked me to do him a favor, to just close my eyes and pretend the man, whoever it was, was Robert Redford.''

The rage that rose in Nick's gut was so strong he had to squeeze his hand into a fist before he slammed it against the door frame. "Son of a bitch," he muttered.

Carly nodded in agreement. "I think that's what I called him, actually." She stared down at the cork again, as though looking for answers there. "I remember walking out of the restaurant. And then—'' Frowning, she left the sentence unfinished.

Nick walked over to her and removed the cork from her hand. "And then what?" he prompted, setting the cork on the counter and facing her.

She gazed up at him with wide amber-colored eyes, but he could tell she wasn't really focused on him. "Nothing. Blackness." She stared through him for a long time, lost in thought. Then her eyes darkened with realization. "Of course. That's why I was given the drug. Richard knew I'd say no when he asked me."

She bit her bottom lip, then went on, the flow of words pouring out of her picking up speed as she did. "He knew me too well. I was too straight, he always said, too law-abiding. I had to learn to play by street rules, he always said, not be so nice."

"Carly." Nick placed his hands on her shoulders. She was quivering.

"That's why we divorced," she went on, her agitation obvious. "It was a lot of things, but mostly I hated his morals, or lack of them. He lied so easily, refused to take responsibility for the messes he got into. He's one of those people who always blames someone else for whatever goes wrong. I couldn't respect him." Nick gripped her arms tightly as her voice rose in pitch. "You should respect the man you're married to, shouldn't you?"

"Carly, it's okay. Calm down. I'm here."

At his words, she stopped speaking, shooting a startled look at him. Then she shook her head as though to clear it. "Anyhow, I remembered. That part, at least. I suppose that means I was…oh, God, someone's toy for a while."

"Hey, you don't know that for sure. Come on, sit down."

"No," she said with surprising force, wrenching herself from his grip. "I'm too upset." Her gaze darted restlessly around the kitchen, settling on the phone. Snatching it up, she punched in a series of numbers, waited, then said, "Richard, where are you? Call me back." She repeated Nick's phone number then hung up. "He'd better come up with some pretty good answers."

Raking her fingers through her hair, she paced the length of the counter and back, her head lowered in deep thought.

Nick leaned back against the refrigerator door and watched her, eager for her to keep talking, while he kept on the lookout for signs of incipient shock. But he didn't think that was likely, not this time. He'd seen this intense kind of behavior in some crime victims—it was focused blessedly outward. She was angry at Richard, which, to Nick's way of thinking, was a lot better than feeling like a victim.

"Why can't I remember?" Carly muttered. As she walked back and forth, she rubbed her hands up and down her arms. "If what Richard wanted me to do actually…happened, then I must have been raped. But if I was, I can't remember it." She glanced at Nick briefly. "Shouldn't I remember it if I was raped?"

"I don't think you were," he said evenly.

"How would you know?"

"There would be signs. You would be bruised if anyone had been rough with you. I've been around a lot of rape cases."

She stopped pacing. For a moment, a look of hope flashed across her face, but it evaporated just as quickly. "That doesn't mean nothing happened, only that I didn't fight it."

"You were given drugs, remember? So you would be more pliable. You're not responsible for any of this."

"You mean, slip a little something into the lady's drink so you can get her to do whatever you'd like? Do you know how horrible that thought is?" She held out her hands. "To be so powerless, to be at someone's mercy and have no say about anything?"

Clenching her fists, she brought them to her thighs. Her small, slim body shook with emotion. "Can you even possibly imagine the thought of being…intimate with someone, without being willing?"

Could he imagine that? Nick asked himself. He'd never thought about it. For a moment, he tried to put himself in her place, but he couldn't do it. As a man, he had no idea how it would feel to be used that way. No idea at all.

Then the full impact of what she'd just said hit him. *Being intimate with someone without being willing.* He felt his body stiffen. Was Carly talking only about what had happened *before* they'd met? When she'd been with him, had she been unwilling?

Had he used her, even unknowingly? The question had been in the back of his mind all day; he'd been wrestling with it, he realized, without being aware of it. Now he was fully aware.

Muttering a curse, he sank into one of the kitchen chairs.

Carly had been so caught up in her own distress, she'd hardly noticed Nick's reaction. Until now. His abrupt movement indicated something was wrong. "Nick?"

"Yeah?" He didn't look up at her.

"What is it?" She walked over to the table and sat down across from him. "Did I say something—"

"I don't know, it's probably stupid, but—" He sat up taller in the chair, as if he wasn't about to be caught slumping. The muscles around his jawline tensed defensively. "Did you mean me? When you said that about being intimate without being willing? Did you mean what happened with *us?*"

Her hand flew to her mouth. "Oh, God, no. Did you think I meant you? I didn't. I'm so sorry."

"Don't."

"Don't what?"

He scowled. "Don't take care of me, dammit. I'm fine."

He was embarrassed, she realized. He was uncomfortable with letting her see him being human. Exposed. Without thinking, she reached across the table and stroked his cheek. He had evening bristles, and the feel of them on her palm was rough...and extremely sensual. It reminded her of how his skin had felt on hers last night.

"I think—" She stopped, determined not to equivocate. "No, I *know* I was willing with you. Whatever drug I had in my system was wearing off by then. Please, I didn't mean you. I'm sorry."

He gripped her hand tightly to stop its movement on his cheek. "Stop apologizing, dammit," he snarled. "You're the one all this happened to, not me. Why do you keep saying you're sorry?"

With a sudden move, he dropped her hand and got up from the table. He walked over to the doorway into the living room and stood there, his back to her, his posture rigid with silent tension.

Carly felt helpless, at a loss for words. In one part of her brain, she understood. He'd lashed out because he was feeling ill at ease, raw. Most men didn't like to be caught at those moments.

But what should she do about it? What did normal people do with angry men, how did they respond? When, as a child, she'd made any attempt to stand up to her father, she'd been laughed at or yelled at, both of which usually reduced her to tears. Then he would sneer at her for crying. It was what they called a lose-lose situation. Eventually she stopped trying to get through.

She was up against it now, she thought, just the way it used to be. The brick wall, masculine version. No matter what you said or did, no matter how much you tried to explain yourself, to be listened to, you just kept hitting that wall till you hurt yourself.

All right, she thought, she didn't know how to respond to anger. But that didn't mean she had to stay put for any more of it. She pushed herself up from the table and faced the food they'd bought, spread out on the kitchen counter. Onions, fresh garlic, olive oil. A few spices. Potatoes, two steaks. A round loaf of sourdough bread, a tub of butter.

She would concentrate on these things, on anything but the angry man in the room. Smoothing her hands down her clothing, she said, "Why don't you go back to watching TV for a while, Nick? I have a dinner to prepare. Did I tell you I'm a good cook?"

"Yes, you told me. And I'm not leaving."

She glanced over her shoulder and saw him watching her. His face was unsmiling in the kitchen doorway. His right elbow leaned against the door frame, his left hand was at his hip. Portrait of one hard, tough cop, she thought, then shrugged. "It's your place."

She turned on the oven, then opened and shut several cupboard doors before she found a large iron skillet, which she set on the stove. A little olive oil, she told herself. Peel the potatoes. Chop the onions, mince the garlic. Keep your back to Nick and focus on the task in front of you.

But another part of her mind was racing off in a different direction. Richard had drugged her so she would have sex with someone he owed money to. Somehow, he'd gotten her to California, redid her hair and clothes...

No, someone else had done that; Richard wouldn't have recognized a hair roller if one had hit him in the face. A second person, then, must have been involved, somewhere along the way. She'd been brought to Demeter's yacht. Was Demeter the second man? Was he the one Richard owed money to?

What had happened once she was on board the yacht? Had she actually had sex with Demeter? Once, twice? More?

Again, she shuddered at the thought, but pushed ahead with what had to be faced.

Had she killed him?

Closing her eyes, she tried fiercely to remember anything that had happened before the picture of Demeter saying "Amanda," before the picture of Demeter getting his head blown away. Anything at all.

"Has something else come back to you?"

Startled by the sound of Nick's voice, Carly dropped the knife she'd been using on the onions. It clattered to the floor. She stared at it, then bent over to retrieve it. But Nick was there before she was. He picked up the utensil and set it back on the counter. He remained there, unnervingly close, instead of returning to his lookout post in the doorway.

"Did you hear me?" Nick said, a slight edge to his voice. "You just remembered something. Care to share it with me?"

She didn't answer him. Instead she tried to ignore his proximity, tried to tamp down her pounding heart.

She wanted to tell him. Wanted to pour it all out. Yes, she wanted to say, I remember a man. A dead man. And I might have killed him. But I don't know, because I still can't remember that part.

"Carly?" he said again.

Sure, she thought. Confess right now. Nick would have no choice but to whisk her off to jail in the flick of an eyelash. And why shouldn't he? She was nothing to him, just a one-night stand who'd become something more—a puzzle for him to solve. He would turn her in. They would lock her up. Behind bars. With no way out.

Just the way it used to be, she and Nina, in their pink dresses....

No. That was history. It was over.

She bit her lip to make herself stop thinking about the past and searched for some way to reply to Nick's question. Finally, she shook her head and went back to making dinner.

Frowning, Nick studied her as she moved around his

kitchen. Had she remembered something else or was her with-drawal just a way of reacting to his little display of temper? Man, did he feel stupid. He'd blown it, but good. Why had he lashed out at her like that?

Because she'd touched some sort of nerve, that was why. Somewhere deep inside, he must have been worried that their incredible night together had been drug-induced. That she would have been that way with any man, not just him. That it hadn't been…personal.

So? he asked himself silently. Even if that had been the case, so what? Was his ego bruised, his pride in himself as a hotshot lover at stake? No, he was past having to prove himself in bed. The truth was that Carly had, in that instant, wounded him, and the sudden realization that he was vulner-able—God, he hated that word!—to her, surprised him. And disturbed him.

Carly could hurt him.

He'd thought he'd learned his lesson about letting a woman get too close, but this one had taken him by surprise. She really had gotten under his skin, hadn't she? She was more important to him than he wanted her to be. Much more im-portant. The recognition of this truth stunned him, even now as he watched her fuss over the dinner, watched her keeping a wall between them so thick he could practically touch it. He barely knew her, for God's sake! But that didn't seem to mat-ter.

She'd said something that had hit a nerve and he'd struck back. Should he apologize? For what? Blowing up at her? Or caring too much?

At a loss for an answer, he remained silent, watching her make their meal. Her actions were competent, experienced. She did terrific things with salad, chopped and shredded all kinds of vegetables he never usually thought to eat. She was a whiz with his carving-knife set, which he'd bought a couple of years ago and mostly used to cut up lemons.

He decided to make himself useful by setting the table. He

took out plates, silverware, napkins. They worked in uneasy silence for a while, then Nick said, "I have a suggestion."

When she didn't answer, he went on, wanting to offer some kind of olive branch to her. "I know this guy, Neil Mishkin. He's an M.D. who's also a hypnotherapist. The department's used him a few times in the past and he was a real help. How about I give Neil a call in the morning, see if he can jiggle your memory? Why put yourself through this? If you know for sure what actually did happen to you during the blackout, you'll at least know what you're dealing with. What do you think?"

"Maybe," she said with a shrug of her thin shoulders.

"I could call him now, but it's Sunday night and I only have his office number. Should I try to get his home number?"

She shook her head. "No, it can wait till morning."

It was something, he told himself. A thinning of the wall. A small weight lifted from his chest.

The shrill ringing of the phone made both him and Carly jump. If it was her ex, Nick thought, he wasn't letting the bastard near Carly, not until he'd finished with him. He snatched up the phone. "Yeah?"

"Hey, don't kill me, I'm just calling to see if your head is as fuzzy as mine is."

"Dom." He chuckled, relieved to hear from his friend. "Sorry. I'm not in the best of moods. Hold on." He put his hand over the mouthpiece. "How long till dinner?" he asked Carly.

"Fifteen minutes."

"Hey, Dom, what's up?" He took the phone into the living room and collapsed into the easy chair.

"Who were you talking to?" Dom asked.

"A friend."

"Female-type friend?"

"You could say that."

"I could say she's a female type or she's a friend?"

"Both, butthole, now why'd you call?"

"You mean you still got that kind of energy, after what we soaked up this afternoon? Oh, sorry, I forgot who I was talking to."

Nick chuckled. "Just don't forget again. And remind me not to do that anymore. I'm too old to do that many brews."

"Yeah. So, what'd you think of Miguel?"

"Okay. Quiet."

"Not always. He clammed up around you."

"Me? Why?"

"Oh, I've told him a couple of stories—about the time you took on three gangbangers and brought them all in without a shot being fired. And the stakeout on that drug deal last year, when your knee got shot up and you crawled to the car and called in the license-plate number before you passed out. You know, supercop crap like that."

Embarrassed, Nick rubbed a thumb along the seam of the chair's fabric. "So where's my supersuit when I need it?"

Dom laughed. "Anyhow, look, the kid's determined to join the force. Will you help him out? Show him the ropes, tell him about the test, like that? If you got time, of course. I figure you got lots of it now. You're practically retired, and it's my job to make sure you don't get bored."

Nick felt a quiver of discomfort in his belly. "Who said I was going to retire?"

"Hell, Nick, it's just common sense," Dom said reasonably. "How much more punishment can your body take?"

"For your information, I plan to go back on active duty."

He heard Dom take in a breath then release it on a hiss. "You're nuts." His friend no longer sounded amused. "What is this, some kind of macho thing? Your knee is never going to be okay and there's nothing that can be done about it. Didn't you tell me that just today?"

"I wish I hadn't. Anyhow, I can handle it."

"Sure," Dom said sardonically. "Except for when you're chasing some lowlife and you fall on your ass and not only can't you bag the bad guy, you can't back up your partner, either. Sure, my friend, you can handle it.''

"I don't want to hear this, Dom."

But he wasn't through. "You won't ever get a medical release, and you know it. Who you trying to fool?''

The arrow hit home, and Nick winced. He really didn't want to hear this, really didn't want to face the truth about the rest of his life. He liked being a cop—hell, he loved it, couldn't imagine doing anything else.

He slumped lower in the chair, tired of the conversation, and depressed as hell about it. Absently, he shuffled through the pile of mail on the table, fingering the envelope from El Camino College. It had arrived on Friday. He'd read it and left it there, refusing to think about it since.

"Nick? You still there?"

"Yeah. But look, let's not talk about my knee, okay? Not now.''

Dom lost his aggressive tone. "Why?" Nick could hear the sly smile in his friend's voice as he went on. "Gotta get back to your woman?''

At that moment, Carly appeared in the doorway and Nick looked up at her. She signaled that dinner was ready.

His woman. Dom had, kiddingly, of course, called her his woman.

Which was nuts. Nick had known her, hell, not even twenty-four hours. No one could be his woman in that short period of time. No one.

"Nick?" Dom said.

"Gotta go."

"What about Miguel?"

"Have him call me tomorrow."

"Hey, thanks." A beat went by, then Dom said, "We okay, *paisan?*"

"Yeah, even if you are a creep." Dom chuckled, but Nick was already hanging up the phone. He rose from the chair, stretched and headed for the kitchen.

Sounds of fat sizzling, the smells of fried onions and garlic and a couple of spices he couldn't identify filled the room. Pans, potato peelings and utensils were spread all over the white counters. For the first time since he'd lived here, his kitchen felt warm and homey, downright domestic. It was a change, for sure.

Noticing his place settings were no longer on the table, Nick looked at Carly with raised eyebrows. Her shrug was hesitant. "The evening is so beautiful," she said, "I thought we'd eat outside."

"Works for me."

On the balcony, Nick breathed in deeply. The night was especially clear, with just a hint of a cool breeze. Stars were visible in the dark sky, surrounding a pale crescent moon. Below, on the marina, soft yellow lights shimmered, boats bobbed in the harbor.

Nick pulled Carly's chair out for her and she smiled her thanks at him and sat. He eased himself into the chair across from her, wondering how she'd made a white wrought-iron table and chairs—all of which usually seemed barely large enough for a child's party—look so elegant. A small votive candle flickered in the center. Where she'd found it he had no idea, then had a vague recollection of having bought several of them as part of earthquake preparedness. Next to the candle was the opened wine bottle and two wineglasses. Small plates heaped with salad were set on the larger dinner plates. A napkin-covered basket smelled of warm, crisp garlic bread.

"Hey, this is terrific," he said.

"Thank you." She seemed pleased, if a little stiff, carefully unfolding her paper napkin and placing it on her lap.

Smiling at the precision of her manners, he did the same, then picked up the bottle. "Wine?"

"Just a little."

He filled her glass halfway with the ruby-colored liquid. The light from the candle transformed it into a glistening dark pink. Pouring a small amount in his glass, he said, "I want to toast the chef.'' He raised his glass and waited for her to raise hers. ''To you. Thanks for the home-cooked meal. I appreciate it.''

''And to you,'' she replied. Again she seemed to be keeping her distance. ''I'm grateful, Nick, really I am, for helping me get through—'' she waved a hand vaguely ''—all of this. You've been very generous. I'll be no more trouble to you after tomorrow.''

Her words sent an arrow of unease through him. No. He wasn't ready to hear about her leaving. ''I have a suggestion. Let's not talk about tomorrow. Let's have a nice dinner and put that other stuff away for now. Agreed?''

She gazed at him solemnly, her large eyes tawny in the glowing candlelight, but didn't reply.

''And,'' he went on, ''I'm sorry I lost my temper before. It had nothing to do with you.''

Surprise, then a softening of her expression let him know he'd said the right thing. She touched her glass to his and nodded. ''Apology accepted.''

Whew. He wasn't sure he could cope with any more polite, removed conversation.

The feeling at the table turned cozier. He was starving, he realized, so he tore off a hunk of bread then dug into his salad. His taste buds rejoiced at the first bite. ''Hey, this is delicious.''

''It's just salad.''

''Yeah, but you've done something with it. What's that tang in the dressing?''

She shrugged modestly but he knew she was pleased. ''A little olive juice. Tarragon on the croutons and some pine nuts.''

''It's really good.''

''You have to stop complimenting me,'' she said, but favored him with a small gratified smile. ''I'll get a swelled head.'' She chewed thoughtfully, then cocked her head. ''Listen, do you know any good jokes?''

''Excuse me?''

"I feel like laughing. I need to laugh, Nick. Tell me a joke."

He scratched his head, but could come up with nothing but the usual sick, twisted cop humor. "Sorry, I wish I could."

"Oh, I know one. Let's see. I have to make sure I say it right." She took a moment to go over it in her head, then nodded. "Okay, here goes. What did the Zen Buddhist say to the hot-dog vendor?"

"I have no idea."

"'Make me One with everything.'"

Clapping her hands like a child, Carly erupted in rich laughter; it was a full, no-holds-barred sound and it pleased him no end.

He sat back and grinned at her. "Yeah, it's a good one. And you have a great laugh. First time I've heard it. Okay, I remembered one—a female bartender told it to me today, and it's only a little raunchy. Still, it's the cleanest joke I know."

"Raunchy's good," she said eagerly. "I like raunchy."

"All right, then. This man and woman get married. On their wedding night, he finds out she's a virgin. 'How can that be?' he asks her. 'You've been married three times.' 'Well,' she says, 'my first husband was a philosopher—he just wanted to talk about it. My second husband was a photographer—he just wanted to look at it. My third husband was a stamp collector…and boy, do I miss that man.'"

Carly's eyes opened wide and her hand flew to her mouth, but she let out a whoop of laughter and was soon giggling helplessly. He chuckled right along with her.

Who was this woman? Nick asked himself. This was a whole other Carly than the one he'd seen so far. In fact, his cop's instinct told him this was probably closer to the real Carly—domestic by nature, good-humored. This was the woman beneath the tension and fear of her present predicament, the woman she'd have been if they'd met under other circumstances.

Would he have been attracted to that Carly? he wondered.

He gazed at her while she ate. Small bites, perfect manners, an occasional sip of wine. Her hair was pushed back behind her ears and she wore no makeup. But she didn't really need any; her eyes were bright, her cheeks flushed from cooking. There was a thin sheen of olive oil on her upper lip and when she ran her tongue over her mouth to lick it away, he felt his body stir with desire.

She was still dressed in his oversize purple sweats, the sleeves pushed up above her elbows. The outline of her pert little breasts, unrestrained by a bra, was barely visible beneath the general bagginess of the clothing. Still, the memory of those breasts in his hands washed over him, as did the feel of her skin, smooth and silken, every part of her. His body hardened some more until he was forced to shift in his chair.

Would he have been attracted to her if they'd met before her blackout? It really didn't matter, because he was attracted to her now. Most definitely. Earlier, she'd made it clear she intended to sleep alone tonight—had she meant it? Because, sometime soon, he intended to taste her again.

Carly couldn't help noticing how Nick watched her, saw the masculine appraisal, even the hint of sexual hunger in his eyes. It sent a thrill of excitement all through her. She'd tried to keep her distance from him before, now she tried to fight down the pleasure she felt from his attention. Both attempts were doomed, and she'd just as well admit it.

Maybe it was her current state of terrified limbo, but she grabbed on to Nick's obvious approval as if it were a hand pulling her out of quicksand. It felt so good to be desired, to have her cooking praised, her joke laughed at. Did this attraction between them muddy the waters? Maybe. But right now, tonight, she wanted not to care. She wanted—needed—to suspend reality. Heaven knew she needed a break from it. How good it felt to have this beautiful man sitting across from her, not being tough and hard, but generous, easy, teasing her.

They traded some more jokes and laughed. She drank a little more wine, but it didn't make her tired. He praised the crispness of the fried potatoes, declared the steak perfection, ate most of the bread and most of her dinner, too. Continuing to bask in the glow of his compliments, she realized she'd been starved for this kind of attention her entire life, even though she hadn't even been aware she'd been missing it.

Something tightly wound up inside her loosened up. Maybe the wine helped, but it was okay to act more freely than usual. She didn't feel shy tonight or hesitant to say what was on her mind. It was such a lovely change, she didn't even want to question why it was happening.

"Tell me about you, Nick," she said. "I mean, you know a lot more about me than I do about you."

He wiped his mouth with his napkin. "What do you want to know?"

"Age, where you were born. The usual."

He sat back in his chair, his hands crossed over his stomach. "I'll be thirty-seven next month, was raised in Oxnard—that's north of here, up the coast, joined the marines out of high school, came down here in my early twenties. For two or three years I did odd jobs, played beach volleyball, worked on my tan, shared a house with a bunch of guys, partied pretty constantly." He grinned. "Basically, I was a bum, which was terrific, for a while. Then it got old. So I joined the force."

"Why?"

She watched his face while he thought about that one for a bit. "At first, I think it was because it was something I thought I could do. I was a pretty tough kid, coming from the neighborhood I grew up in. I was used to being physical, had the military training, wanted a steady paycheck."

"That was at first, you said. Then what?"

"Yeah, well—" He shrugged and she sensed he was less at ease. "Then I found I liked it. I know you'll have a hard time accepting this, but I liked getting the bad guys."

"Why wouldn't I accept that?"

"In the car, you made it pretty clear you don't trust cops. And, sure, there are some who are on a power trip—you get some violent types on the force, as you probably know, guys who like to use their muscle and their badges to get whatever they want.''

She knew. Oh, yes, she knew.

"But most of us aren't like that," he went on.

"I know that, Nick," she said quietly. His pride in his profession, his need to defend it made her realize just how much she'd allowed one man's brutality to turn into a generalization. "Tell me what else you like about being a cop? Really. I'm interested."

He spread his hands, then let them fall to the table. "It's fun hanging out with other cops. I like, I don't know, making a difference, I guess. Not a lot of difference, but some. A lost kid found, a wife-beater locked up, putting away some hood who's selling nickel bags to fourth-graders. It makes the rest of it—the long hours, the cases we lose because some high-priced lawyer gets his client off—it makes those times bearable." He scowled, obviously self-conscious. "I sound like some damned do-gooder."

"No, you sound dedicated, and that's nice."

Nick wasn't like her father at all, was he, Carly admitted to herself. They might both have worn the uniform, and Nick might be quick to anger the way her dad had been, but really, the two men were nothing alike in other ways. Underneath the gruff exterior, Nick had a heart and a conscience. It was such a relief to see it so clearly, she let out a huge contented breath.

"What?" he asked.

She shook her head. "Nothing. I'm just glad you told me all this." Resting an elbow on the table, she propped her chin in her hand. "So, am I being pushy? I might have had too much wine."

"Nah. You're okay."

"Then tell me more. What kind of childhood did you have?"

"You really want to know all this?"

"Very much. It takes my mind off me."

He gave her a look that said he really wasn't used to talking about himself this way, but if she insisted.... "It was okay," he said. "My mother ran off when I was six, and it broke my dad's heart."

"Oh." Distressed, Carly put her hand over her chest. "How awful for you."

"Probably. But I don't remember. Dad was okay, except when he drank. He didn't beat me or anything, just cried a lot. Mr. Self-pity. Not a pretty sight. He's still around, moved to Philadelphia to be with his brother. I talk to him on the phone once in a while."

He pushed himself back from table and stood up, stretching his arms to the side. "I've been sitting too long. I need to move. So, okay?" he asked hopefully. "Have I told you enough?"

Not nearly enough, Carly thought and realized she wanted to cry. She was becoming maudlin, but how could she help it? There were layers and layers in this man; was he even aware of it?

There was one more area she wanted to know about—oh how she wanted to know. The old Carly wouldn't have dared ask; the one tonight dared. "I'm curious..."

His hands were clasped over his head. "Yeah?"

"I want to know about your marriage, but you don't have to talk about it if you don't want to."

He chuckled, then let his arms drop. "Nah, it's all right." He walked over to the railing and leaned his elbows on it. Looking out on the night, he said, "Lenore was a cop groupie, loved men with guns. We met on the beach—I was in the volleyball championship and she was barely wearing a bikini. It was lust at first sight. I was twenty-six or so, but still a kid in a lot of ways."

Angling his head, he smiled cynically at her. "I believed her when she told me I was special, the only one." He returned his attention to the night sky. "We married, bought a house, talked about having children, or I did, I guess. And then she decided I wasn't fun anymore and found another cop to do her number on. She also cleaned me out financially—she'd been transferring funds from our savings account for months. I must have been putty in her hands, and she probably had a good laugh. It taught me a lot, though.''

Carly rose from her chair and stood next to him at the railing, facing him. There were lights and some noise below them, but here, on Nick's balcony, all seemed hushed, intimate. "What did it teach you?"

His quick chuckle was self-mocking. "Protect your investments. Watch your back. Put away lust when making important decisions."

"And never trust a woman," she added softly.

A frown creased his forehead. "I guess it must sound that way, huh. I'm not sure. I don't think it's about not trusting. It's more about...taking some time to see if they can be trusted."

"Have you reached a verdict on me yet?" The minute she said it, she realized she was only half kidding. She held her breath while she waited for his answer.

Nick met her gaze unsmilingly. "I've changed my mind about that a few times."

"I know." Her reply was equally serious. "And I haven't made it any easier."

She needed physical contact, wanted to touch him, had to touch him. Reaching out, she set her hand lightly on his bicep, but just that small movement sent a quick jolt of electricity up her arm and right through her bloodstream. Danger, she thought. Don't send messages you don't intend to keep.

She snatched her hand away. "I'll get the coffee."

As she headed for the kitchen, her heart was beating a little more quickly than usual, and this time it wasn't from fear. Keep busy, she told herself. It works.

When she returned with the coffee tray, Nick was seated again at the table. It was such a lovely night, she thought wistfully. If only it didn't have to end. For a while, she and

Nick had managed to put away the anxiety, the unanswered questions, the underlying mystery of how she'd wound up here. In its place were two people getting to know each other.

And wanting each other.

While they drank coffee and ate store-bought coffee cake, Nick's gaze continued to warm her with its approval. With this man, she didn't have to act or put on paint, she realized; she had to do nothing except be herself. So much of her life had been spent trying to be "the good one"—so she could feel "safe"—that playing a role had become second nature.

Not now.

After setting down his fork with a contented sigh, Nick rose and stood behind her chair. She reveled in the sense of having his large body in back of her, wanted to let her head fall back against his hard stomach, wanted him to reach around with his long fingers and cup her breasts in his hands. The thought of this made the tips of her nipples harden with desire.

Then he pulled out her chair and said, "Up."

"Huh?" Startled, Carly looked back at him questioningly.

"Stretch out on the lounge—you deserve it. I'm cleaning up."

"No, I—"

"I insist, " he said, and proceeded to clear the table. His tone brooked no argument, so she did as he ordered, stretched out on the lounge and let her body relax into its contours.

How silly she was, she thought as she watched the night. From the kitchen came the clatter of crockery, the sound of running water. All those sexy fantasies about what she'd like Nick to do to her…and he wanted to wash dishes.

She laughed softly, then stopped abruptly as a new thought hit her. What was she doing? She shouldn't be resting, exchanging jokes, flirting, engaging in fantasies. There were questions that needed answers, fears to be addressed.

Somehow, this dinner with Nick had accomplished a miraculous thing—she'd stayed in the present for almost two hours. Her tired brain had been given a reprieve from the insanity of her situation. But it would have to be dealt with, and pretty soon.

The clatter in the kitchen ceased suddenly and she angled her head toward the door. Moments later, Nick was back. He stood over her and stared down at her, his expression thoughtful. Then, seating himself on the edge of the lounge, he said softly, "I've changed my mind. I'm going to clean up later."

"Oh?" Her heart fluttered. What had she just been telling herself? Something about dealing with something?

The night was dark. The candle flickered on the table, but there was very little other light. In the shadows, the planes of Nick's face appeared chiseled by a master sculptor. He was magnificent. Her skin tingled in anticipation.

He stared at her, his eyes glowing green jewels in the candlelight. Then he nodded.

"The dishes can wait. Right now, I need to do this instead," he said, and lowered his head toward her waiting mouth.

Chapter 6

His mouth felt wonderful. The touch of it was gentle, but the feeling behind it insistent, possessive. With a move that was pure instinct, Carly parted her lips and greeted his tongue thirstily, a parched plant receiving sweet water. She heard his surprised intake of breath at the passion of her welcome, then his tongue invaded the inside of her mouth, stroking, tasting, curving over her teeth and the tender skin behind her upper lip.

His assault brought back all the delicious memories of being with him the night before. She squirmed with wanting more, and he gave her more. His hands skimmed restlessly along her neck and shoulders, then he reached under her shirt, pushing the fabric up till her breasts were exposed to the night air.

"Carly," he groaned, shifting his attention down to her breast. He took one firm nipple inside his mouth and suckled her; the other received attention from his palm as he made light, teasing circles over the taut peak.

An ache began between her legs, the muscles there clenched involuntarily. Good Lord, she thought hazily, right now, right at this moment, she wanted him inside her. No foreplay, no love words, just the strong, hard essence of him inside, filling her, completing her.

As though he'd read her mind, he stretched out next to her on the lounge, turning her onto her side so she was facing him, pressed against him. She felt the bulge of his arousal, heard his deep, labored breathing—it matched her own—was aware that his hand was inside the elastic of the sweatpants, traveling down, down, till one finger found the round pulsating knob between her legs. She arched involuntarily, her body swimming in sensation.

So soon? So quickly? The inner cautioning voice spoke to her in a whisper, but she heard it.

What was happening? To be fired up so suddenly, so ready to welcome this man inside with no thought, no logic, just blind female need to be filled to the hilt by him? It was so out of character. So much heat, so quickly. This onrush of the primitive, age-old mating urge was frightening.

Now? the voice asked more insistently, and it unsettled her. In the middle of this nightmare she was involved in—drugs, amnesia, murder—now, she still wanted him?

Yes. An unequivocal yes. She wanted him.

But…how much more confusing could everything be, how much more confusing could she make it?

Nick told himself to slow down, but Carly seemed to be in a major hurry, which made it damn difficult. She was ready for him, he knew it—the slick welcoming moisture between her thighs beckoned him, as it had the night before. The silken-smooth skin of her breasts and arms and belly also called to him. She felt familiar, but she also felt new.

Because this was new, tonight was new. Carly had been drugged last night, at least partly under the influence. Last night she'd been Amanda—he'd taken a stranger to bed. It had been fun, athletic, satisfying.

Today, tonight, she wasn't Amanda, she was Carly, sensible, reliable Carly—or so she'd described herself. He hadn't seen much of either quality himself.

Carly, not Amanda, wanted him. Pretty desperately, from all the signs. And Nick wanted her, no doubt about it. He'd been wanting her intermittently since they'd returned to his place. Every primitive nerve ending pulsed with need, telling him to push ahead, take her, possess her.

But something didn't feel right, although what it was he didn't know. It was a vague sense of—what? Wrongness. A gut thing, cautioning him not to take this any further. So, while his body thundered for more, his brain put the brakes on. When his brain and gut agreed, he always listened. However, if he was going to stop, it had better be now, because he was real close to not being able to.

With a superhuman effort, Nick tore his mouth from Carly's, withdrew his hand from its sensual exploration and rolled onto his back. Breathing rapidly, he swung his legs over the side of the lounge and sat up. He rubbed his eyes with the heels of his hands. Damn.

"Sorry," he said. "This doesn't feel right."

For a moment he thought she hadn't heard him, but he didn't turn around to look at her. He was still trying to recover his breath.

"No, it doesn't," Carly agreed in a small, shaky voice behind him.

Disappointment flooded him. He'd probably wanted her to protest, to disagree, to say he was off base, that what they'd been doing with each other felt totally, one hundred percent right. Irritated with himself, Nick got up, went to the balcony railing and looked out. His brain needed air, his head was foggy and grumpy; it was as if he was being forced to awaken from a dream.

And he was still rock-hard, still wanted her with every fiber of his being.

Then why had he pulled away? The answer swirled somewhere in his head, but he couldn't quite grasp it. He leaned on the railing and inhaled deep gulps of the night. A fog had come in over the coastline, covering the moon with a dark gray mist. Scattered lights from boats and street lamps floated like ghostly stars.

"Nick?" Her voice came from behind him.

"Yeah?"

"Thank you for stopping. I'm...not sure I could have."

She made it sound as though he'd done something noble, but he wasn't noble, not in the least. What he'd done—this much he knew for sure—had been self-protective, to keep both of them from becoming further involved.

Why in hell's name had he brought her back to his condo tonight? Why hadn't he either lent her the money for her ticket, or just left her at the airport to fend for herself? He'd thought it was because his cop's mind required answers to the mystery of her, but that was bull. He'd brought her home with him because of the genuine fear he'd seen in her eyes. She'd needed to be taken care of. And he'd elected himself to do it. Again.

Self-disgust filled him. He was probably making a total ass of himself, being with this woman, with all her stories and her secrets....

Secrets, he repeated silently.

And then, like that, he knew why he'd put the brakes on. Sex with Carly tonight had turned into more than an itch that needed to be scratched. That feeling of being new he'd felt, it had been a sign. Earlier tonight he'd used the word *vulnerable*. Well, just now, he'd been on the verge of losing his heart to her. But not Carly. She still kept her secrets.

She was willing to talk about her past, cook for him, even spread her legs for him, but she didn't trust him enough with what was going on in the present. And if she couldn't trust him, he didn't want to lose his heart, not to her, not to any woman. And that was why he'd put the brakes on.

Your woman, Dom had said.

Hell no. She wasn't his woman, wouldn't be his woman, if

for no other reason than she came with too damn much emotional baggage.

Nick gazed out, far out, trying to distinguish the horizon line. As his body unclenched, he became more aware of his surroundings. Someone laughed on a nearby balcony; from somewhere down on the marina came the sound of a jazz piano.

"Nick?"

He hadn't heard from Carly for a while, but there she was. He turned around to face her. She was curled in a corner of the lounge, her knees bent to her chest, her arms around them, looking at him. "Are you okay?" she asked him.

A sudden cool breeze swept in from the ocean, making the candle flicker. "It's getting chilly," Nick said gruffly, without responding to her question. "Why don't you go on inside? I'm going to take a walk."

"Alone?"

"Yeah."

Now he was anxious to get away from her. He went through the kitchen to the living room, got his windbreaker from the hall closet. By the time he'd zipped it up, Carly was standing close by, looking small and confused, as though not sure what had just happened between them.

"Why don't you go to bed?" he said.

She pointed to the kitchen. "I...I thought I'd do the dishes first."

"I told you I'd do them."

"But that isn't right. You've been so good to me, and you paid for the food, and I just think I ought to—"

"You think I want gratitude? Payment for providing accommodations?" He had to get out of here, now, before he blew up at her again. "Cut it out, Carly. Go to bed, I'll be back soon."

"I have a gun.... I have a gun on you and I will use it...."

"Where the hell is he? He's always on board...."

"Hand me the bleach. Not the shampoo, you idiot, the bleach!"

The dream was all darkness, with no picture, just sounds. Wind blowing, bickering voices, the clinking of glass. A black, dizzying void in her head, as though she wore a blindfold and was falling through space.

"Now be a good girl. Sit still...." A man's voice, irritated, petulant, accusing. Condescending.

"You're hopeless. Why is everyone so stupid?"

"Now be a good girl...."

"I have a gun... I have a gun... I have a—"

Carly burst out of sleep in a thrashing frenzy, sweat pouring down her back. For a moment, she had no idea where she was. It was night, but a lamp was on. A rectangle of light shone from another room. The kitchen. Nick's kitchen. She was still at Nick's place.

She'd washed the dishes, even though he'd told her not to, then, exhausted, she'd sat down on the inviting armchair in the living room, just for a minute, to rest her feet. She must have fallen asleep. And had some sort of dream or flashback. But what had it been?

The voice in her dream came back to her. *"I have a gun."*

It had been a man's voice, but whose? She struggled to identify it, but couldn't. The timbre had been unpleasant, harsh and raspy. The voice had sounded irritable, like a grown child. A creepy-sounding grown child.

Too vague, she thought. What else? She concentrated, hard. What had the voice said? The words were there, but just out of her reach. She sought to hold on to the memory but, like a body drowning, it slipped away from her and left her feeling cheated.

She spent the next moments taking in deep, cleansing breaths, getting herself calmed down again. She wished more would come back to her. Maybe she should go to that doctor Nick had mentioned. The idea of hypnosis didn't thrill her, but it might be the best thing to do.

The front doorknob rattled, making her tense up. Before she had time to move, the door opened and Nick came in, pulling his key out of the lock. Cool air followed him into the room.

Earlier, they'd kissed, and more. He'd been the one to put the brakes on. Her reaction had been equal parts gratitude and frustrated disappointment. When he'd stormed out, he'd been strung tight as a string bass.

She eyed him as he closed the door behind him. He seemed thoughtful now, much less testy; in turn, Carly felt some inner tightness dissolve now that he was home. Even the waking-up fear from the dream lessened. Briefly, she wondered why his presence made her feel safe, when it should have made her feel unsafe. It was an enigma, but she had too much else on her plate at the moment to dwell on it.

"Hi," she said hesitantly, not sure what to expect from him. "I must have fallen asleep. How long have you been gone?"

"About an hour."

The walk had cleared Nick's head. He was better now, calmer, more in control of the situation. His knee hadn't bothered him once—it never did when he was just walking. It was when he broke into a run that it acted up.

He'd made some decisions about Carly, or some nondecisions. Basically, he would let her go tomorrow morning, even lend her the money, if need be. Whatever the hell had her terrorized was her business and not his. He needed to take care of himself, not get himself involved with her. The cop in him wanted answers, but, as far as he knew, she hadn't broken any laws, and didn't seem to want his expertise. She was free to leave him.

And he would let her.

She was curled in his chair, her arms wrapped around herself as though she was cold. Her face was soft, her eyelids heavy. She seemed relieved to see him, and he ignored the small rush of pleasure he felt at that fact.

He hung up his windbreaker, then went into the bedroom

and got a blanket from the foot of the bed. Returning to the living room, he tossed it to her. "Here. You're shivering."

She wrapped herself in the blanket and snuggled more deeply into the chair. "Thanks. I woke up suddenly, you know, not sure where I was. There was this voice in my dream...."

"Oh?" Not that he cared, but he asked anyway. "Did you remember something else?"

"Voices, that's all." She frowned. "But I can't remember what they were saying. I had it right after I woke up, but now it's gone—you know how that happens? But, for some reason, I think I need to call Richard one more time."

Nick felt his jaw clench, so he walked toward the kitchen. "Why bother? He's probably home right now, listening to all your messages and not calling back."

"You may be right. He was always real good at avoiding unpleasantness."

He stopped, shook his head, then turned in the doorway and looked at her. "Why the hell did you marry him?"

She seemed momentarily thrown by his question, but thought about it for a moment. Then she surprised him by chuckling ruefully. "Because I thought he was a safe choice. Can you believe it? Talk about being naive."

Nick propped a hand on the door frame. "Why was he safe?"

Carly had to give that one some thought. It had been a long time ago, she'd been just out of business college and totally alone. "He was nice to me," she told Nick. "He had a steady job—his father owned two dry-cleaning stores and he managed one. His life-style seemed modest, he had a home. And, I guess, I was pretty young and needy."

Nick stared at her thoughtfully for a moment, then he nodded and went into the kitchen. "You did the dishes," he called out.

"Washed them," she replied, wondering if she was about

to receive a reprimand for not following orders. "You get to dry."

She got up from the chair and followed Nick into the kitchen. He had a dish towel in his hand and was wiping a plate. He didn't seem in a reprimand-giving mood. "Were you in love with him?" he said, not looking at her.

His question was not what she expected; indeed, it seemed to come out of nowhere. But Carly figured she owed him the truth. "I don't think I knew what that meant."

She'd been alone at fourteen, when her parents had been killed in a car crash. Nina had taken off, even before the funeral, and Carly had gone to live with her father's older sister. Aunt Fan and she had stayed out of each other's way until Carly left at eighteen for college. She'd met Richard there.

"When I first met Richard," she told Nick, resting a hip against the counter near the sink, "he seemed so solid, so reliable. He was to be my under-the-dining-room-table, my refuge." He'd wanted the same things she'd wanted, or so he'd said—a quiet life, no angry chaos and yelling. What a fool she'd been.

"Did you know about the gambling?"

"No. He managed to keep it a secret from me for years."

He looked up at her, one eyebrow raised. "What was he into—numbers?"

"Numbers, horses, even cockfights. I didn't even know they had them in New England. I feel so stupid—how did he fool me all that time?"

Absently, Nick wiped off the iron skillet, then set it down on the counter. "Hey, Lenore was robbing me blind the whole time we were together, and I didn't know a thing about it till it was too late." He shrugged and picked up another plate. "We know, but we don't want to know."

He understood. The thought brought a warm glow with it. "Yes."

"So, how did it end?"

"His father found out first, and it broke the poor man's

heart. Literally, he died of a heart attack. Richard inherited and went on a major spree. I found out and threatened to leave, but he cried and begged me to stick with him and I did, four, five times. He kept promising and I kept giving him one more chance. Can you believe it?''

"Sure. I used to see stuff like that every day on the job— women and men remaining in dead-end situations. But there comes a time when one of them has had enough.''

Carly boosted herself onto the counter, her legs dangling over the side. Something about the domesticity of being in Nick's kitchen with him, something about waking up from the dream had released a need to talk and talk—a kind of exorcism, she supposed. "It was when I discovered he'd taken out another mortgage on his business, with our house as collateral, and the bank was foreclosing on both. I wasn't even surprised by then. I told him to get help, go to Gamblers Anonymous again, but that I was through. I got out and filed for divorce that night.'' She shook her head. "Talk about a wake-up call. It was the best thing I'd ever done for myself, quitting that marriage.''

"Amen.'' Nick closed the silverware drawer sharply.

But it hadn't all been Richard's fault, Carly knew it. She'd kept herself ignorant, even allowed it, because she was so terrified of life. She'd buried her head like an ostrich, and she'd had to pay for it. Which was why the past year she'd gone in for a complete overhaul—her encounter group, self-defense classes, writing in a journal every night. It had been a year of revelation.

"I've really had a lot of growing up to do,'' she told Nick. "And I'm not there yet, but it's not for lack of trying. I'm still quiet, of course—'' her hand flew to her mouth "—except for now. Good Lord, here I am, going on and on again. Honestly, it's not like me.''

He smiled, but she got the sense he didn't want to. "I'm enjoying it.''

"Yes, well, enough about me.'' Her glance darted around

the room, then her eye fell on the leftover cake sitting on a nearby counter. "Want some cake?"

He shook his head, loading two clean plates into the cabinet.

She hopped off the counter, tore off a hunk of cake, placed it carefully on a napkin and hoisted herself back onto the clean countertop. Not only had she washed the dishes, she'd scrubbed all the tile till it shone. Back home, tile-scrubbing was a surefire relaxation technique.

She broke off a corner of the cake, put it in her mouth and chewed thoughtfully. "Not bad, really. We don't have this brand back East."

Nick was watching her now, his hip propped against the counter right near her, but he didn't reply. As a matter of fact, she realized suddenly, he'd been pretty terse, noncommittal, keeping his distance from her, since he'd returned from his walk. And she'd been so full of herself—her reflections on the past, the voice in her dream—she'd not really noticed.

Carefully, she wiped her fingers on the edge of the napkin and set the cake down on the counter next to her. "Did you have a nice walk?"

"Yeah." She had crumbs around her mouth, damn her. Three or four small white bits of cake that just ached to be licked off. By his tongue. Nick stared at that full, pouty mouth of hers and he couldn't seem to tear his gaze away.

She noticed, of course, how could she not? A flush came to her cheeks. Wide-eyed, she seemed to be waiting for him to say or do something.

His groin area tightened up again and he cursed it silently. Decisions and follow-through had never been a problem for him before. Until now. He kept firmly making up his mind to have nothing to do with Carly, and his traitorous body kept laughing at him. With supreme effort, he turned away from her and slammed a cupboard door.

"Well," Carly said, seeming to sense his mood, "maybe it's time to turn in. I mean, for me to turn in. I mean, you know...."

He whipped around and faced her. "I'm not going to jump you."

"Oh, you're not?" She seemed both relieved and upset by his declaration, then her hand flew to her mouth again. "I can't believe I just said that. But…well, tell me. Why did you stop before? Oh, God, I sound like I'm, you know, coming on to you or something."

He tried to bite back the smile, but he couldn't. She was so damn sweet when she was flustered. The coiled tension left him as quickly as it had come up.

It was all that unfamiliar tenderness she aroused in him, he figured. It had a way of softening his hard edges. Resting his hand on the counter next to her, he leaned in slightly. "So then, let me get this straight. I'm not to think you're coming on to me."

"No. Oh, Lord. Get me out of this before I dissolve in a puddle at your feet." She started to jump down, but he moved to place a hand on the counter on either side of her, effectively restraining her.

It was time to be serious. "I stopped for the same reason I went on a walk," he told her. "Something didn't feel right, and I needed to work it out."

"Oh. What did you come up with?"

He decided to give it to her with both barrels. "I don't want to get involved with you, Carly, because you won't tell me what's going on. That's the truth. And what's also the truth is that I'm still attracted to you, as I guess you can tell. I want more, a lot more, of what we had last night. But I won't initiate anything. It will be on your say-so, and only when you feel you trust me enough to come clean—" Pushing himself away from the counter, he shrugged; it was out of his hands. "If you ever do. If you don't, I'll say goodbye, and that will be the end."

Shock widened her eyes, then they clouded over with sadness. Folding her hands in her lap, she looked down at them. She nodded slowly. "I understand."

Gazing at the top of her head, where the pale blond hair parted to reveal pink scalp beneath, he clenched his hands a couple of times. He'd let her have it. Why didn't he feel better?

Because sometimes it was like that.

He let out a sigh. "Good. Time for both of us to go to bed."

After another moment or two, she seemed to gather her composure around her. Without making eye contact, she hopped off the counter, swiping at the back of her sweats. "Where are some sheets?" she asked brightly. "I'll make up the couch."

"I'll do it."

Hands on hips, she faced him. "Are we going to do this again, Nick?"

Again, he couldn't help smiling. "Okay, we'll make up the couch together." He followed her to the next room.

She folded the sheet corners the way they did in hospitals, he noticed, making sure everything was even and neat. "You had some pretty good training there."

"Some training you don't forget."

"Your father?"

"Yes sir," she said emphatically. "The original tow-the-line-or-else dad."

Troubled, Nick shook out the blanket and let it fall onto the couch. "Couldn't something be done about the abuse?" he asked her. "Someone be told?"

"My father had a lot of influence in town." She fussed with the ends of the blanket.

"Why? What did he do?"

She said nothing for a moment, then met his gaze with a startling directness. "He was the chief of police."

The breath left him then, as if he'd been sucker punched. "Good God."

She nodded slowly, as though she understood his reaction, then unfolded a clean pillowcase and stuffed a pillow into it.

"We lived in a pretty small town, inland from Cape Cod. He was completely in charge of law enforcement. There were ten officers under his command and, no, there was no one to go to."

"The mayor? Social Services?"

She shrugged, fluffed up the pillow. "His friends. But I never even thought I had a right to complain. When you grow up in a house like that, you think that's how it is everywhere. I never talked about it to anyone, so I had no way of knowing it wasn't."

"Where was your mother in all this?"

Carly hugged the pillow to her chest and smiled wistfully. "She made us promise not to tell anyone. It was to be our secret. She would be shamed, she said, in front of the town. So it went on until—" she gave a dry laugh "—fate intervened and they were killed in a car crash."

How much should someone have to go through? Nick wondered. How many obstacles could a person overcome before they no longer possessed the strength to fight back? That curious tenderness toward her rose again in the vicinity of his chest. "Well, that sure explains why you didn't exactly leap with joy when I told you what I did for a living."

Frowning, she perched on the arm of the couch. "About that, listen—"

He held up a hand. "Tell me you're not going to say you're sorry."

"Are you kidding?" Her smile was rueful, but lacking in humor. "I'm never going to apologize for anything, ever again. Believe it or not, it's something I've been working on. It feels like I spent my whole life being sorry for my very existence. I'm in this woman's group, you know, assertiveness training and all that."

He raised his eyes to the ceiling. "God help us all."

"No, it's really great," she said earnestly "They've made me aware of how much I apologize. In fact, I thought I'd stopped doing that—they applauded me one time when I'd gone a whole two hours without saying it. But the group leader told me once that when you get into rough situations, or your stress level is high, you tend to revert to old behavior. And, I guess—'' she offered another wry smile ''—since Friday night, I've been under a lot of stress.''

''You could say that.''

Suddenly, Carly yawned, covered her mouth and smiled drowsily at him. ''I think I need to sleep now.''

She was totally drained, it was obvious. ''Bedtime,'' he said. Taking her hand, he led her into his bedroom, but she stopped at the doorway, her body stiff with resistance.

''I'm sleeping on the couch,'' she said. ''Remember?''

''No, take my bed.''

''Nick, I meant it.'' She yawned again. ''It's my turn.''

Her eyes were wide-open in the dark. There was very little light, just a glow from the windows, casting phantom images over everything and giving them strange shapes. She stared at one dark silhouette then the other, at the dancing shadows on the ceiling for a while. Finally, she sighed and sat up.

Carly had tried to sleep for the past couple of hours, but it was useless. Even dead tired, as she knew she was, there would be no sleeping any time soon. Maybe that quick nap was responsible. Or maybe she was afraid to fall asleep, afraid to remember any more.

Rubbing her eyes, she reached over to turn on a lamp. Before she did, her hand stopped. Nick's bedroom door was open. The light might disturb him. She scrambled off the couch and stood. What was she wearing? she wondered. She grabbed a piece of material and looked at it. Oh, yes. One of Nick's undershirts and nothing else. Because she had nothing else. Why, she asked herself, during all the time she'd spent wandering around that day, why hadn't she at least bought a pair of panties or a bra? It felt strange not to have the protection of underclothes.

She wrapped the blanket from the couch around her and

walked over to the door of Nick's room. Faint moonlight shone through his curtains and she could see that he was sprawled across the bed, lying on his stomach. By squinting, she could discern the dark outline of his body, bisected by a much paler strip—his briefs, she assumed.

He was a large man, quick-tempered, rough in so many ways. But surprisingly gentle sometimes. She felt a sudden yearning in her chest to be close to him, to crawl into bed with him, to run her hands over that tanned skin, those firm muscles. The surge of longing that went through her was part lust and part the need just to be held.

But he'd set the terms, and he'd been right, she knew it. It was up to her.

Still, it would be nice if she were the kind of woman who could get into the bed of a sleeping man and seduce him into waking up. But, all recent evidence of Saturday night to the contrary, she thought, she wasn't that kind of woman.

Careful not to make a sound, she closed the bedroom door. Then she switched on the lamp next to the couch and looked around for something to read. There was a *Law Enforcers' Quarterly,* a *Sports Illustrated,* a few paperbacks by Robert Ludlum and Joe Wambaugh. Not quite the thing to relax her mind, she thought with a smile.

The room was so stark. If she lived here, she would add some color. Cushions, a woven wall hanging. Hey, she told herself. Stop decorating. This is Nick's condo.

Shaking her head, Carly turned on the TV, kept the volume very low and clicked through all the stations till she found news. She sat cross-legged on the floor so she could see the picture clearly, hoping that something would come up about Pete Demeter's murder.

After about fifteen minutes, she was rewarded. A man with white teeth and perfectly sprayed blond hair spoke about the murder. On screen there were pictures of the yacht, then of the bloodstained floor. Carly's stomach lurched at the sight. Yes, it was the same room she'd pictured in her flashback.

There were the same small windows in the background, the white wooden floor, a hassock with a checkered pattern to the right.

The camera showed a lone wooden armchair on a raised platform, standing in the middle of the room and facing the bloodstain. She'd sat in that chair, she was pretty sure. Alone on the chair, with no nearby table, no footrest, just a chair. Raised. A throne. As though she'd been royalty; no, as though she'd been on display.

She closed her eyes for a moment to aid her concentration; she needed to flesh out the memory of sitting on that chair. In the background she heard the newscaster droning on about Demeter's rise, how he'd been arrested but never tried, his suspected associations with other underworld figures. Carly opened her eyes in time to see a videotape of him waving confidently at reporters as he was being led into court, then again as he left a free man, a battalion of lawyers by his side.

A still shot of a bride and groom were next. There was Demeter, his expression serious, looking intently at the woman, his Amanda, by his side. She wore a white, formfitting suit, her jacket open to reveal a low-cut blouse with a generous amount of cleavage. Her blond hair swung loose to her shoulders, and her smile was smugly amused.

Carly froze for a quick second, then she moved in a little closer so the picture could come into complete focus. It was true, she thought wildly as her body went rigid.

The bride was Nina.

The late Amanda Demeter had been Nina, her sister.

She stared at the TV screen. It was like seeing a fuller, sexier version of herself. The two of them had always been very alike, physically, if not temperamentally.

"Authorities are still baffled by a piece of the puzzle," the newscaster was saying. "After the death of his late wife, Amanda—"

Nina was dead. Tears stung her eyes, even as she tried to listen to what the blond image on the screen was saying.

"Demeter rarely left his yacht, which was watched at all times by two onboard bodyguards. Both have been cleared. All known close associates have been questioned and released by police today. It is assumed to be a gangland revenge killing, or part of a turf war. All that police will say is that the investigation is ongoing. When asked if reports that a woman was seen fleeing the yacht shortly before midnight are true, police spokeswoman Joan Tremayne stated…"

The image on the TV screen jumped to that of a competent-looking black woman as she spoke into a sea of microphones. "A neighboring yacht owner, who asks to remain anonymous, said he heard gunshots, saw a woman in a short dress fleeing, and then called police. When asked if he'd seen any suspicious activity earlier, he said he had not."

The newscaster returned with a bland white smile. "And now, on a lighter note, today was Hog Day in—"

But Carly had stopped listening. She'd been the one fleeing, she realized. She was the woman in the short dress.

And Nina was dead.

She'd tried to find her a few years ago, hired a detective to scout around. But there wasn't enough money for a really thorough investigation. Carly had assumed her older sister didn't want to be found because Carly might remind her of how awful their childhood had been. She used to block it out pretty effectively herself and hadn't really blamed Nina.

More tears flooded her eyes and she jabbed at them with the palm of her hand. A now-familiar wave of desolation came over her, even as another piece of the puzzle clicked into place—somehow, her looking so much like Nina had figured in whatever had happened on that yacht.

She tried to think through what that suggested, but she was too overwhelmed by her sense of loss. She turned off the TV and returned to the couch, where she huddled in one corner and cried softly. For her sister, and for herself. They'd never been close, but Nina had been the last member of her immediate family. Now she was truly alone. No siblings, no parents, no mate. The sense of abandonment deepened and a wave of loneliness hit her like a strong wind.

She stared at Nick's door. All she had to do was get up, walk to it and open it. How she wished she could cry herself to sleep on his broad shoulders.

But…Nick still knew nothing about her connection with the Demeter murder. Thanks to her runaway mouth, he knew a lot about her past, but she'd kept the present situation to herself. The tenuous communication they'd built up this evening would crumble into pieces if he knew all she hadn't told him.

And he would have to turn her in, she reminded herself. She would be locked up. It was an option that was unthinkable.

She thought briefly about running away, as she had this morning. But where would she go? And there was still the man with the gun…. Maybe he'd followed her here. Maybe—

The voice in her dream! It had been the man with the gun at the airport. What had he said? What were the words? She tried to remember. Please, she prayed, come back, help.

But they were gone.

And so was her sister.

Nina. Carly had hated her, resented her, loved her—her older sister, her only sister. Often, she admitted, she'd admired Nina for standing up to their father—the only one in the family who had. Their mother would cry and Carly would hide. So Nina had taken the brunt of their father's rage, had run off at age seventeen, had changed her name and had wound up married to a gangster.

Carly's eyelids were swollen from too many tears, too little sleep; they felt weighted with sandbags. She lay back down on the couch, pretty sure she'd have no trouble sleeping this time.

She sits in a chair, dressed in that tiny dress. A man kneels before her, worshipfully kissing her bare foot. "Amanda," he keeps calling her. He is crying. The tears run down his face in small rivulets.

Someone else is in the room—Carly can't see anyone, but she senses it. It's Richard! He has this annoying habit of clearing his throat with a series of three quick dry coughs, and he's doing that now. She'd know that sound anywhere.

She turns around in her chair to see where Richard is.

A shot rings out, then another. She turns front in time to see the crying man fall over. Part of his head is missing. There is so much blood. Her stomach recoils and she thinks she's going to throw up. But she is grabbed from behind and a gun is put in her hand. She stares at the gun. The person in back of her takes her hand and lifts it, aiming the gun toward her head.

Suddenly, there's a thumping noise to her right, and the gun skitters across the floor. Her hand is released. Behind her there's scuffling; she turns around to see Richard, wrestling with someone on the floor. Carly can't see who. "Go, go, go!" Richard is saying as he struggles with the other person.

She does as he says, gets up from the chair, runs barefoot up the stairs to the deck, down the gangplank.

Running, running, for what feels like hours.

Headache. Chilly. Dream state. Confused. Who is she? Where is she? Heart thumping. "Amanda." Her name is Amanda. She runs some more. Running for her life.

Chapter 7

At the sound of moaning, Nick was through his door in a heartbeat, crouching and coming in low while his gaze searched the living room for signs of an intruder. All his animal senses were on alert, but, as his vision adjusted to the light, he could see that Carly was alone, on the couch, crying in her sleep. He went to her, bent over and shook her shoulder gently. "Carly, wake up. You're having a dream."

She sat bolt upright, a startled scream followed by more moans issuing in a tumult of sound from her gaping mouth. He sat on the edge of the couch and pulled her quaking body to him. "Carly, it's okay. I'm here."

"I didn't kill him." She sobbed into his bare chest.

"What?" Now that his attack-defense response mechanism was no longer required, his still-tired brain was having difficulty functioning.

"Nina is dead," Carly said next.

"Huh? Your sister?"

She sobbed again. "Not me. Not me."

It got through to him then that something was terribly

wrong. Under his touch, her arms trembled then tensed into rigid iron. More alert now, Nick shook her again. Her head bobbed back and forth like a rag doll as he did. "Carly? Who didn't you kill? What about Nina? Tell me!"

Pulling away from him, she stared as though looking through him. Her eyes were dry, both wild and vacant at the same time. He grabbed her chin. "What are you seeing? Tell me!"

Awareness crept back into her gaze gradually until she was able to focus on him. She blinked her eyelids several times, then said, "I was dreaming."

Relieved, Nick let go of his iron grip on her chin. "No kidding."

"It's okay," she mumbled. The words came out slurred. "It was just a bad dream." She got that faraway look again, and tears filled her eyes. "Nina is Amanda. Amanda's dead."

Nick felt completely lost now. Nina was the sister. Amanda? That was how Carly had introduced herself Saturday night. What was she talking about? Was she hallucinating, babbling as an aftereffect of the drug? Or—he had to ask himself—was it possible she really was schizophrenic? Two people in one body? No. Not possible, this he knew, dammit, if he knew anything.

Maybe, after all, Carly's wild words were simply the result of a nightmare. Hey, he'd woken up mumbling after a few pretty bad ones of his own. But could he take the chance?

He stood up, pulling her with him. "Come on, we're going to the hospital."

She pushed him away and sat down on the edge of the couch. Shaking her head, she looked down at her lap. "No, it's not necessary. Just a dream, that's all. Promise."

"But, look Carly—" he scratched his head "—you talked about not killing someone—what did you mean?"

Her body seemed to freeze for a second, then she lifted and dropped her shoulders in a shrug. "Did I?"

She didn't raise her head, didn't make eye contact with him.

She was hiding again, but at least she seemed more awake, more in control now, no longer a candidate for the emergency room.

"Tomorrow morning," he said firmly, and his tone brooked no argument, "you're going to the doctor." He crouched down again and took her hand. It lay limp and cold in his, as though the life had drained out of it. He took both her hands and rubbed them between his, trying to give her the warmth she so obviously needed. "Hear me? Tomorrow morning. End of discussion. You're going to have to trust me, Carly."

Images, fast, terrifying images swept through Carly's mind and pulled her toward some unknown void. Still, somehow she managed to hear him through the mists in her brain.

Trust him.

But she was so cold. And disoriented. Her mind kept leaping from one subject to the next.

Richard had been there... Someone else had killed Demeter, but she'd seen him die... Death.

Nina was dead.

Could Richard be a murderer?

There had been another voice... A man. She knew that voice....

The man at the airport. He'd been on the yacht.

"Amanda," the crying man kept calling her. He thought she was Amanda. She looked like Amanda. She had been *made* to look like Amanda. Like Nina.

Nina was dead. Oh, Lord, how that hurt.

Trust him, Nick had said.

Could she? With superhuman effort she tried to focus on that very question, tried to imagine trusting him. Telling him, all of it—the dream...

No, not a dream, this had been a flashback, a memory. She'd been on a chair, Demeter had been killed by someone— Richard? No, not Richard, Richard had told her to run.

Carly was not a murderer... But Nina was dead. It was more than she could handle.

"I'm so scared."

She wasn't aware she'd said it out loud until she felt the cushions dip as Nick lowered himself onto the couch. He leaned over, the upper part of his body covering hers as he drew her into his arms, engulfing her. She'd wanted that, wanted it so badly earlier, and now he was here, offering shelter. The heat from his body warmed her, made the shivering and shaking slow down.

"Tell me," he whispered.

Tell him. Part of her wanted to. *Let him help you.* He was one of the good guys, he wasn't her father, not a brutal cop. Nick was here and he offered a broad shoulder and a clear head. He'd been so kind to her. She wasn't used to such kindness from men.

Her mind shifted in a new direction. "What happened to Richard?" Again, she hadn't been aware she'd said it out loud until she felt Nick stiffen.

"Don't tell me you're worried about him?"

"Only because he was on—" But she could not go on. Nick would take her to the police and they would have her and she would be locked up, put in a cell, with no way out.

No way out....

In that instant she was six years old again, sitting at the dinner table with her parents and her sister. Her father was smiling, his eyes glittering with his latest triumph. Down at the station they'd managed to "misplace" some evidence that might have cleared the man they were holding. They'd railroaded him into a confession, so now they had enough to file charges. He was a loser anyway, her father had told them, so who cared? *Why look for the bird in the bush,* he'd said with a laugh, *when we have the bird in the hand?* Wasted energy, he'd called it.

A primitive wave of fear washed over her. She would be locked up, again. Would Nina be there with her? She was so little. Someone else would have the key and she wouldn't be able to get out. This time she would die.

No, her tired brain insisted. *Stop this.* Carly wasn't six years old anymore. She was an adult. And she wanted to tell Nick... But she couldn't tell Nick. So she said nothing, just lay back down on the couch and turned onto her side, away from him.

She felt him ease his body onto the couch, so that it lay side by side with hers. She stiffened for the briefest moment when Nick's arms enfolded her. Then she stopped fighting and gratefully let herself be enveloped by him. Oh, Lord, he was so large, his embrace so all-encompassing. How she needed this. For a few moments, Carly lost herself in him, wishing she could curl up somewhere inside that large, strong, warm body and seek oblivion from everything.

His arms held her fast. "I'm all right now," she mumbled sleepily. "Really. It was just a dream."

"Good. Go to sleep. I'm not leaving you."

But he would. She had secrets, so many secrets that she must keep from him if she was to save her own life. And to protect him. She'd come to care for him. Yes, even in the middle of this horrifying ordeal, she knew her feeling for him was strong. Perhaps too strong.

Her brain was on overload. Too many thoughts, too many questions. And then she stopped thinking at all.

Monday morning

Fear sucked the breath from her lungs as she awoke. She was trapped, a prisoner. She was suffocating; she couldn't get any air.

Then some of the weight crushing her shifted and reality intervened. It was Nick, stirring in his sleep, she realized. He was lying half on top of her on the couch. The tension ebbed away; she even smiled. It was Nick's heavy, warm body keeping her safe, not some half-remembered demon crushing the life out of her. And she was having trouble breathing because her face was buried in the back of the couch. Shifting her head slightly, Carly allowed oxygen into her lungs.

Lie still for a moment, she told herself. Let your heart slow to its normal rhythm. She breathed deeply, several times. In, out, in, out, as she'd learned to do when the panic hit her. It worked. Her head was clearer now.

Last night, she'd remembered so much more—especially that she was not responsible for killing another human being. Thank heaven for that, she thought.

Now she had to think, to plan. She had to stop feeling so lacking in control. Action was what was needed now, not passivity, if she was to get to the bottom of this mystery.

But first, she had to get to the bathroom.

She wished she didn't have to disturb Nick, but he was pretty firmly planted. She pushed her elbow into his ribs. "Nick?"

"Hmm?"

"Could you move?"

His hand did just that, moved up from her waist to cup one breast possessively. "Too early," he mumbled, his thumb tracing her nipple. Even as her flesh hardened, she could feel his arousal against the back of her thighs, felt it growing as the seconds ticked on. Even in sleep, she thought with wonder, he wanted her.

"Nick." She put her hand over his and withdrew it from her body. "Nick, I have to get up."

She felt him stir again, and suddenly the weight of him was gone. Behind her, a loud thump was followed by a muttered expletive.

She turned over, her stiff body protesting the movement. Nick lay on the floor between the coffee table and the couch. Rubbing the back of his head, he slanted her a puzzled, groggy gaze. "What happened?"

She just had to smile. He looked so grumpy, so offended to be taken by surprise this way. His hair stuck up in black spikes, his eyes were heavy with interrupted sleep. A faint beard shadowed his chin and jawline. The rest of him, covered only by his briefs, was tanned and strong, the stuff dreams were made of. He was all man.

"Did you hurt yourself?" she asked. "You fell off the couch."

He rubbed the back of his head again, then shook it. As he sat up, he shouldered the coffee table away. "What time is it?"

"I don't know."

He blinked a couple of times, then awareness dawned. Swiping his hand over his face, he said, "Hey. The hell with me. Are you all right? You had a pretty rough night." There was such concern in his question that a lump of emotion gathered in the back of her throat. He cared about her, too, although the whole thing was a miracle to her.

She nodded. "Much better this morning, thank you. I want to call Richard and Margie again. I'm really worried."

"Yeah, okay." He rose, offering his hand.

Why in hell did she keep talking about Richard? Nick wondered. She seemed concerned about the man's welfare, not angry, the way she should be. Richard had been the one who'd slipped her the drugs, after all.

Maybe she was more hung up on her ex than she knew or admitted to herself. No, he thought quickly. Not after what she'd told him about her marriage. This wasn't about being hung up on him. But she was still connected to him, in some mysterious way, and Nick didn't like it.

She accepted his hand and stood, making sure to smooth down the man's T-shirt she wore, so it covered her thighs. Still modest, he noted. Still the lady.

He dropped her hand. "Sure you're okay? You were pretty scared." Hell, *scared* was hardly the word. She'd been terrified. She seemed calmer this morning, more in control, but it was hard to forget the screams, the moans of despair of a few short hours ago. "No more bad dreams?"

She smiled briefly. "Not that I remember."

He stared after her as she hurried off toward his bedroom.

As he heard the bathroom door shut, he stretched his arms over his head, groaning as creaking muscles protested. Why the hell hadn't he carried her into his bed instead of making the effort to balance on that narrow couch all night?

Not to mention the effort of pretty much keeping his hands to himself. It had been a trial, a night-long one. It sure hadn't been easy, but he'd made up his mind. Several times during the night, with her soft, rounded flesh thrust against him, he wished he hadn't.

Hey, he told himself. Time to stop dwelling on body parts and get down to business. He shook his head to clear it once again, then went to the small desk by the window and pulled out his address book. After looking up Neil Mishkin's phone number, he put in a call. His service answered. Dr. Mishkin would be in at ten, the operator told him crisply, one hour from now. Nick left word that he would be bringing someone in to see him about eleven, and that it was important.

As soon as Carly came out of the bathroom, he went in himself while she made her phone calls. He made an appearance ten minutes later, showered and dressed in jeans and a long-sleeved shirt. Carly was sitting at the kitchen table, staring at the phone.

"Any luck?"

She looked at him with a puzzled frown. "Richard's still not home. Margie got held up at customs and has bad jet lag, but she promised to go to his place and check up on him, then call me back. She's also going to call my boss and tell him I'll be out sick for a few days."

"You're staying?" Elation roared through him so swiftly, he was caught off guard. But he kept his tone casual. "I thought you wanted to get home."

"I don't feel right doing that." Her smile was sheepish. "It would be…running away."

She wasn't leaving, not yet. He would have more time with her.

Cut it out, he warned himself. This changed nothing.

"Good," he said. "If Margie or Richard calls while we're gone, my answering machine will pick it up."

"Where are we going?"

"First I'm buying us breakfast, then we go to the doctor." He walked over to her, grabbed her elbow and helped her out of her chair. Steering her toward the bedroom, he said, "It's a beautiful day, the sun is shining, and we could both use some fresh air. I've already showered. Your turn."

"Still giving orders, aren't you?" she said with a smile.

"You got it."

While Carly was in the bathroom, he spent several minutes on vigorous knee exercises. When she returned to the living room, she was wearing the purple sweats again. "We need to get you some clothes," he said.

"I have a closetful back in Hull."

"I thought you weren't planning to go back."

"Well, not yet, but eventually."

Of course, he reminded himself, of course she would go back. Eventually. "Well as far as I'm concerned, you're not going back to Hull until we know how you got here. And I don't want to hear any arguments, okay?"

"Excuse me?" Her look was a combination of surprise and resentment.

He had to grin; even he wondered where that little piece of caveman chest-pounding had come from. "I'll put that differently." With one arm across his waist, he offered a mock bow, then rose. "Today, Ms. Terry, you and I are going to make every attempt to understand what happened to you. I have a few ideas that I'd like to discuss with you over scrambled eggs." He grinned. "How does that grab you? Better?"

Her answering smile was reluctant. "Better. You have possibilities, Mr. Holmes. Definite possibilities."

It was a beautiful, breezy morning, with just a hint of autumn in the air. Sun, ocean, gulls, boats. The smells, the sounds of a busy boardwalk. As he and Carly strode toward the docks, Nick realized he loved it here on the marina—it felt more like home than anyplace he'd ever lived.

As they passed Con's Bait Shop, Nick felt the back of his neck tighten. That was where his cop's sixth sense usually made itself felt and he'd learned to trust it. He grabbed Carly's hand, then turned casually as though to murmur something to her. The reflective flash from a pair of sunglasses caught the corner of his eye. He whipped around, just in time to see a form dart behind the small shack.

"What is it?" Carly asked.

"I think we're being followed." Her hand tensed in his and he squeezed it. "Keep walking. Act naturally, Carly."

The wind picked up as they walked along some more. Nick pointed to something nonexistent and steered them around the corner of an old warehouse, now being refurbished into a nightclub. Once there, he pushed her up against the wall, shielding her with his body, and focused his attention on the direction they'd just come from.

A small man sporting sunglasses and a baseball cap rounded the corner. He wore white tennis shoes, a pair of chinos and a short-sleeved plaid shirt, buttoned all the way to his neck. The moment he saw Nick and Carly, he ducked his head and turned on his heel in one movement, and sped off.

"Stay here," Nick ordered.

Carly was not about to stay anywhere. As soon as Nick took off, so did she, wishing she had something other than rubber thongs on her feet. By the time she turned the corner, Nick was yards ahead of her; ahead of him was a blur running for its life. Carly squinted as she ran, trying to make out more details, but it was hopeless.

She saw Nick's hand reach toward his waistline. Then he must have realized he didn't have his gun because he sped up even more, yelling, "Hey, you! Stop!"

But the man kept on going. Nick turned into another alleyway and she followed him. She did not want to be alone.

They rounded one more corner. Now they were on the dock

itself. Hundreds of boat masts bobbed in the water of the harbor, their spires reaching high into the sky. Nick was leaning against a wooden signpost, rubbing his knee and cursing.

The man they'd been chasing was nowhere in sight.

"Damn knee," Nick said as Carly caught up to him. She could tell he was in pain by the effort he was making not to give in to it. His eyes were closed and his jaw was tight, as though he was gritting his teeth.

"You're hurt," she said.

He ignored her. "Did you see where he went?"

"No."

"He just disappeared on me." He struggled for breath. "The little weasel must run marathons."

Carly, too, was panting pretty hard. "Are you sure you're not hurt?"

"Nah. Mad."

"Please stand back," someone shouted. "Please stand back."

Nick looked up toward the sound, which came from farther south along the harbor. Fifty yards away, a small crowd gathered at the edge of a boat slip. Blue lights atop a sheriff's department patrol boat flashed, while a loud voice told onlookers to keep back.

"Looks like an accident," Nick said, his natural policeman's curiosity aroused. "Let's check it out."

Carly hung back. "I'll stay here."

"Come on." Nick grabbed her hand again, shook his leg one more time to make sure his knee would function and headed toward the boat slip. When he and Carly got there, he pushed his way through to the front of the crowd. At the edge of the slip, two men in scuba gear were hunched over a lifeless form.

The uniformed officer urging the onlookers to keep on their side of the taped-off area was someone Nick recognized. "Hey, Kuzinski," he called out.

The blond, crew-cutted policeman looked up at the sound of his name. "Nick? What are you doing here?"

"Happened to be in the neighborhood."

A Harbor Patrol vessel chugged in next to the first boat. By now, the scuba divers had given up and the body lay on the dock, facedown. Carly seemed strangely fascinated by the sight. Nick wondered if it was a good idea for her to look. It was obvious the floater was dead, and, as a civilian, she wouldn't have seen a dead body before. But, he figured, she was a grown-up.

"So, what's up?" he asked Kuzinski.

The patrolman jerked a thumb toward the harbor. "Some woman saw a hand rising out of the water and screamed bloody murder. We just got here. Coroner's on his way."

"Oh. Any idea who it is?"

"Nothing so far. It's a man, white, probably in his thirties. He's still in one piece, so he hasn't been down there too long."

Nick felt Carly release his hand, then she edged closer to the tape and bent over, squinting, as though studying the body. "Any connection to the Demeter thing?" Nick asked. "His yacht's over at pier 44."

Kuzinski shrugged. "Possible. The homicide guys'll know something."

Nick was about to caution Carly about getting too close, but at that moment one of the scuba divers rolled the body onto its back while the other placed a tarp over the still form. Carly put her hand over her mouth in horror. She began to fall back, but before she hit the ground, Nick was there, lifting her in his arms.

"Hey," the patrolman called out. "She okay?"

"I'll let you know in a minute." Murmuring, the crowd parted for them and Nick carried her to a nearby bench several yards away. She lay still in his arms, but at least her breathing was regular. Her first sight of a dead body, he assumed, and she'd fainted. A common reaction.

Lowering himself onto the bench, he held her close, rocking her and patting her cheeks lightly. "Carly, it's okay, I'm here."

She stirred. "Richard," she moaned.

His jaw tightened again. "The name's Nick."

"It was Richard." Her eyelids fluttered open.

"Who was—?" Comprehension hit him like a fist in the gut. "You mean, the body?"

She nodded, tears in her eyes. "It's Richard. They killed him."

"Who killed him?" When Carly didn't answer, he found her chin and tipped it so she was facing him. "Dammit, who killed him?"

"I...don't know."

He wasn't sure if he believed her. "All right, who is 'they'?"

"I don't know. Honestly."

"But you're positive it was Richard?"

"He was wearing the watch I gave him, and his awful plaid bowling shirt and black socks with the tennis racquets on them, and—" She put her hand over her mouth as though to stop a cry from escaping, then went on. "And it was bloated, but it's his face."

"Are you sure? Without your glasses?"

"Yes, it was Richard."

"Then we'd better get over there and let them know you can ID the body."

She tensed. "No."

"Huh? Why not?"

She pushed against his chest. "I'll deny it."

"Excuse me?"

Carly's sudden attitude change, from being overwhelmed by her ex-husband's death, to fierce defiance at reporting it, took him completely by surprise. He wondered if he was hearing her correctly. "You'll deny what?"

"Let me go." She continued to push at him, trying to make him release her. But he held her tightly.

"What in hell are you hiding?"

Instead of replying, she increased her struggling; it was as though she were a caged animal fighting for its life. This time he loosened his grip. She stood up, weaving slightly. He could see the enormous effort it took to bring herself under control. "I can't stay here, near his body. I can't."

Frowning, Nick stared at her. The tension poured out of her in waves. She was quivering again with obvious terror, but remained stubbornly unwilling to disclose anything that might help him understand its cause. He felt his anger rising. He was tired, tired of asking questions and not getting any answers. Tired of being patient. Tired of watching her tear herself into little pieces rather than let him in.

He rose from the bench, his hands fisted at his sides, and looked right into her eyes. "Okay, here's the deal," he said, keeping his voice level. "Either you tell me what you're hiding, and I mean all of it, or I'll haul you into the police station so fast you'll think you're on a spaceship."

She flinched at his tone and closed her eyes. Then, slowly, she nodded her agreement. "Yes. All of it," she said in a small voice. "But not here. Please."

She was ready. He could sense it in his bones. Hell, if she didn't spill her guts soon, she'd implode. All right, then, if she needed to be away from Richard's body, fine. The restaurant he'd planned to take them to was nearby, so he grabbed her elbow and steered her toward it. She had about five more minutes of secrets left, and then she ran out of time.

It was a weekday, past the breakfast rush, so Marina Muffin wasn't overly crowded. The usual California beach types were there—surfers who'd already put in several hours at the nearby oceanfront, freelance writers, directors and actors taking meetings or reading *Variety*, businessmen with the *Wall Street Journal* folded by their plates and a few gawking tourists.

Nick sat Carly down at a private corner table, ordered bacon, eggs, hash browns and coffee for both of them, then leaned his elbows on the table, steepled his hands and looked at her. By now, she'd regained her composure enough so the cornered look had left her eyes. Soft rock music and conversation filled the air, but as far as Nick was concerned, there was nothing else in the universe that required his attention.

"All right," he said bluntly. "Let's have it. All of it. Now."

Carly's heart was racing, but she knew she was at the end of her rope. Richard was dead; if she felt anything at all about that, she'd have to deal with it later, when she had the luxury of her emotions. Right now, it was time to talk, to let one other human being in on what she'd been struggling with, alone—so alone!—for what had only been a couple of days but felt like a lifetime.

She desperately wanted to take a moment and gather her thoughts, but Nick wouldn't let her. "I'll wring it out of you if I have to," he warned. "If you don't like my manner, fine, but you're going to talk to me. Dammit, you can trust me."

Trust him. The man who had been there from crisis to crisis in the past thirty-six hours. Trust him. A cop.

A cop who was not her father.

The waitress, a fortyish woman with permed gray hair, came over with their coffee, giving Carly a little reprieve from Nick's insistence. By the time she'd put in cream, stirred it with a spoon, and had a sip, she was ready.

"You're right," she said. "But maybe when I explain, you'll understand a little better. I hope you will anyway. I remember little bits and pieces and they add up to something pretty awful."

"How awful?"

She swallowed. "Murder."

He went very still. She could see the surprised, even shocked, look on his face. But he recovered quickly, then understanding dawned. "Demeter," he said. "You were there?"

When she nodded, he looked to his right, then to his left, as though checking on possible eavesdroppers. "Go on."

Willing herself to speak as matter-of-factly as possible, she said, "I think I'm an eyewitness, but I'm not sure about a lot else. I saw him die."

Again Nick went still. "You saw it?"

She nodded. "I was on his boat—it's the first thing I remember since being at the restaurant with Richard. I suppose I was…waking up from whatever stupor I'd been in." The relief of coming clean with Nick was overwhelming. The pace of her words picked up till they spilled out of her. "I was sitting. He, Demeter, was kneeling in front of me, kissing my feet, my hands. Crying, calling me Amanda, over and over again. Then someone behind me shot him. I—" she flinched, but finished her thought "—I saw his head blow up."

"Damn." Nick gripped her hand; his face registered the grim understanding of someone who'd been there already and knew the horror.

She bit her bottom lip to keep her feelings in check. The picture was one she'd carry with her the rest of her life, but she couldn't allow it to take over now.

She was so grateful for Nick's presence, for his strong hands on hers. They steadied her and gave her the strength to continue. "Whoever it was that shot him put the gun in my hand, then aimed it toward my temple, I think to frame me, then to make it look like I'd killed myself. But Richard stopped him—"

"Richard? He was there?" Nick was one hundred percent cop now; she could practically see the wheels turning.

"Yes."

"Go on."

"Richard told me to run while he fought with this other person—it was a man, I'm sure, but I didn't see him. I did as he said, and wound up at the bar with you. The rest of that night, well—" she shrugged self-consciously "—you know about that."

His grip on her hand gentled and he seemed to gaze inward for a moment. She knew he was evaluating her story, turning over the details, preparing more questions for her.

"Why didn't you tell me all this earlier?" he said.

"Because I thought I might be a murderer."

"You thought *you'd* killed Demeter?"

She nodded. "I kept seeing this...picture in my head—me with a gun in my hand and a dead man. Then, last night, when I was having that nightmare...? That's the first time I knew I hadn't killed him."

Releasing her hands, he picked up his coffee cup, as though needing time out to digest what she'd told him. Before taking a sip, he shook his head slowly. "Whew, this is not what I expected to hear this morning."

"It's all true." If she sounded defensive, it was because she was afraid Nick thought she was inventing the whole thing; maybe he hadn't lost his suspicions of her. The thought of that bothered her, but she was determined to go on. "I'm not through yet."

Setting his cup down, he met her gaze grimly. "I'm listening."

"On the news last night I saw a picture of Demeter's wife, the one who died in a car crash. It was Nina, my sister. We'd always looked a lot alike—dressed and acted totally differently, but still, the resemblance was there. Hair, eye color, facial structure. She was more...curvaceous and more outgoing. And, I guess, since I'd seen her last, Nina had changed her name to Amanda, had gotten a lot blonder and had married Pete Demeter. Amanda died six months ago. Which means, of course, Nina's dead."

Carly swallowed a lump of pain; like so much else she'd been hit with, further mourning for Nina would also have to wait until later. But despite her resolution, a feeling of melancholy swept over her, for her sister and for herself, for the innocent, frightened children they'd been.

Nick saw Carly's face crumble with the onslaught of emotion. He grabbed her hand and squeezed it. "Hey, I'm sorry," he said softly.

She managed a small, dispirited smile. "Thanks," she said, then seemed to will herself to keep going. "Anyway, I'm pretty sure that I was chosen for whatever happened because I look so much like Nina."

He nodded slowly. "So, that's why you woke up last night saying Nina was dead."

"Did I say that? I wasn't sure if I was dreaming. Anyhow, I guess whoever shot Demeter won the fight with Richard after I left. This…other man must have killed him and pushed him into the water. So, just now, when I saw Richard's body, I…" As a twist of pain crossed her face, she clasped her hands together tightly and brought them to her mouth. Closing her eyes, she seemed to take a moment to gather whatever resources she still had, then raised her lids again. "I realized," she went on, "that, well, Richard might have set me up for this, but he died saving my life."

"If he hadn't set you up in the first place," Nick said bluntly, "it wouldn't have happened at all."

"I know. Look, he was an awful husband, and the gambling made him a pretty dreadful liar, but I can't hate him. Saving my life might have been the only decent thing he ever did." Glancing down at her coffee cup, she shook her head. "Poor Richard, he always made such a mess of things." She returned her gaze to Nick, unclasping her hands and resting them on the table. "So, that's the story, as much as I know of it anyway."

Nick's head was spinning, bouncing all over the place between compassion and rage, but he held on to the clearheadedness he always had when he was on a case. He wasn't on a case right now, not officially, but he needed that clearheadedness and he knew it. Carly was in a mess, and in danger, too.

There were a million more questions he wanted to ask her. Soon, he thought, he'd lead her through the whole story, step by step. And with it all, Nick couldn't help being impressed. She'd been through a hell of a lot and had survived. She was brave, in a way that he'd never associated with the word before. Real bravery wasn't battling adversity, but courage in the face of fear. She'd had so many battles to wage during her life, and so much to slog through on the way. But she'd persisted, hadn't given up. He'd seen inherently stronger, tougher people go through this kind of thing and not have even an ounce of the resilience Carly had.

Expelling a loud breath, he shook his head. "You've really been through it, haven't you."

Neither of them spoke for a moment. Then Carly started picking on the edges of her napkin; his cop sense told him her anxiety level was on its way up again.

"What else?" he prompted.

"I wish I could remember more," she said, gazing at him with worried eyes. "Like where I was from Friday night to Saturday night. If anything happened to me that I need to know about, apart from someone completely redoing my hair—" A laugh that was part mocking and part agitated escaped, but he saw her bite it back. "I don't mean to sound like a broken record, but if I was someone's plaything, Demeter's, or this other person's, the killer, whoever it is, or even Richard's, I want to know. It's the not knowing that's making me crazy."

The waitress chose that moment to arrive with their food. She set their plates in front of them, then, propping a hand on her hip, asked cheerfully if they needed ketchup, jam, more coffee?

Glancing up at the gray-haired woman, Nick shook his head, then went back to concentrating on Carly. "Neil Mishkin will help, promise. Okay, right now, is there anything else I should know? Anything?"

"I don't think..." She hesitated. "Yes, there is one thing. The man who was at the airport yesterday, his voice was familiar, so I think he was there."

"Was that the guy I chased earlier? He was short, pale, like you said he was. Was it the same one?"

"I don't know. Anyway, without my glasses—" She shrugged. "Sorry."

"Could you describe him to a police sketch artist?"

"I honestly don't know."

Nick was about to ask another question when he glanced down to see two full plates of steaming food on the table. He picked up his fork. "Eat," he told Carly, "before it gets cold."

"I'm not hungry."

"Eat anyway. You need your strength. I don't want you fainting on me again."

"I've never fainted before in my life."

He looked up at her indignant face. "And you've never cried. Broken a couple of records, haven't you?"

She managed a smile, then began to eat. After a few moments of clattering utensils, Nick said, as though no time had passed, "So, let's assume you were followed yesterday to the airport and this morning here to the marina. Both times he must have tailed you from my place. Which means he followed you from the boat on Saturday night, because that's the only way he'd know where you'd wound up—at my place. So he was on the boat with you and Richard and Demeter."

"Do you think he's anywhere around, I mean, now?"

"Nah. I've been keeping a lookout. We'll get him, the little creep." She was wolfing down her food and he smiled. "I see your appetite's come back."

She swallowed a mouthful of eggs. "Telling you all this has helped. I feel a lot better."

"Good." In one way, he felt better, too. That invisible barrier of secrets she'd kept between them was history. All kinds of new possibilities for the future were conceivable now. But first they had to take care of the present. Briskly, Nick said, "Finish up and then we need to go."

"Go where?"

"There's a sheriff's department substation right near here, on Fiji Way. You'll tell your story, we'll look at some pictures, see if we can get a make on this guy, track him down." He glanced around, caught the waitress's eye and signaled for the check. "Don't worry, I'll be there with you."

"No."

Both her answer and the determined way she said it surprised him. "You don't have a lot of choice."

The fear returned to her eyes briefly, but she seemed to be making an effort to stay in control. "Are you sure it will go the way you think it will? Are you sure I'll be treated as an innocent party, or even that I'll be treated fairly?"

"I'll see to it," he said confidently.

"It's not enough, Nick. Remember, I told you my dad was a cop. I know what happens. He used to brag about it—if they have someone in custody, and any kind of a case can be made for their guilt, they stop looking. They're shorthanded, or caseloads are too large, or maybe they're just lazy, but if there's enough evidence to turn it over to the D.A., they stop looking. That's how it is in Massachusetts, and I imagine it's the same in California."

"That won't happen."

"How do you know?"

"I said, I'll be there."

Damn, he hated when people ran down his profession, even though what Carly said was—on occasion—how the system worked. If she turned herself in, the authorities would have a woman who admitted to being on the scene of a murder and whose fingerprints probably matched the ones found there. They might or might not book her and throw her in a tank, but whatever happened, she'd wind up having to deal with lawyers, bail, notoriety. Her life would be changed forever.

Still, there really was no other option. "Sorry," he said as the waitress set down the check. He fished in his pocket for money then peeled off a twenty. "If I could spare you the ordeal, I would, but I can't. Besides, it's probably the safest place for you to be right now."

"Nick." The intensity in her voice made him glance up. Her jaw was set stubbornly. "I don't have to go to the police station, not if I don't want to. I'm a witness, not an accessory, and I also know that no one can force a witness to come forward. So, I'm sorry, but I just won't."

"Carly—"

"At least, not now." The determination in her eyes softened slightly. "Give me a little time, please, twenty-four hours. Maybe I'll remember something else, maybe the police will make some progress on their own. It's a lot to ask of you, I know, but I'm asking." She swallowed, then added, "If by this time tomorrow you still think I should turn myself in, I will."

"This is crazy," he said with equal intensity. "If nothing else, you belong in protective custody. You're in danger. You're an eyewitness to one of the biggest gangland murders in southern California history."

"And I'm with a man I trust with my life. I feel safer with you than I would with seven bodyguards patrolling outside my jail cell. Twenty-four hours, that's all I'm asking."

Don't even consider it, his brain told him. Sling her over your shoulder, do what has to be done, but take her in and get the wheels rolling.

Do as she's asking, said his gut. She's right—there's no law that says she has to go in. Give it your best shot, give her one day.

Welcome to the war zone, he thought bitterly, for a change. The woman always got to him, made him bend rules. Why would this moment be any different?

"Twenty-four hours," he agreed reluctantly. "But that's it." His mind was racing now. "Neil will look you over. I'll do a little footwork, make a few calls and find out what the cops have right now. By tomorrow, we can bring you in with all kinds of ammunition."

She emitted a relieved sigh of gratitude. "Thank you."

He wasn't through. "But, if I give you twenty-four hours, I need a promise from you. If you remember anything, I mean *anything,* I want to hear it right away."

She nodded. "I agree."

"And one more thing. I'm the professional here. I take over from now on. Whatever I say, goes."

She frowned a little, then said cautiously, "Within reason, I agree."

He had to pound it home, nothing halfway would do. "I need your trust, Carly, your total trust."

She met his gaze with equal directness. "And I need yours," she answered quietly.

As the full meaning of what she'd said hit him, he stared at her. No more doubting her sanity or her motives. No more second-guessing. *Trust.* A word that had slipped from his vocabulary, as far as women were concerned, a long time ago.

The moment resonated with seriousness. Nick looked into Carly's eyes and saw the openness he needed to see in them. He offered his hand and she took it. The skin of her palm was soft in his, her hand small, the bones fragile-seeming. But her handshake was firm, and so was his.

"Ms. Terry, we have a deal."

Chapter 8

"**D**om!" Nick said into the receiver. "Hey, I found you."

"You found me fast asleep," his friend mumbled. "Call back later." He yawned loudly. "I was on a stakeout all night and I'm dead."

Nick was keyed-up. He might have been out of action for a while, but the rush of excitement he always felt on a new case was flooding through him. Phone to his ear, he paced from the refrigerator to the sink and back again, while Carly sat at the kitchen table, her eyes following his every move.

"Yeah," Nick said, "that's what they said at your store, but I need a favor and it can't wait."

After letting out another huge yawn, Dom said, "This better be good. What's going on?"

"I may or may not know something to do with the Demeter murder."

"Oh yeah? Demeter?" He sounded more awake now.

"You assigned to that?"

"No. It's Carlusky and Ryan's. What do you mean you may or may not know?"

Nick glanced again at Carly. They'd returned to his place after breakfast so he could make phone calls and set everything in motion. Her hands were folded politely on the tabletop, and she seemed composed, but she was listening to every word with fierce concentration. There was tension emanating from her, but not fear. Not now that she'd let Nick in on the situation.

It was up to him now. He had to play this conversation with Dom just right. He didn't want to bring up Carly's involvement in the incident yet, not if he could help it, but he also didn't want to compromise his friendship with Dom. He'd have to do tightrope walking with words.

"Here's the thing, Dom. I was down at the marina, near my place, when they brought a floater out of the water. It may be connected to the Demeter murder, but I need to check out a couple of things before I get involved. Okay?"

Dom didn't answer right away. Finally, he said, "You're being kind of mysterious, buddy."

"Just go with me on this, huh, Dom?"

Again, there was silence on the other end of the phone. Then, "Okay..." But he didn't sound enthused.

Nick realized his pacing was making him sound agitated, so he leaned against the kitchen counter and expelled a breath. "Can you tell me what you guys have on Demeter so far? What you found at the crime scene, suspects, like that?"

"You know Ryan—why don't you ask him yourself?"

"Right now, I'd like to keep this between you and me." He waited, then added more quietly, "I wouldn't ask if it wasn't important, Dom."

Dom exhaled a breath. "Ah, why not. Sure. Give me a few minutes. You home?"

"Yes. Thanks."

Nick clicked the phone to Off and set it on the counter next to him. "He's finding out and he'll call me right back."

Carly nodded, her eyes bright. "But you don't have to involve me?"

"Not yet."

"Good."

He really couldn't stand still, so he paced again, deep in thought. There were angles to be worked out, questions to consider. He wanted to be ready for whatever popped up. Carly had put her trust in him and he didn't want to let her down.

Carly. He stopped pacing and glanced over at her. "So, you holding up okay?"

With a hint of a smile, she said, "Better than you are at the moment. Would you like me to make us some coffee?"

"Nah. I'm too hyped." He headed for the coffeemaker. "But I can make some for you."

"No. I think I'll just sit here and watch you work off both our breakfasts."

Her tone made him stop in his tracks. He turned to her, nodded ruefully, then made himself lean back against the counter. "That bad, huh?"

"Not really. You're enjoying yourself, aren't you?"

"Yeah, I'm revved. It's been a while."

She gazed at him as though trying to understand, then said, "Tell me, why didn't you call one of the people you work with instead of Dom? Didn't you tell me he's in a whole other department?"

"Yeah, L.A. County Sheriff's. See, my precinct—Manhattan Beach P.D.—it's too small to deal with anything really heavy-duty. We get the stuff like pickpockets and warrants for parking tickets. Once in a while, when we get an armed robbery or a murder, we call in the big guns—the county. I was working a holdup a few years back, when it turned into a drug-related thing that involved some local gangbangers. Dom was assigned to the case. That's how I met him." Nick chuckled. "Dominic D'Annunzio. Born and bred in Brooklyn, and he talks like something out of a gangster movie, but he's okay."

"Is he a good friend? Can he be trusted?"

"Absolutely." He glanced at his watch. It was ten-fifty.

They were supposed to be at the doctor's office in ten minutes. Nick was debating whether or not to call Mishkin and say they'd be late when the phone rang again. He grabbed it. "Dom?"

"No." It was a high-pitched woman's voice. "This is Carly's friend Margie. Is she there?"

He handed over the phone, then forced himself to sit down on the table's other chair. To relieve the tightness in his neck, he rotated his head and shoulders while he listened in on Carly's conversation.

"Oh?... Thanks... Uh-huh. I see." She nodded, closed her eyes for a moment and sighed. "Yes."

This friend of hers, Margie, spoke quickly and at length; Nick heard the sounds of female babble without making out any of the words.

"Yes," Carly said again. "Well, thanks." More rapid words, then Carly glanced at Nick, smiled sheepishly and listened some more. "Yes, it was... No.... Well, sometimes, but... Yes.... I promise." She laughed and nodded again.

Nick sure liked that laugh of hers, liked the way her eyes lit up and her cheeks grew rosy. He wondered how he'd ever thought her almost plain—had he? Sure, just yesterday morning when she'd greeted him in the kitchen in his robe, looking for all the world like a homeless war orphan. He'd been one hundred percent off base. As he came to know her better, with each passing moment, she became more and more beautiful.

"All right," Carly told her friend, nodding some more. "Yes, I'll call you later. Now stop clucking at me. Bye." She hung up. When Nick raised an inquiring eyebrow, she shrugged. "Margie means well, and she's the best friend I've ever had, but she tends to take care of people a little too much."

"What did she say?"

She seemed slightly embarrassed. "She wanted to know if you're as gruff as you sounded, and I said sometimes."

"Yeah? Am I?"

"Uh-huh. And she wanted to make very sure that you were treating me nicely. I assured her you were, but I had to swear it, or else I think she might have called out the militia." She bit her bottom lip, as though trying to hold back nervous laughter. "Of course, doing that would be redundant, as you *are* the militia."

He raked his fingers through his hair. "Not quite, although I wouldn't mind the backup. What else?"

Her smile faded. "She called because she went by Richard's place and he wasn't there, then she checked at the dry cleaner's and he hasn't been seen since Friday morning." A brief spasm of pain crossed her face. "I didn't tell her the reason he's not there. It didn't seem the smart thing to do. Not yet."

"Good thinking." The phone rang again. Both of them jumped, then looked at each other and smiled. Nick picked it up. "Yeah?"

"Here's what they got," Dom said without preliminaries. "Demeter was shot twice in the head. With a .45-caliber. They got latents all over the place, most of them Demeter's and his bodyguards'. A couple of other prints on some of the furniture, no ID on them yet."

"Do they have the gun?"

"Nope. They got divers on it—probably thrown overboard."

"Okay, what else?"

"Woman's clothing, size ten, in the closet, belonging to the late wife. And some others, a size smaller, folded up in a pile in the head." The sound of paper rustling let Nick know that Dom had taken notes and was reading them to him. "A blue silk suit, a white blouse, a printed scarf, silk. Bra, 34-B, panty hose, size small, heels, size six."

All of which corresponded with what Carly said she had worn to dinner with Richard. Her story matched the evidence in every particular, but Nick no longer needed to be convinced she'd told him the truth. "No purse, car keys, anything like that?"

"Nope."

"How about eyewitnesses?"

The paper rustled again as Dom read. "Only the guy who called it in. Old guy, almost eighty, but alert. He owns the neighboring yacht. Said he and the wife were sleeping, heard two gunshots, wife buried her head, he peeked out and saw what he thinks was a woman running away, but he's not sure—the fog was kind of thick. He stayed below, didn't want to get shot, and called 911. That's it."

"Thanks."

"Now, give."

Nick glanced quickly at Carly then told Dom, "The body they pulled up this morning?"

"Yeah?"

"His name is Richard—" He put his hand over the mouthpiece and asked, "What's Richard's last name?"

"Fallows," Carly said, her voice cracking slightly.

"With an *a?*"

She nodded. Lifting his hand, he relayed the information to Dom. "He's from back East—Boston area. Can you pass it on? Say you received an anonymous tip."

"Why don't you call it in?"

"It's not…the best move at the moment."

Dom digested his answer. "Okay," he said slowly, "then how do you know who this guy is?"

Nick paused. Again, he wanted to tell his friend the truth, but had to be careful not to give too much away. It struck him suddenly that this must be how Carly had felt all day yesterday and this morning, before she unloaded the whole story on him.

He did his best. "Say he's a friend of a friend and leave it at that."

The muttered expletive at the other end of the line told him just what Dom thought of the suggestion. Then he said, "Is that friend female?"

"Dom, I'll tell you all about it in a day or so, okay?"

"Hey, you in trouble, Nick? Anything I can do?"

Nick smiled, grateful for his friend's concern. In Dom's place, he wasn't sure how trusting he'd be. "Not a thing. Thanks, Dom. I owe you a beer."

"Beer, hell. You owe me a six-pack."

"You got it. Talk at you later."

He clicked the phone to Off, then sat staring at it for a while longer, digesting what he'd learned.

"Nick?" Carly said.

"I'm thinking." Drumming his fingers on the tabletop, he laid it out for himself. They had her fingerprints, her clothes, someone who saw a woman running away after gunshots. Not an innocent-looking scenario, for sure. Potentially, it was as incriminating as Carly had thought it might be. Potentially, she was in deep, deep trouble.

Not to mention that now, he, too, was involved up to his eyebrows. In more ways than one.

"Nick?" Carly sounded more upset now. "What did Dom say?"

He jumped up, grabbed her hand and pulled her out of her seat. "Let's go. I'll tell you all about it on the way to the doctor."

In the car, Nick gave it to her straight, with no sugarcoating, and Carly made herself listen to every detail. None of what he said was a surprise, she thought with a sinking heart, but now it was reality. Everything she had worried about was true. They might not know her name yet, but she was probably, even now, wanted for questioning, if not yet murder.

She felt a hint of incipient panic at the realization, but it was eased somewhat by Nick's taking her hand and squeezing it. She was not alone, she reminded herself. Nick was there. It wasn't quite time to take it to the worst possible place her imagination could come up with.

"Thanks for being honest with me," she told him.

He squeezed her hand again, then released it, peering quickly into the rear- and side-view mirrors, as he'd been doing since they'd been in the car. Looking out for a tail, he'd explained. But, he'd added, he was pretty sure no one was following them.

They sped along the marina north, toward Venice. Carly gazed out the passenger window, needing some respite from her troubles. The sky was slightly overcast, but the sun was struggling to peek out through the gray clouds. They passed tall white apartment buildings and parking lots with ocean views. There were so many joggers, Carly observed, and in the middle of a workday. She knew that people in California were health-conscious, but they seemed to have such odd hours. And they were all dressed in the latest workout clothing—spandex and bright colors—instead of the old high-school sweatpants and shirts most of the people back home wore for exercise.

Her musings were interrupted by Nick's no-nonsense tone. "How do you feel about laying it out, everything we know so far. You game?"

"Yes, I am," she said emphatically, grateful for his positive energy.

Nodding, he held up a thumb. "Number one, Richard was in debt and wanted to use you as payback. Question—Who was the contact, the debt collector?"

"I wish I could help. I never knew who Richard owed money to. He never mentioned it and I didn't try to find out." Another example of hiding instead of facing a hard truth—how blind she'd kept herself during her marriage.

"All right. Two—You were to look like Demeter's late wife, Amanda—who was really your sister, Nina. Question—Did Demeter know about the setup? Did he arrange it? Or did someone else arrange it, someone in his circle or a rival's?"

"Also," Carly added, "how did someone find out about my existence and how much Nina and I looked alike?"

Nick nodded. "Good. That's three. How *would* they know?"

She took a moment to consider. "Through Nina...or Richard. I can't think of any other way."

"Yeah, makes sense." A quick perusal of the mirrors again, then eyes back on the road.

He was looking out for her, Carly thought, and she had to swallow a sudden lump that formed in her throat. She was so *emotional* today, she thought helplessly—well, the last two days. The fact that someone wanted to look out for her, was on her side, made her want to weep.

"Okay, four—"

Again, Nick's voice brought her back to the present moment. She swallowed again, determined to stay there.

"You were given a drug, probably by Richard, that caused a twenty-four-hour blackout. During that time, in no particular order, your hair was done up like Amanda's, you were dressed in Amanda's clothing, transported to Los Angeles—how, we have no idea—and onto Demeter's yacht."

She shook her head with disbelief. "Doesn't the whole thing sound surrealistic?"

His chuckle lacked humor. "I'll tell you some stories sometime that make this one sound like a fairy tale. Okay, we know the creep who came after you at the airport was involved, at least somewhere during your blackout, and we know that Richard, and at least one other person, was there on the yacht when you regained consciousness."

He frowned momentarily, then shrugged. "Maybe those are all the players, actively involved, at least. You, Demeter, Richard, this other person, the airport guy. The last two might be the same person. All right, next. Five—Demeter got knocked off. Question—Was that the purpose of the whole scheme, or did it happen without being planned? And if so, why were you there?"

Carly was remembering her first waking moments on the yacht. "He kept kissing my foot and crying."

"Demeter?"

"Yes. It was like I was being worshiped, like he honestly believed he was seeing Amanda." She turned and faced Nick. "Would he have set that up himself? Doesn't it seem more likely that someone else did it and surprised him with my appearance?"

He made a maybe-yes, maybe-no gesture with his hand. "It's been done. You've heard about kinky-sex stuff—" He lifted an eyebrow. "Or have you?"

"Hey, I read magazines, thank you," Carly protested, but felt herself reddening slightly nevertheless. "I do know something about the world."

"Well, this could have been where someone pays someone else to dress up as a person from their past, so they can play a game—acting out some little scene that turns them on. It can get pretty ugly. Whipping, being whipped, worse, especially when they hated the person."

"But that involves pretending, a lot of it. I didn't get the feeling he was pretending. It was like he really thought he was seeing Amanda, like it was a complete surprise."

"Then let's go with that. It makes more sense that he was set up, too. So, what number are we on? Five?"

Something to Nick's left caught her attention. "Six. What's that?" she asked, pointing. "I can barely make it out, but it looks like a Ferris wheel."

He glanced over, then said briskly, "Santa Monica Pier. Some fishing, mostly tourists. Lotta kids, lotta drinking on Saturday nights."

The world through the eyes of a cop, Carly thought, but his next words drew her attention away from the Santa Monica scenery and sent a cold shiver down her spine.

"Okay, six—You. After Demeter was killed, you drifted in and out of reality for the next few hours, most of which was spent with me."

"Oh, Nick, I'm so glad it was you. Just think what could have happened if someone less—"

"Don't, Carly." They pulled up at a red light. Taking his hand off the steering wheel, Nick reached over and took her clenched one in his. "Don't," he repeated quietly. "It *was* me, not someone else. Don't drive yourself nuts with might-have-beens."

She met his gaze and nodded. "You're right. Thank you."

He surprised her then by bringing their entwined hands to his mouth, turning hers over and kissing her palm. Her flesh tingled from his touch, and she gasped.

"Yeah," he said in that same breathless tone, and she knew just what that one-word reply meant.

It was still there, always there in the background, that fierce attraction they had toward each other—and it continued to amaze her. In the middle of this nightmare of drugs and gangsters and blood and dead sisters and ex-husbands, she could and did feel outrageously attracted to this man. And, apparently, he felt the same. Amazing.

It was the only bright spot Carly could find, but it was strong enough to make the nightmare bearable.

The light turned green. The car started up and, again, Nick's voice, all-business once more, broke into her reverie. "Now we're on seven. Lucky seven. Someone is following you, someone tried to kidnap you at the airport, someone was behind us at the marina this morning. Let's assume it's the same person, and let's also assume this person was closely involved in the whole thing, because you remember his voice as part of your blackout period and from the airport. Question—Who is he? And why is he still after you?"

"Because I know something?"

"Or because he thinks you can ID someone, maybe him. Or, there could be something else that we have no information on at the moment."

"Wonderful," she said grimly.

"Hey, that's how it works. You lay out what you know, then you start filling in the missing pieces. So, what have I forgotten?"

"Richard's death," she said quietly.

"Yeah." Offering an apologetic grimace, he said, "Sorry, I know he was once important to you, but he's still scum, as far as I'm concerned. Okay, eight—Richard is dead, so that source of information is dead, too. Is there anyone he would have told about this? A good friend?"

"I don't think so. He didn't have many friends."

Nick turned the car into the parking lot of a tall medical building, grabbed the automatic ticket and drove down a long, crowded row of parked cars. "He was killed sometime between midnight on Saturday—when Demeter was killed—and we don't know how many hours later. So we have two dead bodies, a woman with a blackout and a man following her."

"Do you think...?" It was hard to treat any of this, but especially her ex-husband's murder, so dispassionately, but Carly made the attempt. "I mean, was Richard's death part of the plan or incidental? Was my suicide setup part of the plan or incidental? Was Demeter's death part of the plan or incidental?"

"And how do we make sure everyone knows you're innocent?" He maneuvered the car into a space. Again, he looked in his rearview mirror as he turned off the ignition. "The man who followed you, he's the key. I haven't seen him since he took off. I wonder where he went."

Dr. Neil Mishkin was in his early forties, medium height and slim, with thinning hair, thick glasses and the nicest smile Carly had ever seen on a doctor. On his office desk stood a silver-framed portrait of himself, a petite brunette and three young boys with the same smile. She relaxed with him immediately.

Nick, on the other hand, was far from relaxed. Neil had insisted on giving Carly a full physical examination before deciding if hypnotherapy was called for, and had also insisted that Nick wait in the reception area. Instead, while Carly was being poked and probed, he found a pay phone and called a reporter he knew and set up a meeting. Then he returned to the waiting room and flipped through magazine after magazine without registering a thing he read.

Apart from his concern about Carly, he couldn't escape a nagging sense that he needed to hurry. A murderer was on the loose, Carly was in danger, and Nick wanted answers—now. When, finally, the female receptionist told him he could go into the doctor's office, he leaped up so quickly, one of the other patients who had been dozing jumped with surprise.

"Sorry," Nick said, and followed the crisp white uniform to Neil's office. The doctor was alone, seated at his desk, a file spread out in front of him, when Nick entered. "Where's Carly?"

"Changing."

"Thanks for seeing her on such short notice, Neil," he said.

Dr. Mishkin waved away the gratitude. "Don't worry about it. Sit down, won't you." He had a precise, formal way of speaking, one that belied his basically friendly nature. "Ms. Terry said it was all right to fill you in on what I've already told her. I take it you two are quite close friends."

Nick smiled. It had been the quickest close friendship in history. "Yeah, you could say that." He lowered himself onto a chair that faced the doctor, but leaned in eagerly, too keyed-up to sit back. "So?"

"According to Ms. Terry, she's pretty sure she was given a drug on Friday night, and has suffered a memory blackout. From her description of symptoms, it's possible she was given an illegal version of Rohypnol or gamma hydroxybutyrate."

"'Roofies' or 'Scoop,'" Nick said, using the street words. The rape pills. His jaw tightened.

"Yes." The doctor consulted his notes. "There has been recent intercourse, a little soreness in the genital area, but no signs of forced penetration or violence. Also, there's no spermatozoa present, so either there was no completion or he was wearing a condom."

"He was. It was me."

The doctor glanced up from his file and said with a small smile, "So she said."

"Are there signs that anyone...other than me, I mean..." Nick shrugged.

"Had intercourse with her? It can't be ruled out. In a mature woman, without sperm samples, it's impossible to tell how many partners she might have had recently."

"So, we still don't have an answer on that."

He shook his head. "Sorry."

The office door opened and Carly entered, sliding into the seat next to Nick. He glanced at her to see if she was all right; she gave a small smile that signaled she was. Then she folded her hands on her lap in that way she had of wanting to appear self-possessed.

Nick turned his attention back to the doctor. "Go on."

"I drew blood. The lab will test it for all the known narcotics, although the drugs I mentioned leave the body pretty quickly."

"When will you get the results?"

"Preliminary toxicology should be in by tomorrow morning. I've put a rush on it." Picking up a piece of paper, Neil read again. "Her heart is fine, her blood pressure is slightly elevated, but she assures me it's usually normal, so we can assume that's due to the recent stress she's been under. Her memory, while spotty, seems to be returning. Basically, she is in good health."

"What about hypnosis? You know, to help it along. That's what I thought you would be doing."

The doctor steepled his hands and looked from Nick to Carly and back again. "It's not always reliable. It's preferable, and less traumatic for the patient, if the memory returns on its own."

"Dr. Mishkin thinks I should wait a couple of days," Carly told Nick.

He scowled. "We may not have a couple of days."

"Oh?" The doctor raised an eyebrow. "No one has contacted me from your precinct. I'm sorry, I didn't realize there was a time element operating.''

''Let's say this is more of an unofficial request,'' Nick said. ''But it's still an emergency.''

The doctor studied him, then nodded. ''Tomorrow, possibly. Ms. Terry has already recalled a lot of what happened. If her blackout period was actually a drug-induced coma, she might never remember anything else.''

''But do you think I'll be okay?'' Carly asked, folding and unfolding her hands on her lap. ''Will there be any lasting damage?''

''Doubtful, but we'll have to wait for the test results to determine that.''

Nick scowled again, drumming his restless fingers on the arm of his chair. ''So, we don't know a hell of a lot more than we did when we came in.''

''Nick.'' Carly placed a restraining hand on his arm, as though to keep him from jumping out of his seat.

''Some things take more time than others, Nick.'' Dr. Mishkin's smile was understanding. ''I wish it could be otherwise.'' He rose from his desk chair. ''Now, if you don't mind, I have a waiting room full...''

Carly stood and offered her hand. ''Thank you so much.''

He shook it, then studied her. ''I recommend you do something to take your mind off this—walk, go to a movie. Better yet, get some sunshine. The brain is an amazing organ, it prefers to heal itself.''

Carly sat in Nick's car, watching him as he slid into the driver's seat, overcome by a sense of gratitude...but more than that, a closeness, a connectedness to this man. The sensation was unfamiliar to her, but it churned up her emotions all over again, bringing a tightness to her throat and chest.

''Nick?''

''Yeah?'' He glanced up as he was putting his key in the ignition. She could see by the way his forehead was creased that he was frustrated by the doctor visit and its nonanswers. His shoulders were tight with tension.

"Thank you," she said softly. "From the bottom of my heart. Being examined by a doctor was the intelligent thing to do, of course, and I've been in such a state it was the furthest thing from my mind. So, thank you for insisting on it. And it was...so good having you there. I still don't have a lot of answers, but somehow I feel less terrified."

It was true—her predicament hadn't changed, and she might still face a rocky road ahead, but that sense of being alone with her fears was over. She had been so alone—and so afraid—most of her life.

One side of his mouth quirked up. "You feel better? Really?" he said distractedly, then seemed to actually focus on her. He shifted in his seat so he faced her. His gaze roamed all over her face, and he smiled. "You do look a hell of a lot more relaxed. What an amazing change." He reached out and stroked her hair, then cupped her cheek. "You've really been through it, haven't you?"

The gentleness of his touch made her pulse quicken. She brought her hand up to cover his. Then, as though he were a magnet and she a piece of metal, she leaned into him, setting her elbow on the armrest. The feeling of his flesh against hers, warming her, was like something almost mystical—a transfusion of his strength. "It doesn't seem so bad now."

"Good," he said quietly, but made no other move.

"Please," she said.

"Please what?"

"Please kiss me." She hadn't planned to say that, but when his mouth covered hers—gently this time, softly, not with the aggressiveness she associated with him—it felt so right.

Her lips parted for him and he groaned, shifting the angle of their mouths so he could delve into hers more deeply. But still he kept the kiss gentle, and she was grateful. He seemed to know it wasn't hot, raw sex she wanted right now.

On the other hand... The lovely soft pressure of his mouth

and tongue created sensations in the rest of her body that were just as arousing, in a subtler way. In truth, everything about Nick was arousing, and she might as well face it.

When she slid her arms around his neck and kissed him harder, he responded with another groan. The kiss deepened until their breaths mingled in short, hot gasps.

Carly was the one who broke away—she needed air. The expression she saw on Nick's face must have reflected her own—equal parts wonder and passion.

"Man," he said, breathing heavily. "Talk about timing."

He frowned as though disappointed, and started the car. "Let's go."

"Where to?" Dizzy with sensation, Carly managed to fasten her seat belt as he backed out of the parking space.

"My place."

She felt her mouth fall open with surprise. "Now?"

"Huh?" He chuckled. "I wish." With another glance in his rearview mirror, he pulled into the aisle and headed for the exit. "No. I'm locking you in so you'll be safe. I'll get someone to come stay with you."

Her euphoric dizziness disappeared immediately. "No."

"Hey. You said you'd take direction from me."

"If it was reasonable." Her heart thumped loudly, but her senses remained sharp. "This is not reasonable. This is my mess, not yours, and I want to be part of getting myself out of it."

He pulled the Camaro into an empty slot and slammed the gear into Park. "Listen, if that guy is following you—"

"Is he?"

"Not so far as I can tell, but that doesn't mean you're not in danger. He could have accomplices. We have no idea who we're dealing with. I'll feel a lot better if you're behind a locked door."

"Where will you be?"

"Out in the field, working on the case, doing footwork."

She crossed her arms over her chest and stuck her jaw out.

"I'll feel a lot safer with you than without you, Nick, that's the truth. So, you're not getting rid of me."

At first he glared at her; then his expression turned troubled. "You're putting a hell of a lot on me, Carly," he said.

"Am I?" She was instantly contrite. "I don't mean to."

"Hey, I'm only human." He raked his fingers through his hair. "I'm a good cop, got a pretty good brain, but I'm not some all-powerful cartoon hero. I can't promise to keep you safe."

"I haven't asked for promises, just to stay with you." A deep surge of emotion made her bite her lip to keep it from taking her over. She felt her eyes filling, but managed to say, "I'm a little claustrophobic, I guess. I don't want to be locked up." Her voice shook; she couldn't help it. "In your apartment, in jail, anywhere."

She took a couple more deep breaths, swiped under her eyes in case any of the tears had escaped, then faced front again, focusing her attention on whatever blurry object was beyond the windshield. "So," she said with determination, "now that we're not going back to your place, where *are* we going?"

Out of the corner of her eye, she saw Nick shake his head either in exasperation or reluctant admiration, or both. "Man, when you start to develop teeth, you really start using them, don't you?" He put the car into reverse and backed out of the space. "All right," he said. "Here's the next part of my plan—it's time you got to see again."

On Main Street in Venice, Nick took Carly to an instant eyeglass place where she was given an exam, tried on frames, chose the cheapest ones she could find and was told to return in two hours.

"I thought this was a one-hour place," Nick complained to the clerk, a curly-headed young man busily snapping gum.

"We're backed up."

He gazed around; they were the only customers in the place. "Make it an hour," he said. "I'll pay extra."

"Listen, mister—"

He flashed his badge and said confidentially, "We need this young woman to ID a lineup ASAP."

The clerk stopped chewing and stood up straight. "Yessir, you got it."

"The perks of power." Carly chuckled as they left the store. "If you got it, flaunt it."

Neil Mishkin had said Carly should get some sunshine, and the weather had cooperated. If it wasn't for the fact that Nick had to keep looking over his shoulder at every moment, he might have enjoyed a stroll along Main Street with Carly. But strolling wasn't the smart thing to do—it made them too much of a target.

He guided her down the street, one hand on her back, checking out their surroundings at all times. As they were passing a large used-clothing store named Aardvark's Odd Ark, Carly stopped and peered into the window. Nick stood behind her, his attention drawn by a coat that seemed to be made of fake polar bear fur.

"I love places like this," Carly said happily. "I'm a thrift-shop junkie. You can find the most amazing bargains." She squinted at a dress that looked to Nick like something out of an old Sandra Dee movie.

"Come on." He took her elbow. "Let's get you something new."

"But old clothing is much more fun."

"I hate shopping," he grumbled.

Angling her head, she grinned at him. "You really are a typical male, aren't you?"

"I sincerely hope so." He grunted. "Okay, let's go in."

While Carly checked through the racks, Nick kept an eye out. His gut told him the stalker from this morning was history—either he'd decided to get lost, or something else had come up to take him away from his pursuit of Carly. But Nick wouldn't let down his guard—all it took was one moment of inattention for violence to strike.

Something on one of the racks caught Nick's eye, and he pulled it out. It was a low-cut, semitransparent black dress. He went over to Carly and tapped her on the shoulder. When she glanced around, he held up the dress, smiling suggestively. "What do you think?"

Her eyes widened, then she gazed at him sorrowfully. "I wish I were like that, but I'm not." She was serious, he realized, actually regretful that she wasn't comfortable being on sexual display. Come to think of it, he was glad she wasn't.

"Hey, I'm kidding, really." When Carly's face relaxed with relief, he checked out the dress one more time. "So, you find this too obvious, huh?"

"About as subtle as a For Rent sign."

She chose a lightweight green sweater and matching slacks. A small well-used black leather purse brought the total to nineteen dollars. After that, they picked up a toothbrush and underwear—sensible cotton, to Nick's regret. But, he figured, now was probably not the time to extol the virtues of silk and lace next to skin. Maybe later, when the threat of danger was history. Maybe then.

The glasses were ready when they returned. Carly put on the round black frames, peered around the shop, then into a mirror. Her very own, nonfuzzy face stared back at her. "I can see!" Turning to Nick, she wrinkled her nose. "Do I look awful?"

"No. Actually, you look kind of cute."

She made a face. "Spare me. But, oh, Nick, this is wonderful. Do you realize I have yet to see, I mean, really *see*, anything? What's next?"

He glanced at his watch. "We get information. This reporter I know is meeting us in fifteen minutes."

"Reporter?"

"We do each other favors sometimes. I supply an extra detail or two on a case, Bobbie gives newspaper space to something that needs publicity. She's bringing along pictures and background on Demeter."

The sense of letdown was immediate. Carly had been in-dulging herself, enjoying a brief respite from tension. Engaging in banter with Nick, and window-shopping in the sunshine, she'd actually been able to leave the terror in the shadows.

But, of course, Nick was right. Now that her immediate physical needs were taken care of, it was time to focus all their attention on the case.

The clock was ticking.

Chapter 9

The morning clouds were gone. The fabled Venice Beach boardwalk, Nick observed, looked her best. As it was past tourist season, the wide stretch of sand that ended in a sun-dappled ocean seemed clean and relatively free of debris. There was, as always, still a lot of foot traffic on the board-walk—dogs, in-line skaters, bicyclists, joggers, the elderly with walkers, mothers and fathers with babies in strollers—but Nick was able to steer Carly close to some of the stalls that lined one side of the street.

He should have set the meeting with Bobbie in a less public place, he thought. He should have brought his gun. If he hadn't been off the force all these months, he would have automatically taken it with him when they'd left the house that morning. He'd lost his edge, and he knew it. So he was super-vigilant in protecting Carly, sticking close and constantly checking their surroundings. The merchandise was all junk to him, but Carly seemed to find the tacky T-shirts with slogans, racks of sunglasses and cheap jewelry, swimwear and souve-nirs thoroughly fascinating.

The woman was definitely a shopper. Nick added this facet of her personality to the small store of information he already had on her. She was also, he discovered, a basketball fan. She knew her game—years, she told him, spent rooting for the Celtics. He was a Lakers man, but who cared, as long as she was a fan.

When Nick steered her to the Venice basketball courts, which consisted of several playing areas divided by chain-link fencing, Carly decided she had never seen so much testosterone in one place. Black, white and brown athletes, mostly men, but a few women, communicated with each other using the most astonishingly foul language Carly had ever heard. As Nick and she found an empty bench to sit on, he explained that was just the way they talked—it was part of the tradition and meant nothing personal.

The games were fast and furious. Onlookers hooted their encouragement. Even though she knew they'd come there to meet the reporter, Carly found herself so caught up in a one-on-one challenge, she barely noticed when a woman sat down on the other side of Nick and said hello to him.

"Carly," Nick said, "meet Bobbie Kim."

Bobbie's round face creased in a smile; she reached over Nick and gave Carly a hearty handshake. She could have been anywhere between thirty and fifty, Carly thought, liking her instantly. Her features were one hundred percent Asian, but her accent was that of a California native, except that she spoke much more rapidly. Carly had to really work to keep up with the woman's flow of words.

Bobbie had gathered all that her newspaper's files had on the late Mr. and Mrs. Peter Demeter. To the background noise of thudding basketballs, running feet and colorful insults flying back and forth as quickly as the ball changed hands, Nick looked over the information about Demeter while Carly read about what had happened to her sister.

Nina Terry had become someone else, had undergone a total transformation, leaving behind the small-town girl of her youth. The reborn Amanda Terrence had been a dancer in Las Vegas, then gone on to Hollywood. Some modeling, some "acting"—roles in a couple of X-rated films. Marriage to Pete Demeter, a big-time gangster, a huge home in the Silver Lake area near downtown L.A., great sections of which had nearly been destroyed in the '94 earthquake. After that, they'd lived aboard Demeter's yacht. He had been wild about her, they'd thrown lavish parties. Who was this person, this Amanda? Carly wondered sadly. Had she ever known her sister at all?

In the car crash six months earlier that had killed Amanda, Demeter had been driving. It had not been his fault; the other driver, who had been drunk, was also killed. Nevertheless, Pete Demeter had been racked with guilt over his wife's death and had become a near hermit since, grieving in seclusion.

Bobbie had also brought along some clippings with pictures of Demeter's associates. Still dazed and troubled by the story of her sister, Carly looked through them, then, disappointed, shook her head. She didn't recognize any of the faces. Bobbie shrugged, smiled, said she was glad to help and took off, walking away as rapidly as she'd spoken.

Bobbie's data confirmed what Nick already knew: recent underground scuttlebutt was that Demeter was losing control over his drug-trafficking empire. The sharks were circling. There were rumors of a possible takeover from within while his enemies nipped at his heels. But there was nothing new in all this information, nothing that would cast a light on the mystery of Carly's involvement and the man who was after her.

He'd been hoping for a break, but it hadn't popped up yet. He glanced at Carly and noticed the wistful expression on her face. "Hey, what is it?"

"Nothing, really," she said with a sad smile. "It's just that I guess I never really knew my sister, and now I'll never get the chance."

Squeezing her hand, he said grimly, "If she could live with Pete Demeter, believe me, you're better off not knowing her

better. The man was a vicious killer—the world is better off
without him.''

She nodded, letting him know she was all right, so he went
on. ''I need to access the sheriff's department database. Their
organized-crime section has everything we're looking for.''

''Can you do that?''

''No, but Dom can. It's time to bring him on board. Come
on, let's find a phone.''

Most of the public phones were out of order, so Nick
grabbed Carly's hand and they ducked into a trendy coffee-
house that stood adjacent to a pool hall. He called Dom from
the pay phone, managing to reach him at his desk.

''So, what's up, Nick?'' Dom asked.

''I need mug shots of everyone concerned with Demeter.''

''Yeah? Why?''

''Because I'm asking you.''

''Not good enough.''

Nick muttered an expletive. ''Why did I know you would
say that? Okay, here it is.''

With Carly by his side, her gaze locked on him, he spent
the next five minutes, pitching his voice low, laying out the
situation for Dom. His friend's only reaction was what
sounded like brief spurts of rapid gum-chewing.

''Okay,'' he said when Nick was done. ''I'll need an hour
or so. Meet me at, let's see, somewhere out of the way. I got
it. The kid? Miguel? His family runs a restaurant in Santa
Monica, Casa Griego on Tenth near Colorado. Meet me there
at six.''

''We have an hour,'' Nick told Carly when he hung up.
''You hungry? Need to do any more shopping?'' He was
buzzed, impatient. He wanted action. Now.

She put a hand on his arm and said softly, ''What I'd like
to do is sit on a cliff and look down on the ocean. Do you
mind? Something about the waves and the sand makes me
calm down, and I really need to do that.''

So did he, and both of them knew it. "I know just the place."

They drove to the palisades that stretched all along and above the Santa Monica beachfront. Rugged cliffs rose high over the Pacific Coast Highway, offering a view of the vast ocean. Along the grass-filled palisades were oddly shaped pine trees that had been sculpted by the winds. In the late afternoon, people were gathering blankets and boom boxes, leaving, making their way back to their regular lives.

A low wooden fence, perfect for leaning on, ran the entire two-mile length. After checking the area and deciding it was safe, Nick stood next to Carly and watched die-hard surfers to the south, dolphins to the north, sailboats way in the distance. For a short while, he tried, really tried, to allow his nervous energy to let down.

Carly's suggestion had been a good one. When you looked at the ocean, just looked at it, thought about how it had always been there and always would, things got put into context. He'd always been drawn to the water for that very reason.

It was one more thing they had in common.

Monday night

At six, they walked into Casa Griego, which was small and intimate, with four tables in the middle and three rounded and high-backed booths on each side, facing center. All except one of the booths were full, but conversation was muted by the mariachi music playing in the background. Just past the entrance stood a colorfully decorated cubicle where a round, gray-haired woman—the blood of an ancient American Indian tribe inscribed on her face—was hand-rolling tortillas from ground cornmeal, then setting them on a hot griddle to bake.

At the first whiff of the restaurant's wonderful smells, Carly heard her stomach growl. Realizing they hadn't eaten since breakfast, she told Nick, "I'm starving."

"Yeah?" He seemed distracted, but revved up again, the

way he'd been all morning. The ocean view had helped her, a little anyway. But it hadn't worked its magic on Nick. His barely contained restlessness radiated from him like static electricity.

A slender, dark-haired boy of twenty or so came up and led them to a booth. "Carly, this is Miguel," Nick said. "Miguel, meet Carly."

The boy smiled shyly at her. "Welcome to my family's place," he said with a faint Hispanic accent.

"It's charming," she said. "Do you have a large family?"

"My aunt and uncle are in the kitchen. That's my *abuela,* my grandmother, rolling the tortillas, and my mother is watching from the cash register. I wait on tables, and my little brother is the busboy. Now, what can I bring you?" he said once they were seated. "A glass of beer? Maybe some nachos?"

By now her mouth was watering. These were not familiar East Coast smells, but they were enticing. She glanced at Nick, then back at Miguel. "Well, we hadn't planned on eating…" She let it trail off.

"But you will," Miguel said with a grin. "Dom told me you were meeting him here." His eyes glowed with excitement. "You two are working on something undercover. Very important."

"Yeah? Is that what he said?" Nick asked.

"Not really, but I can tell when he's hyped. He's been my Big Brother a lot of years. Okay, sit back and I'll bring something *delicioso* while you're waiting for him."

Dom walked in just as they were drinking beer and eating hot fresh corn chips smothered with melted cheese and chiles. He was shorter than Nick and stockier, Carly noted, although none of it was fat. He had black curly hair, a nose that looked as if it had been broken a few times and an unsmiling mouth with a small scar across one corner. He wore dark wraparound sunglasses and chewed gum rapidly. He scared her to death.

"Um, hi," she said when Nick introduced them.

Poker-faced, Dom nodded at her by way of return greeting, but said nothing. As his glasses completely covered his eyes, she couldn't see his expression—but it wasn't friendly. She wondered if he disliked all women on principle or her in particular, for putting Nick in a difficult situation. Whichever it was, it didn't make for a pleasant atmosphere.

Seating himself next to Nick, Dom tossed a thick manila envelope on the table. As though on cue, Miguel appeared with an open bottle of beer and a chilled glass, and set it down in front of him. "Your favorite, Dom."

Dom almost cracked a smile. "I like the service, kid."

"Will you excuse me, please?" Carly said, getting up and escaping to the bathroom. She needed to give herself a little talking-to.

Both men watched her walk away, then Dom turned to Nick. "Hey, my friend," he said, "what kind of deep doo-doo are you into? You got to bring her in."

"I will. Not yet."

"She's a witness to a homicide."

"Not technically—she didn't see who did it."

"Don't give me that technically crap. Hell, she should go in for her own safety, if nothing else."

"I'm taking care of it."

"Oh? Pardon me, I forgot I was talking to supercop. Why haven't you brought her in?"

Nick let out a sigh. What Dom was saying reflected what his brain had told him already, repeatedly. He shouldn't have agreed to the twenty-four hours. But, since meeting Carly, he hadn't listened to his brain. "Because I've promised her she doesn't have to, not yet."

"Excuse me?" The black eyebrow rose in an arch. "You 'promised'?" He made the word sound ludicrous.

Defensive now, Nick's temper flared. "Hey, I gave her till tomorrow morning, Dom. Get off my back. If you don't want to help me, say so."

Dom continued to stare at him, assessing. He chewed his

gum rapidly, then stopped. Finally, his natural pugnacity lessened and he allowed one corner of his mouth to quirk up.
"All right, for now."

"And, for my sake, lighten up a little on Carly."

"Yeah, yeah, okay." Shaking his head at the shame of it
all, he added, "Amazing what happens to a man when a
woman is involved."

"It happened to you, too, Dom," Nick said quietly. "With
Theresa."

At the mention of Dom's late wife, his friend took in a quick
breath of surprise. He was thoroughly subdued, his expression
serious. "No way. Is it like that, Nick?"

"Could be."

Dom whistled softly. At that moment, Carly returned to the
table. He snuck another look at her, as though deciding to
really check her out this time, maybe even give her another
chance. Good, Nick thought. The tension at the table would
lessen now.

"Ready," Carly said. She'd taken a little time to gather her
resources. Dom had intimidated her, but she was determined
to get past that. She had no intention of viewing pictures of
criminals while her hands shook.

"Look at these, okay?" Dom said, pulling out the stack of
pictures from the envelope and setting them on the table. He
sounded almost pleasant, for that moment. While she studied
each one, he went on. "I ran a check on all known associates.
The two goons that guarded Demeter are in that stack too, in
case they look familiar. Both of them were found unconscious
belowdecks, one with a major conk across the temple."

He pointed. "That would be Sam 'the Shift-Man'
O'Connell. The docs aren't sure if he'll make it. The other
one—Fast Frankie L'Bonza—he just had a mild concussion,
but he ain't saying squat."

Wide-eyed, Carly glanced at Dom, then at Nick. "Do they
really have names like that? Shift Man and Fast Frankie?"

Nick chuckled. "Yeah, it's a status thing. If you don't have a nickname, you're not part of the inner circle."

Dom pointed to the picture Carly held in her hand—a brutal-looking man with a shaved head. "I also threw in a few for-hire types, in case some rival gang set Demeter up. I got a whole book of these crooks down at the station." He directed this pointedly to Carly. "If you want to come in, you could look through them."

"Tomorrow, Dom," Nick said easily, perusing the pictures over Carly's shoulder. "Like I told you."

Carly had just rejected one of a surly-seeming ape of a man when she picked up the next one and froze. Her stomach muscles clenched with fear.

The man had a narrow face with sunken pits under his cheekbones, and pale, eerie eyes. His hairline was receding, but he didn't seem older than thirty-five or so. True, she hadn't seen him with her glasses on, but she hadn't needed to. "That's him," she told Nick and Dom. "The man at the airport. And he was on the yacht, too, at some point, although I can't say just when."

Nick grabbed the picture, studied it and nodded. "Yeah, that's the one who followed us this morning."

"Bingo," Dom said.

Nick turned the photo over and read the information on the back. "Eddie Monk," he said out loud, "aka Lance Monk aka Lawrence Edwards... Born in Boyle Heights, here in L.A. Two arrests, in L.A. and Vegas. One conviction—served nine months in Nevada for selling drugs. That was eight years ago. Moved back to L.A. afterward. Last-known address is Kittery Island, Maine."

At last, Carly thought. A lead, something concrete. But... "Maine?" she repeated with surprise. "Nice, peaceful, serene Maine? They have men with nicknames on an island in Maine?"

Nick smiled at her naiveté. "These guys are anywhere

there's people and money and a way to take advantage of both.''

Dom drank his beer, then wiped his mouth with the back of his hand. ''Demeter's operation has been infiltrating New England the last couple of years. This guy might have worked for him on the East Coast.'' He took the picture from Nick and perused it. ''Eddie Monk. Don't know him.''

He took a final slug of beer, then slid out of the booth. ''I'll call in, get someone to run an updated check on him.''

After Dom left, Carly's eyes were wide as she said to Nick, ''Boy, I thought you were tough. He's like the Godfather.''

''Nah, inside he's a pussycat.''

''Jungle variety, I think.'' She put her hand over her heart for emphasis. ''He chews gum as though he's chomping some-one to death.''

''He stopped smoking a couple of months ago and it's driv-ing him crazy. Dom's one of those guys who was raised in a neighborhood where the kids either become priests, cops or crooks. He didn't have a strong enough belief for the church, but he swears it was a toss-up between the other two.''

''I can believe it.''

''But he's good people. And he's with us, all the way.''

She put both hands up in a gesture of surrender. ''Then I take it all back. The man's a saint.''

Nick smiled, but already his mind had left the conversation. Eddie Monk. Nick silently repeated the name. Eddie Monk. Boyle Heights. Vegas. Maine.

Nick's excitement level, which had been up there all day, was now approaching the top of the scale. It was that feeling he always got when they were closing in on a perp, wrapping up a case, fitting together the last pieces of a puzzle. It was a buzz that could never be matched anywhere else, and only cops understood it.

Not that he'd stopped worrying about Carly. She was still in danger, and all kinds of things could happen to the case later, in the courts, in the press. But this part of an investigation was the high. He drummed his fingers on the tabletop, his mind busy calculating his next move.

Then he snapped his fingers.

"What?" Carly asked.

Miguel walked up with a platter of food just as Nick rose and said, "I need to make a call."

"You can use the phone in the office," Miguel told him. "It's private."

"Thanks. Will you keep Carly company? I'll just be a few minutes."

"Sure." He set the large platter of quesadillas, beans and rice in the center of the table. The spicy aroma of hot chile peppers and something even more exotic wafted into her nostrils. As steam rose from the platter, soft cheese oozed out of the sides of the quesadillas. Her mouth watered. "I guess I'll have a bite or two," she said.

Miguel grinned. "Bet you can't stop at a bite or two."

By the time Nick returned, she'd downed an entire plateful of food and made friends with Miguel. She'd heard all about Dom being a Big Brother, and Miguel's dreams of being on the police force, and the pointers Nick had given him the previous day. There was some hero worship going on, she thought with a smile.

Nick spoke as he slid into the booth. "Lucky break. I just talked to Ken Millett, friend of mine, used to work Boyle Heights. His wife had asthma so he transferred to Phoenix. He was home just now. He knew this Eddie Monk."

At the mention of Monk's name, Carly's jitters started up again. But she made herself concentrate on every word Nick had to say.

"Monk was a small-timer. Used to be a hairdresser, can you believe that? Then a blackjack dealer in Vegas, then got involved in porn magazines. On the side he always ran a little dope. He left L.A. about three years ago and no one's seen him since. There was no connection to Demeter that Ken knew of, but that didn't mean there wasn't one. He gave me the name of another cop who knew Eddie a lot better. He wasn't in; I'll try him again later. More background, anyway.''

Nick had noticed that Miguel had been hanging on every word. "You, all you cops, you know each other. It's like a fraternity.''

"You see each other in court, hang out at bars." Nick shrugged. "Yeah, most of us know each other.''

Miguel rose reluctantly. "My mother's giving me the eye. I have to get back to work. Is there anything I can do, Nick. Any way I can help?''

"Yeah, go to college.''

"I meant now—on this case.''

"I know.''

They stared at each other, then Miguel said quietly, "No matter what you and Dom say, I want to join the force, Nick.''

"You can join, after college. Listen, amigo, they got an incentives program for college grads—fast track to getting your stripes. It's the smart move. Think about it.''

Miguel frowned, then stared down at his feet. "Yeah, okay.''

"Hey," Nick said. "Thanks for looking out for Carly.''

The young man glowed, then with an embarrassed nod, walked in the direction of the kitchen. Nick turned back to Carly. "So, how are you holding up?''

She gazed at him, the rounded glasses and large amber eyes giving her face a serious, studious look. "He's a nice boy. It's hard to imagine him in uniform.''

"Yeah. So, answer my question. You okay?''

She shrugged. "Is it going like it's supposed to? I know you can't give me any guarantees, but it's just that every time I think about Eddie Monk, I get the willies. What happens now?''

He covered her hand with his. "We get Monk, bring him in for questioning. You tell the D.A. what you know, we make the connections, build a case. I'll be with you every step of the way. And so will Dom. Homicide is under the jurisdiction of the sheriff's department. Hell, Dom will probably get credit for the collar.''

"What if you don't get him?"

He saw the flash of fear in her eyes, saw her trying not to give in to it. She was fighting her demons with every weapon she could muster. A need to comfort her, to surround her with safety, made him bring her hand to his chest and hold it to his heart. "I'm not leaving you till we do," he said quietly.

She searched his gaze, and whatever she found there made the fear in her eyes diminish. She smiled, seemed about to say something, then shook her head.

"What?" he asked.

"I...don't understand why you're so good to me."

"Don't you?" he said softly. "Haven't you figured it out yet?"

Carly was struck speechless. Dom chose that moment to hurry back to the table, so she had to drag her gaze away from Nick's sea-green eyes and remove her hand from his fast-beating heart so she could pay attention to whatever Dom had to tell them. But new thoughts whirled in her head, sensations that had nothing to do with solving a murder case. She felt a totally inappropriate giggle trying to come up, but she clamped her mouth closed and bit down hard to stop it.

This time Dom slid into the round-backed booth on her side instead of Nick's, and even offered her an encouraging smile. Still reeling from that moment with Nick, she nodded at him, but didn't trust herself to say anything.

Suddenly, with Nick on her right and Dom on her left—each, in their way, equally imposing—she felt a little like a very small sardine stuck in a can between two huge fish. But it was more of a comfort than a threat.

Dom grabbed the platter from the middle of the table, set it in front of him and dug in. "Man, this food is good."

Nick covered Carly's hand with his as he asked Dom, "So? Anything from DMV?"

"Yeah," he answered in between bites. "Monk didn't renew his license, but they got an old address for him—in West Hollywood, on Lexington. And the Department of Water and Power says he still pays for utilities there.''

Nick was out of his seat before Dom finished his sentence. ''Let's go.''

Dom shoveled one last mouthful in, wiped his mouth with his napkin and stood. ''She stays,'' he said, pointing to Carly.

''She goes,'' Nick said. ''I don't want her out of my sight.''

''Miguel can keep her company. She'll be safe here.''

''Excuse me, gentlemen.'' Carly slid out of the booth and planted herself between both of them. ''Didn't anyone ever teach you it's not polite to discuss someone in the third person, as if she wasn't in the room? I'm going.''

Dom glared at her for a moment, then cracked a smile. ''Pushy, ain't she?''

''Some women,'' Nick said, ''they think they wear the pants.''

''If you're both done preening,'' Carly said tartly, ''I'd sure like to get moving.''

The drive to West Hollywood took about a half hour. While Nick filled Dom in on what he'd learned from Ken Millet, Carly's head flip-flopped between wanting to capture Eddie Monk tonight and never wanting to see the man again. Whatever had happened to her on that yacht, she knew he'd played a large part in it. He was evil, and dangerous...although her imagination just might be going in the direction of high melodrama.

Instead of dwelling on it, she listened to Dom's police scanner, receiving an insider's earful on reported incidents, Los Angeles style. There seemed to be an endless stream of wife-beatings, gang warfare, armed robberies. Life seemed cheap, somehow; people pulled out machine guns and killed indiscriminately. She knew, of course, that if you hung around with cops, you heard only the bad stuff. You didn't come in contact with goodness or kind deeds, or even happy children. But it was a violent world Nick lived in, one that she doubted she could adjust to.

Hold it, she told herself silently. Why was she even considering adjusting to Nick's world? But she knew the answer; in that moment back in the restaurant, there had passed between them a feeling that she'd never experienced before. In fact, since that morning when she'd finally unburdened herself, she'd felt so close to him, so connected to Nick in a way that let her know she'd never really been intimate with anyone before in her life.

She wanted more. She wanted him…or so she thought. Always prudent, Carly reminded herself that these feelings might not stand up under the less hectic, less dangerous, just plain normal light of day-to-day reality. But, for the moment, it was so comforting to have this harbor of warm feelings to dock in.

The house on Lexington was one of many similar ones on the tree-lined street. Built in the 1930s California-bungalow style she'd seen in magazines, it was a one-story wood frame with a covered front porch. A pathway beside the house led to a small guest apartment over the garage in the rear, which, Dom explained, was where Eddie Monk lived.

Again Dom wanted Carly to wait in the car, again Nick refused to allow it. He was serious about his vow not to let her out of his sight, she thought, and thank God he was.

It was eight-thirty now, and overhead lamps lit the city street, but there was no illumination in the rear of the house. The windows of Eddie Monk's apartment were dark. Nick and Carly stood back several feet, under a large avocado tree while, with gun by his side, Dom walked up the stairs to the door and knocked, moving quickly to one side afterward. There was no answer. From a nearby yard came the high yipping sound of a small barking dog. When Dom knocked again, louder this time, another much deeper bark joined the first.

Carly couldn't suppress a nervous shudder. "I guess the silent approach is out," she quipped. Nick squeezed her shoulder; his grip was hard, and she could imagine that the muscles in his shoulders were also bunched with tension.

Dom waited another few moments, then tried to turn the doorknob. It was locked. He gave up and hurried down the stairs. "He's not there."

"Kick the door down," Nick whispered.

"Come off it. With no warrant, no official witness? No can do. The guy's not in."

"Ask the neighbors. Ask the owner of the house. What kind of car does he drive? Is it parked anywhere near?" he asked, his rapid-fire questions delivered in a tight voice.

"A twenty-year-old Cadillac. It might be in the garage, but I didn't see it parked on the street. Hey, cool it, huh?" Dom's voice had a warning edge to it.

Nick ignored him. "We need to put out an APB."

"Dammit, Nick, you know we can't put out an APB, not on the basis of what we got. You need to bring her in."

Carly, who had been watching this exchange in worried silence, put her hand on Dom's arm. "It's my fault, Dom, not Nick's, so don't blame him. He's just—"

Nick cut her off. "Don't, Carly. Look, Dom, we made a deal. She goes in tomorrow. Now, you want to drive us back to my car, or do I call a cab?"

The two men stared at each other, reminding Carly of two large stags sizing each other up. She held her breath, afraid they might get into a fight. But, amazingly enough, as though some guys-only signal had passed from one to the other, they each exhaled a slow breath.

Nick said, "Forget I said that," at the same time Dom came out with, "Okay, I hear you." Then they grinned at each other, nodded and walked her back to the car.

They were closing in, Nick thought all the way back from Santa Monica to his condo. But until Eddie Monk was in custody, the possibilities for danger were still rampant. One more night, Nick thought, then he wouldn't have to feel so responsible for Carly's safety.

Before putting his car in the garage, he drove around the block a few times, searching for Monk's Cadillac, or for anything that even looked out of place.

But the neighborhood seemed as peaceful as ever. Working people lived here, and Monday nights were always relatively quiet. There hadn't been a sign of Monk since that morning—where was he?

He let Carly into the condo then had her wait in the living room while he checked the other rooms and the balcony. There was no one and nothing to suggest he'd had any visitors. When Carly excused herself to wash out some things in the bathroom, he made sure all the windows and doors were locked, then went to his closet and got his gun from the top shelf. Quickly and efficiently he took the .38-caliber bullets from their case and loaded the weapon, grabbed the holster and stuck them both in the drawer of the nightstand.

The phone rang. Nick sat on the edge of his bed and answered it.

"Eddie Monk booked a flight to Boston that went out at 3:00 p.m." Dom said without preliminaries. "He checked luggage through, two suitcases, and, as far as we know, was on the flight. We're still making sure, though. I'll call you with updates."

"Thanks again, Dom. Especially for staying with it like this. I know I haven't made it easy—"

"Forget it. As long as the ending is a good one, who cares how we got there? Give Carly a kiss for me. I like her. She just may be a keeper." Dom hung up before Nick could reply.

Water was running in the bathroom sink and Carly was humming, her voice softly melodious. Smiling to himself at Dom's final words, Nick returned to the living room, thinking there was one more thing he'd meant to take care of, but couldn't remember what. His glance around the room stopped at the letter lying on the table by the easy chair. The smile left his face. The letter was not something he'd meant to take care of; it was something he'd been hoping to forget.

Reluctantly, he walked over to the chair, picked up the letter, read it again. The offer was a good one, and he knew it. He even knew he was lucky to have received it. His decision about retirement was getting close. He knew it and hated it. Even the personal note scrawled on the bottom, from the man who'd been his first partner on the force and now ran the police academy, wasn't enough to lighten the load of his decision.

He lowered himself onto the chair and stared at nothing.

After Carly finished rinsing out her new underthings, she found a sponge and wiped around the tile in Nick's bathroom. She genuinely enjoyed cleaning—loved to see porcelain shine. Absolutely hopeless, she thought with a smile. Baking, cleaning, even a little sewing on her old Singer—these were the things that gave her the most pleasure. A throwback, that's what she was. A dinosaur.

But she did her best thinking when busy cleaning. And her thoughts were now traveling in two directions, both having to do with Nick. She was a huge burden on him—possibly compromising him, endangering his friendship with Dom. The sooner she was out of his hair, the better.

But she also remembered the look tonight in the restaurant. And something Nick had said to her—heavens, was it just last night? He wanted her, but would wait for her to make the first move.

The first move. What did that entail? Announcing what she wanted and going after it? What she wanted was definitely Nick; the thought of lying in his arms again had been popping into her brain for most of the day. But how did someone "go after it?" She'd never initiated sex, another example of how she was a throwback. Except, of course, last Saturday night, and nothing about that night could be considered normal behavior for her.

Would she appear ludicrous? Would she please him? Fear

and self-doubt again—they'd been her constant companions for so much of her life. Wasn't it time to give herself a break? she wondered. And would it be tonight?

When she joined Nick in the living room, the sight of him slumped dejectedly in his chair made all her musings fly out the window. "What is it, Nick?"

"Huh?" He looked up, then sat straighter. "Oh. We have an update. It looks like Eddie Monk flew back East. Dom's checking to make sure."

Relief flooded her. "That's wonderful. Sort of." Nick's expression didn't concur. "I guess it's bad for the case and good for me?"

"Something like that."

"Is that why you're so down?"

"No. It's nothing." He rose from the chair and walked toward the kitchen. "I'm going to have a beer. Want one?"

"No, thanks. You didn't eat any dinner. Aren't you hungry?"

"Nope." He reached into the refrigerator and grabbed a bottle of beer. The very air around him seemed dark with unhappiness.

"Hey, Nick." Carly watched him anxiously. "Something's bothering you and I want to know what it is."

"Let it go."

He turned his back on her, but she moved around to his front and crossed her arms across her chest. "No. In the past two days, I've told you everything you'd ever want to know about me. You've made my problem yours, put a friendship on the line for me. Let me give something back. Please. I'm a good listener. Let me in, please."

Frowning, he took another drink from the bottle. "It's just a decision I have to make, that's all. About whether or not I remain a cop."

"Is there any doubt?"

"Oh, yeah." His short laugh was bitter. "There's doubt." He didn't go on for several moments, seeming to focus inside.

Then he shrugged. "It's this knee of mine, I told you it got smashed up by a bullet last year. I've had three operations on it. Between the hip and the knee…and," he added with self-disgust, "let's not forget the hand."

"What's the matter with your hip? And your hand?"

Nick leaned against the front of the refrigerator, cradling the half-empty beer bottle to his chest. "My hip got screwed up from all the volleyball. It's why I didn't pass the sheriff's department physical. Not that I've been unhappy at Manhattan Beach. No, these have been the best years of my life." He stared thoughtfully into space.

"And your hand?" she prompted.

"I used to use my fists a lot, in the marines, and before I became a cop." He held his right hand out, thumb extended. "There's a pin in there, from when I broke it, all along the thumb line. Believe it or not, except for all that, I'm in great health. Except I've got enough artificial parts in me to set off metal detectors," he added.

How difficult it was for him to let her see him this way, she thought, unprotected and hurting. She wanted to stroke his face, to offer some comfort. "You love being a cop, don't you?"

"Yeah," he said brusquely. "So, I have to make this decision. Do I try to get my knee in good enough shape to slog through another few years, or do I get out now?"

She stared at him, wondering how she could have spent two days with him and not had a hint of this inner turmoil. "I didn't know."

"I didn't tell you. Besides, you've had a couple of life-and-death matters on your mind."

Leaning against the counter, she kept her tone deliberately casual. "So, what will you do? Have you thought about options?"

He stared at her for a moment, as though turning something over in his mind. Then he strode into the living room. Carly followed him. He picked up a letter from the table near the easy chair and handed it to her wordlessly.

Carly read each word closely. It was an offer to teach a police procedures class at El Camino College. It noted Nick's fine record, the fact that he had his teaching credential from his sergeant's training, his leadership ability, and the fact that he'd been president of the police league for two years. She wasn't sure what all these groups were, but it wasn't necessary. This was a side of Nick she knew nothing about, another new dimension to him.

Smiling, she looked up at him. "But this is wonderful."

"A glorified desk job," he answered, dismissing its value.

"Where you'll be training new recruits. Breaking them in the way you want them to be broken in. Rookies, like Miguel. Young men and women who need to know what you know. Who are honest and dedicated like you are, not corrupt bullies like my f—" She interrupted herself. She'd been getting carried away. "I'm sorry," she went on. "I've just always thought that teaching is about the most important profession there is."

Again, his shrug said, So what? "Maybe." He walked over to the window, parted the curtain and looked out. "Lately, I've had this dream."

"Tell me."

"I'm at my old desk, at work. No one's paying attention to me. They're all working on a real important case, but they're horsing around, laughing, like they do when it gets to crunch time. And they're too busy to notice me. I'm back where I belong but no one gives a damn."

Aching for him, Carly walked up to Nick and put her hand on his back. The muscles were rigid with disappointment. "I'm so sorry you're—"

He whipped around and faced her. "Stop saying you're sorry. And I don't need your pity."

She flinched at his vehemence, but refused to let it keep her from having her say. "No, Nick, this isn't pity, just understanding. You can't do something you really want to do, and you know you have to accept it, and it hurts.''

"Dammit, I'm not ready yet." His jaw clenched.

"No, I can see that."

His pain ate at her. She wanted to give to him as he'd given to her. She wanted to take his mind off his troubles. It was the only explanation she could come up with for what she did next.

Slowly, she untied the belt of the robe she had on, pulled the lapels open and said, "Do you think you might be ready for me?"

Chapter 10

Nick felt his mouth literally drop open. As far as he could remember, in his entire life, no one had ever taken him by surprise in quite this way.

At once, the mood in the room changed from being heavy with blackness, even self-pity, into something both lighter and more filled with possibilities. Exciting possibilities. In the space of seconds, his heart rate and blood picked up both speed and heat, and most definitely, his groin area tightened with throbbing desire.

Amazing, he thought. One minute he and Carly were talking about his job crisis and the next, she was doing a strip for him.

Well, not quite a strip. Admittedly, the expression on her face wasn't all that sensual, nor all that confident, the way the face of a woman experienced in the art of seduction would look. But she was smiling, and if that smile held more tentative promise than downright sensuality, it was still a bewitching smile.

As she posed before him, holding the robe away from her

body, it was as though she was offering a present that she hoped would be received with pleasure—not really anxious, but not quite self-assured, either. Still, he saw, she seemed also to be laughing at herself, as though she knew she wasn't doing this too well and found the whole thing amusing.

He moved away from the window to the blank wall next to it, then leaned against it with feigned nonchalance. He returned her smile while his body continued revving up, going into automatic mating mode, masculine version.

"Well, well, what have we got here?" Nick asked, draping his arms across his chest in a relaxed fashion.

"Me, I think." As Carly's hands fell to her sides, her eyes widened with a question. "I didn't wear anything under the robe because you said it was up to me to make the first move."

"Is that what this is?"

"Isn't it?"

"Yes, ma'am," he said softly. "It sure is. And, by the way, I like it. A lot. So, what's your next move?"

She hadn't expected that, he could tell. He watched her face change as she thought about it for a couple of moments. Then the sides of her mouth turned up in a seductive curve. She lowered her eyelids slightly, so that she seemed to be peering at him through eyes heavy with suggestion. Finally, with a few leisurely shrugs of her shoulders, she let the robe slither down over her narrow shoulders and curving hips to rest around her ankles.

He kept his arms crossed, but the muscles in his biceps contracted and he stood a little straighter. The blood in his body seemed to have drained from his veins and pooled between his legs while, in the soft lamplight of the living room, he gazed on the slender, curved, perfect female form standing before him, his own terry-cloth robe draped around her feet.

The breath caught in his throat as his gaze explored her. He began slowly with her glowing, amber-colored eyes, lingered for a hungry moment on that incongruously full mouth, took in her long, graceful neck and elegant collarbone. He paused at the sight of her rounded, peaked breasts—so white, so full, their tips pink and standing at attention. He clenched his fists; his fingers itched to cup her breasts. He ran his tongue around his lips; his mouth yearned for the taste of her.

But not yet.

He continued his personal inventory over and down past her subtly rounded stomach and flaring hips. Again, he ached for the feel of her silken skin, wanted to flatten his palms against her hipbones while reaching with his thumbs to stroke the pale curls between her thighs. Craved the feel of her long legs wrapped around him while he plunged into her slick, welcoming womanhood.

This was bad, Nick thought, as bad as it had ever been. He wanted her with a need so strong, it threatened to erupt in one hot movement. It took all his willpower to clamp down on the urge to grab Carly and flatten her against the wall, rip down his zipper and take her, right there, pump himself into her while she stood, braced by the wall so she wouldn't lose her balance, abandon himself in her and then—finally!—let them both fall to the floor without him letting go.

No, he told himself. He was usually the aggressor with women, but this was Carly's move on him; he would use whatever restraint he could muster, even if the thought was enough to send his body into an impatient frenzy.

He felt his chest heave up and down rapidly in an effort to draw enough air into his lungs, but he stayed where he was. "You're beautiful."

She spread her hands and looked down at herself, then back up at him, her expression shyly pleased. "Am I, really?"

"Yes."

He said nothing else. Waited.

Their eyes locked and messages sizzled back and forth between them, although just what they were was beyond his present capabilities. His head was too filled with sensation to allow any coherent thought. What he did know was that several feet separated them, but the buzz he felt was as strong as if the distance was inches, and he and Carly were poised on some sort of threshold, about to touch after hours of teasing.

He waited for her to walk up to him; he was pretty sure that would be her next move. But, again, she surprised him. With a small half grin, she turned her back on him then walked away slowly, her softly curved buttocks moving up and down suggestively with each step.

"Hey," he said, unfolding his arms. "Where are you going?"

She glanced over her shoulder and raised an eyebrow. "The bedroom. Care to join me?"

That did it. With two long strides Nick caught up with her, grabbed her from behind and pulled her tight to him. She arched against him, the back of her head falling onto his shoulder, so he could smell her clean hair, take in the musky odor of a woman on fire. The bulge between his legs ached for release; while he used one hand to stroke the silken soft skin of her upper body, he splayed the palm of the other over her stomach and pressed her into his ache. He devoured her neck, licking it, biting the skin at her hairline. He heard her moan as, unable to help himself, he thrust his hips against her rear.

"Carly," he murmured, "I like your second move even better than the first one." He played with her nipples, tweaking them between his fingers, his palm smoothing over the slender curves of her. He couldn't get enough of stroking her velvety skin and hearing the small, pleased sounds she made in the back of her throat.

"And the third," he muttered, his mouth against her hot skin.

"Good," she said between strained breaths. "I hoped you would."

He tongued all around her ear and reveled in her quick intake of breath, the loud moan of desire she emitted. "Sure it's not because you're feeling sorry for me?" he murmured.

Her small, answering chuckle was husky with sensuality.

"If I did this with every person I've felt sorry for, I'd be doing it with a lot more skill."

"You're skillful enough for me."

His questing fingers found the moist folds between her legs and he used one finger to rub back and forth till she was moaning and writhing with a need that matched his own. He wanted to hear her scream, wanted to feel her soft interior muscles clench and shudder with release before he took her— because he wasn't sure he could hold out much longer.

"No," Carly said suddenly, breaking the grip of his hands and stumbling away from him.

"What?" Disappointment, more surprise, slammed into him like a boxer's jab.

She spun around to face him. Her eyes bright, her face flushed with color, she announced, "No, it's going too fast. We haven't even kissed yet. I want to kiss you." She put her hands behind his neck and pulled his head down, then pressed her lips to his and plunged her tongue into his mouth. Before he had a moment to recover, her hands found their way under the bottom of his shirt, pushing it up. Halting the assault on his mouth, she whispered, "I don't want to be the only naked person in the room." Then she lowered her head and ran her tongue over his nipples, first one, then the other.

As she heard Nick's breath hissing between his teeth, Carly was filled with a sense of joy that was exhilarating. Not only joy. She felt powerful. Female. Lusty. Desired. It was similar to the way she'd felt when she'd been Amanda, that sense of total freedom unlike anything in her admittedly limited sexual experience.

But that whole night had had a dreamlike quality. This, tonight, was real. Now she wasn't Amanda. She was Carly. For Nick, that seemed to be enough.

He pulled his shirt up over his head, got his arms caught somehow and muttered curses while he untangled himself and got rid of the pesky piece of clothing. And all the while, Carly chuckled quietly and flicked her tongue over his nipples, his chest, the line of black hair that disappeared into his jeans. She could feel his skin trembling; the fine, quivering pulse matched her own. She'd never teased a man like this, had never felt confident enough. But Nick's reaction to her every move gave her all the confidence she'd ever need.

With a groan, he grabbed one of her hands and placed it over the prominent bulge behind the zipper of his jeans. "Better be careful," he said in a hoarse whisper. "I've been carrying this for almost two days and the slightest move—" He shuddered. "Well, I make no promises."

"Two days? Really?"

When he nodded, she added, "The slightest move?"

Falling to her knees, she cupped him between her hands, using one finger to scratch along the base of his shaft. The denim fabric prevented her from actually touching his flesh, but he reacted as though she had.

Grabbing the sides of her head, he gasped, "I'm warning you."

She looked up at him and met his burning gaze, feeling powerful and mischievous and as thoroughly, deliciously aroused as he appeared to be. "This is practice. My assertiveness-training group told me—"

He didn't let her finish her sentence. Instead, he tightened the grip on her head and pulled her up to kiss her thoroughly and aggressively, taking charge. His tongue moved in and out and around the insides of her mouth, showing her without words what he wanted, what he intended, to do to her. Then he broke the kiss.

"What did they tell you?" he asked, not letting go of her head, his gaze lingering on her mouth. His green eyes glittered, ablaze with desire for her.

"That I need to play with fire—" again, she reached deliberately between his legs and cradled him in her hand "—so I can learn how to handle it."

A look of anguish flashed over his face and he closed his

eyes and gritted his teeth. She was about to push him over the edge, she realized with a thrill of anticipation.

Then, with a growl, he swept her up in his arms. "You want fire? You got it."

He carried her into his bedroom and set her down on the bed so she lay sprawled across the width of it. She watched as he ripped off the rest of his clothing. He stood naked before her, his body tense with wanting her, his fists clenched at his sides. He was all sinewy muscle and deeply tanned skin, with a paler band of flesh where his bathing suit marked him.

And there, from the thatch of black hair between his legs, the evidence of his burning need for her projected outward. He was fully erect, and she was fully aware of him, as she hadn't been two nights before. She'd been feeling the effects of a drug then; at this moment, there were no drugs in her system to alter reality. She didn't need them. The sight of Nick sent a thrill through her that made her entire body shudder with longing.

The room filled with the harsh sounds of their breathing as he rose over her. Setting one knee on the bed next to her supine body, Nick pinned her hands above her head. A thrill of fear shot through her system, even as she realized she didn't like being forcibly held down, no matter how titillating it might feel.

"Hey," she said. "I'm supposed to be doing wicked things to you."

He stopped in midmovement, although it seemed a major effort for him to do so. He gritted his teeth again, then gave her a reluctant grin. "Okay. You're calling the shots." He stood up again, reached into the single drawer of the bedside table and took out a small, foil-wrapped square. "You want to do this, or shall I?"

She put her hands behind her head and smiled in anticipation. "You. I want to watch."

"Yes, ma'am." He tore the top off the condom, fit it to the head of his shaft and slowly rolled it down as far as it would go. He kept his eyes glued to hers the whole time, but the slight tremor in his hands belied the coolness of his gaze. When he was done, he opened his hands. "Safe. Now what?"

"Lie down, on your back."

He did as he was told, sprawling next to her on the bed, then raising himself on his elbows. "Ready when you are."

He certainly was, Carly observed. Taking her time, she slowly slid one leg over his thighs and balanced herself on her knees, careful not to touch him. Yet.

"What about foreplay?" she asked innocently.

His chest moved up and down rapidly. "What do you call what we've been doing?" he gasped.

"Having fun."

Grabbing her hips, he brought her down on him, hard. As she cried out with both surprise and pleasure, he said, "So is this."

Like a wild stallion breaking free of its reins, Nick thrust up into her. After her initial shock passed, she found herself meeting his thrusts with equal force and equal enthusiasm. Soon they were joining and separating, joining and separating with such wild abandon that moans of joy keened out of her mouth.

As Carly felt herself climbing, climbing, climbing toward the pinnacle of release, she knew what she wanted her *final* move to be—to give and give and give some more, to present Nick with all the pleasure he could withstand.

She clenched the muscles deep inside her womb, felt Nick quicken the pace, heard him groan. Then he exploded with a sound so primitive, so filled with agony and triumph, that she reared back, opened her arms wide and joined him in free fall.

Afterward, their positions got somehow reversed so that now Nick lay half sprawled on top of Carly. He hoped he wasn't crushing her, but he was way too drained to move. It wasn't just his flesh and bones that felt drained. What he'd pumped into her was more than the product of physical release; he'd given her his very soul. He was vaguely aware of inner stirrings, of all kinds of strange new emotions. This wasn't what usually happened to him during sex.

In his experience, making love with a woman was entertaining, acrobatic, physically pleasing. Titillating, but not...deep, the way this had been. A sudden tightening at the back of his throat warned him that if he kept dwelling on this, he would cry. He never cried.

With enormous effort, he rolled off Carly, turned onto his side and pulled her to him so they lay curled together, spoon-fashion.

"Carly?"

"Hmm."

"You okay?"

She chuckled softly. "Do you have to ask?"

He smiled, felt himself drifting off to sleep. But didn't.

"Carly?"

"Hmm."

"What's going on...between us, I mean?"

There was a pause before she said, "Do I have to answer that?"

"No." Coward, he called himself. Out of some sort of self-protection, he'd wanted her to go first. "The thing is, I...feel things for you, all kinds of things."

Hell, Nick thought. There was probably a better way to say this, to do this, but he'd never been good at sentimentality. Besides, even in the grip of this strong emotion he felt with Carly, his head was in the way, doing handstands to get his attention.

He forced himself to go on. "So, here I am with all these feelings. But isn't it crazy? We've known each other—what?—forty-eight hours?"

"I know."

"But you feel it, too." It wasn't a question, and he held his breath until she answered.

"Yes," she whispered softly.

He smiled, kissed her neck and felt better. Now he had confirmation: they were both in it, whatever it was and whatever the outcome, so there was no rush. No need to talk it to death.

A few moments later, when he thought she'd fallen asleep, Carly spoke again. "Maybe this is the kind of thing they say happens during a war. You know, with the heightened sense of danger and urgency going on all around us, all kinds of emotions are being set off. They may not be real."

"Oh." Something previously warm and filled with hope shriveled inside him. "I see."

Quickly, she turned over and gazed at him, her eyes clouded with confusion. "I don't know if what I just said is the truth, or if I just…said something to be saying anything."

Reaching up, she smoothed some hair off his forehead, then set her palm on his cheek. "Everything in the past two days has been crazy. I witnessed a man having his head blown off, I've been drugged against my will. My ex-husband has been shot to death, and I just found out my sister is dead." Her gaze softened and she smiled. "But all I can think of is being in your arms, touching you, talking with you, even cooking for you, for heaven's sake. You're right. It *is* crazy."

Relief was Nick's primary emotion. Grateful to hear what he was feeling echoed by Carly, he covered her hand with his, slid it over his mouth and kissed the palm. "Are you scared?"

"Terrified."

They smiled at each other.

He did not use the word *love*, nor did she. And that was as it should be, he thought. Love? After two days? Utter insanity.

But the thought of the word revived his depleted condition to such an extent that he found himself reaching for her again. He wanted to express with his body what he could not yet say out loud.

He would make sure it was slow this time. This time he wanted to explore her, all of her, and so he did, starting from the bottom up.

Carly had been on the verge of dropping off to sleep, but Nick changed her mind in a heartbeat. She let out a huge sigh as Nick's hands stroked her shins and knees. She luxuriated in the velvet touch of his tongue playing gently with the toes of one foot, sucking them into the moist warmth of his mouth. She squirmed a little as he laved her instep, then the heel; a deep thrumming pulse coursed through her bloodstream, even as he moved over to the other foot and rewarded it in the same, deliberate way.

He was loving her, she thought dreamily, without the need for words; a steady heat throbbed in her veins. Again, her breath caught on a long sigh.

He uttered a pleased chuckle, then moved his mouth up to where his hands had been, on her legs, licking and kissing her flesh with a languid, teasing, tantalizing thoroughness.

If his intention was to be unhurried, her response was lightning quick—it always would be, she knew. Like a match held to dry timber, his touch set her on fire. Clutching the side of the mattress with one hand, she buried the fingers of the other in the thick, wavy black hair on his head, kneading his scalp and trying to urge him farther up her body, to the already-pulsing, wet center of her femininity.

He chuckled again. "Soon," he said. "Let me take my time. It's my turn."

His fingertips feathered up and down her shins and around to her calves. Groaning, she felt her hips rotating with need, but she tried to be patient. Raising both arms, she gripped the brass headboard with all her might and let him do whatever he wanted to. For what felt like an eternity, he played and licked and stroked her, finally lifting one leg to reach the tender skin on the back of her knees with his tongue. She nearly rose off the bed at her body's swift reaction. He dislodged her hands from the headboard and eased her onto her stomach. Now he had easier access to the flesh of the back of her thighs.

She felt so *hot*. When his tongue reached the top of her

thighs, when his fingertips stroked along the curve of her buttocks, she tried to turn over again, onto her back—she craved having him inside her as he had been before, driving, thrusting, filling all emptiness till there was no more room for anything but the feel of him.

But he whispered, "No. Stay that way."

"Please," she said. "You're making me crazy."

"Soon," he soothed. "Soon."

She had no strength to fight him. The thought of simply doing as she was told sounded lovely right now. She felt him shifting on the bed so that his legs straddled her thighs. He stroked and teased her buttocks and hips, tracing circles on the skin with his fingertips and raising goose bumps wherever they touched. She was aware of his hard, thick manhood pushing into her back and she squirmed restlessly. Her inner muscles clenched with wanting him; she felt another gush of moisture there....

But he wanted it slow, and that's how it would be. He was calling the shots this time. He was telling her, showing her, in fact, that if she had controlled their earlier encounter, he would do the same to her now—but better. A little show of male dominance, she thought wryly. But it was all right with her; he had so much to teach her. If a power play was going on here, it didn't matter. They were both winners.

His featherlight touches set fire to her skin. Oh, Lord, his touch was driving her crazy. She turned her head to the side and groaned, "I don't know how much longer I can—"

"Ssh," he said softly, licking her ear. Then his thumbs traced down the cleft that led to the source of her womanhood, finding and stroking the wet folds between her legs until she shivered with ecstasy. Her breathing grew more labored as she felt herself climbing, climbing... Again? she wondered. Had anything ever felt this erotic? No, not possible.

She pushed herself onto her knees, opening her legs to her lover. Soon she was swept up in more touches and moans, sensations in new places that made her shiver all over again, till he finally eased himself into her and began the firm, insistent, rhythmic journey which would take them both over the edge of the world and into oblivion.

Tuesday morning

There was a murmur of conversation way in the background, so she buried her head under a pillow. No, Carly thought, wanting to swat the sound away so she could remain asleep. She didn't want to wake up, not yet.

She knew where she was—in Nick's bed. Two mornings ago, she'd awakened in this very same bed, but this time there was no terror, no need to bound out of it and lock herself in the bathroom. So much had happened, so much had changed in these two days. Then she'd wanted to run away; now she wanted to stay. In bed. With Nick.

She reached over to touch him, but her hand patted empty cold sheets. Dragging her head out from under the pillow, she opened one eye. She was alone. Nick must be the one talking in the background, on the phone probably, given that it was only his voice she heard, and no one was answering.

Turning onto her back and stretching her arms above her head, she smiled with womanly satisfaction. The pillow felt so soft. More memories of that first morning with him—good old goose-down and feathers, not the sensible, inexpensive pillow she slept on back home. This was Nick's place, not hers. And she felt wonderful.

There had been no dreams. For the first time since she'd awakened here two days before, she'd been able to sleep soundly and in peace.

When she slept, of course. When Nick and she had allowed each other to sleep. Carly crossed her arms behind her head and mused on the fact that, all her childhood, Nina had been the wild, spontaneous one; she'd been sensible, reasonable Carly.

But she must have had this side of her hidden—from the

world and from herself—the whole time. She'd been waiting for the right person to bring it out, and now she'd met him. A tough cop with a midlife crisis who played her like a virtuoso.

She smiled again, feeling like Brunhilde, a pet cat she'd had as a child, all leisurely stretching and purring, waiting for her tummy to be scratched, for her ears to be tugged at and stroked.

Carly wanted more stroking. Hadn't she had enough last night? she asked herself with wonder. But there would never be enough. Nick seemed to have more stamina than she'd thought possible. And the foolish man had claimed that, between his knee and his hip and his hand, he wasn't as physically fit as he used to be. Dear God, what must he have been like then?

Still, she was glad she'd met him now, when he was older, when he'd learned to handle both his fists and his temper. Well, his fists anyway. She frowned. His temper still set off memories of her father, even though she knew they weren't alike in any other way. It was why, from the time she'd started dating, until she'd married Richard, she'd always gravitated toward safe—boring—men.

Nick wasn't safe and he wasn't boring, and still they'd met and been attracted. It almost felt like fate, to have run into the bar that night, seeking shelter, and to have had Nick be the one who offered it. Fate, yes, she thought, even though she'd never particularly believed in the concept. It had to be fate that had swept her up in a strange, bizarre murder adventure which, in turn, had enabled her to meet the man who would change her life, would bring her happiness and acceptance and love.

Yes, love. The word had been hanging in the air between them all night.

She let out a happy sigh before reality intervened. It was morning now, and she needed to get out of bed, find out if there was any more news about Eddie Monk. She should shower, get started on her day. But, oh, she didn't want to. She wanted to just stay here in the bed that smelled of Nick and think about him.

"Oh, good, you're up."

Nick stood in the bedroom doorway, imposing as always, but blurry. Still sleepy, Carly reached for her glasses and put them on. His form sharpened; she could see now that he, at least, was wide-awake. He'd shaved and showered and was dressed more formally than she was used to seeing him, in dark gray pants and a pale gray long-sleeved shirt open at the collar. His eyes shone with excitement.

"What?" she asked.

"Good news." He rubbed his hands together.

She yawned and covered her mouth. "Tell me."

"One of Demeter's bodyguards from the yacht, the guy who was in a coma—"

"Sam 'the Shift-Man' O'Connell," she said, but it came out slurred. She ran her tongue over her dry mouth; it would be a while before her body woke up.

"You remembered." He sat down next to her on the bed. She could sense that cop-on-the-prowl excitement about him. He held her hand while he told her the rest. "Anyway, Sam's conscious now and is spilling his guts. He's positively ID'd Eddie Monk, says Monk attacked both him and Frankie, took them by surprise with the butt of a gun. So, even without your testimony, there's an APB on Monk."

"Oh, good." What a relief! They didn't need her to start the ball rolling.

"This morning, just to make sure, Dom went back to Monk's place and busted the lock on his door. He's not there. In fact, it looks like he's cleared out. But the wheels have been set in motion—East Coast and here. That cop from Boyle Heights? The one I couldn't reach last night? He has a snitch who knows Monk real well, he's ready to tell us all about him. We'll get him. We should have everything tied up soon."

"I'll relax completely when they have Eddie Monk in custody."

He squeezed her hand tightly one more time, then let it go. "It's a matter of time, Carly. So, come on."

He stood and tore the blankets off her, then stopped and stared at her nude body. Masculine appreciation gleamed from his eyes. "I wish I could get back into bed with you." Leaning over, he gave her a quick kiss on the mouth. "But there'll be other days."

"Why do I have to get up?" she complained.

"Because you need to get dressed." He grabbed her hands and pulled her up to a sitting position. Her legs dangled over the side, while she groaned her protest.

"You're not a nice man."

"Come on, Carly," he persisted. "Dom's on his way over." He smiled. "The kid, Miguel, wanted to be in on it, wanted to see how it's done. But Dom told him it's crunch time. Pros only. Now, are you going to get out of there, or would you rather I picked you up and threw you into the shower?"

Holding up a restraining hand, she nodded reluctantly. "No need. I'll be ready to move in a minute." She yawned, then scratched her head and glanced at him sleepily. "Where are we going?"

Her brain wasn't quite functioning yet, or she'd have known the answer to her question before she asked it.

"Down to the station, of course. I'm bringing you in."

Chapter 11

"**Y**ou're what?" All her remaining morning-after glow vanished in an instant. "Why do I have to go in?"

"Are you kidding?"

"No."

Gripping the brass headboard with one hand, Nick frowned while he stared at her. "Carly, Eddie Monk has been ID'd as being on the yacht and knocking out the guards. You can peg him as the man at the airport who threatened you, and I can back it up with him tailing us yesterday. They're working on a match between the bullet that killed Richard and the bullets that killed Demeter. They have an eyewitness who saw you running away from the yacht, another who saw someone dressed in a raincoat running in the same direction a minute later. Everything's coming together now. You asked for twenty-four hours, you got it. Time's up."

It made sense, she told herself. What he was saying was true. She'd promised, in fact, that if Nick said she had to go in by today, she would. She knew with the functioning part of her mind that Nick was right.

But in a deeper, more primitive area of her brain, where reason and logic played no role, something rebelled. Old fears died hard, and this particular fear wasn't ready to be buried, not yet.

But she would not fall apart on Nick again, she would *not* turn into that quaking, panicked woman she'd been for so much of the short time they'd known each other. Not after last night.

Carefully folding her hands on her lap, she locked gazes with him. "Nick? If they already have someone who can identify Eddie Monk, and can place him on the yacht at the time of the murder, why do they need me? I didn't actually see him kill Demeter, you know."

"Because you're the linchpin, Carly. You were there at the start in Boston, up to and through the murder."

"Yes, I see." Carly looked down at her hands.

Nick frowned with confusion. Now what? Maybe his own tension was getting to her. He flexed his fists a couple of times to relieve his pent-up energy. Then he sat down next to her on the bed. "Okay," he said as evenly as he could. "What is it?"

She didn't respond. Then, slowly, she turned to him and said, "Suppose…just suppose it doesn't go the way you think it will."

"Carly—"

"Humor me, Nick," she interrupted him with a strained smile. "If I go with you now, and tell them I was on the boat when Demeter was killed, here's another way it could be interpreted—they'll have me, and my fingerprints, I assume. Nina was my sister, and Pete Demeter drove the car that killed her. Don't you think the death of my sister might look like a motive for me to have pulled the trigger?"

He dragged his fingers through his hair impatiently. "If you want to turn it into—"

"What if they never find Eddie Monk? Who else is going to back up my story? Richard is dead." Her agitation and the fear behind it was more apparent now. She gripped and knotted the bedsheets, as if she could keep herself together by holding them.

"Who's to say I didn't kill him," she went on, "under the influence of drugs or not, except me? Who's to say they won't decide Eddie and I were working together? Or even that I killed Richard? Who's to say they won't book me and lock me up on suspicion of murder?"

"I say it, dammit."

She held out her hands. "Are you that all-powerful, Nick? If you tell them I'm innocent, because you feel it in your bones, does that mean they salute and say. 'Yes sir'?" As the corners of her mouth turned down, she bit her bottom lip in an obvious effort at self-control. "It doesn't work that way."

It was obvious that she was tremendously upset, and he tried to hold on to his temper, but he, too, was near the edge. "Carly, you gave your word. I don't think you have a choice."

"No. *You* don't have a choice, but *I* do."

She jumped up off the bed. Nick's gaze followed her path to the bathroom, where she closed the door. Shaking his head, he got up and knocked on the door. "What are you doing?"

"Getting dressed." In a matter of seconds, the door opened and Carly rushed past him, wearing the slightly damp clothes she'd washed out the night before. "I'm sorry—I have to get out of here."

Grabbing one of her wrists, he pulled her to a stop. "No you don't."

"I have to, Nick." Her eyes were wild with fear. "Unless you'd like to knock me out, drag me down to the station by my hair. Or maybe you'd rather put me in handcuffs?" She brought her other hand up so it was even with the wrist he was holding. "Go on."

Letting her hand drop, he stared at her in disbelief. "Carly—this is impossible. You're being impossible."

"I know it. But I am not going to jail." It registered, in some dim part of Carly's mind, how she must sound. But she was fighting for her life. "I am not spending one minute behind bars! Don't you understand?"

Nick grabbed her shoulders and shook her. "No, I don't. Tell me."

Tell me.

Tell him what? She'd had only brief flashes of memory over the years, like small mental snapshots. Little girls in starched dresses standing behind bars. Dirty knees, dirty cheeks from crying. Mock family photographs in a mockery of an album. But she'd never let it rise fully to the surface, because it was too terrifying to identify the children in the pictures.

It rose to the surface now, in one stunning moment of clarity. Her body stiffened with a child's terror of the dark. She shut her eyes tight, to try to block it out, but it was useless.

"My…my father—it was one of his favorite ways to punish us." The effort to talk made her chest heave; she couldn't seem to catch her breath.

"What did he do?" Nick's voice was low and harsh.

Carly's eyes snapped open and she stared at him. His face was stiff with fury. At her? Why? What had she done? She turned her back on him, tried to curl in a ball inside herself, the way she had back then.

But he gripped her shoulders from behind. "Tell me what the bastard did."

Tell him, instructed a voice from somewhere inside her. And Carly did as the voice said to do, the words tumbling out one after the other. "From the time we were little, he used to taunt us with all kinds of stories about what they'd done to people in holding cells—kicking, punching, beating them where it wouldn't show. And…even uglier things. He would take Nina and me to one of those empty cells, lock us in, turn off all the lights and leave us there alone for hours. Twice he left us there all night…in separate cells. One time it was after a party at the church, it was someone's birthday, I think, and Nina and I had matching pink dresses. We didn't do something fast enough for him. I don't even remember what anymore. Do you know what it's like to be six years old and locked up all night in the dark?''

Behind her, Nick muttered an epithet, but she barely heard him. She was back there, back to being small and helpless and so terrified that she'd used to pray, first to be rescued, and then, to die. ''There were all these strange noises, someone crying nearby, shuffling sounds—mice or rats. Smells—liquor, garbage, urine. It was a lesson, he used to say, to show us what would happen if we didn't listen to him, if we broke the rules, if we were bad.''

She felt his hands tighten their grip, felt the rage pour through him, but this time she understood it was rage at her father. Somehow, even as she relived her childhood through the mists of memory, she recognized that Nick's anger was not directed at her.

Turning, she buried her face against his chest. ''It worked. On me, anyway. Nina just got more and more rebellious, more and more angry. But I wasn't strong like her. I sat in the corner, whimpering. Nina told me to shut up. I was hopeless, she said, I was a wimp. It taught me a lesson—do any kind of dance necessary, play by the rules, show up, be responsible, but never, never get into trouble.''

Lifting her head wearily, she met his stormy gaze with a sad smile. ''I've pushed this out of my mind for years, but I've never forgotten that lesson. I've been so careful, I've practically ceased living. But it's left its mark, Nick. I can't be in small places, I can't breathe if I'm locked up.'' Her hands balled into fists against his chest. ''I've tried to overcome it, Nick. I've worked on the fears, I told you, but this—'' She couldn't even finish the sentence. Bowing her head, she murmured, ''I can't go there, Nick. Sorry, I can't.''

Nick felt rage pour through him, red and black and strong. Carly's father—what a bullying, sadistic son of a bitch. Nick wanted to hurt someone; he also wanted to cry for Carly. He wanted to put his fist through a wall.

''Dammit!'' he raged. ''All along you've been set against

going in, and now I know why. Why the hell didn't you tell me any of this before?''

With a startled look, she backed away from him as though he'd breathed fire in her face. ''What?''

''Do you realize what kind of position you've put me in? I've probably set myself up for disciplinary action, I've gotten Dom involved, all because you said you'd go in. You also said you'd told me everything, that there was nothing else I needed to know. You trusted me, you said.'' He was yelling now; he couldn't seem to stop himself. ''And I believed you, idiot that I am. What else have you been keeping from me, huh? Tell me. What other secrets have you been hiding?''

The hurt flashed across her face as though he'd slapped her. ''Nothing.''

It came out weakly and he saw her try to swallow. On her face, the determination not to be cowed by him fought for dominance over the residue of childhood memories. ''I guess...I didn't tell you because I didn't even know it myself. But that's it. That's the very last intimate secret you'll ever need to know about me.'' Her face crumbled with despair. ''I can't, Nick. I can't go in. I'm sorry.''

She dashed by him, out of the bedroom, headed for the front door. The sudden whirlwind movement startled him for a moment, then he took off in pursuit.

Carly flipped the lock and made it out the door. ''Carly, wait!'' she heard Nick call, but ignored him. Stairs, she decided, not the elevator. She hadn't put her shoes on yet, so once again, she was barefoot, running away from Nick. Also, again, without money. But there was no time to dwell on the irony of the situation. She *had* to get away.

She tore down six flights of stairs, running, running, the cold concrete hard on her arches. In the lobby, she glanced quickly at the front door, decided against it and headed for the rear of the building, where the cars were parked. Nick had to be right behind her, she knew, even though she didn't hear him.

Just as she burst through the rear door, fingers dug into her left arm and pulled her to an abrupt stop. She turned to see who had done it, and found herself staring into the cold, pale eyes of Eddie Monk.

His dead-white skin was pitted with old acne scars. An incongruous pug nose turned up in an otherwise downward-turning countenance. Before she had a chance to cry out, he'd reached in his pants pocket and pulled out a gun. She stared at it—it looked like, might even be, the one she'd held in her hand, the one that had killed Demeter.

No, she thought, this can't be happening.

Eddie slammed her against a wall and stuck a piece of tape across her mouth. Pointing the gun at her, he grabbed her arm again with his free hand and dragged her along the alleyway. He was small, but he was strong. She looked around for anyone to help her—where was Nick?—but the only other alley occupant was a dirty calico cat that scurried across their path and disappeared over a short brick wall. Eddie hustled Carly along till they reached the huge garbage bin at the edge of the alley. Partially hidden behind it was a long, rust-colored car with several dents in the fender. Without saying a word, he pulled open the back door and shoved her in. Then he twisted her arms behind her back and clicked handcuffs on. Locking the back door, he slammed it shut.

She had a momentary urge to laugh out loud. Nick's handcuffs would have been preferable, she thought wildly, to these. Under the tape she screamed, the screams rasping in her throat. The car suddenly lurched forward and Carly's mind spun away into raw panic.

Nick held on to the sides of his front door and gritted his teeth in pain. He hadn't gotten two feet in his dash after Carly, when his damned knee had given out. Furious at his traitorous body and at himself, he leaned his head against the door till the pain subsided enough for him to put some weight on his leg. When he could walk again, he limped into the bedroom, grabbed his loaded gun and holster, and headed out the front door.

He got to the street just in time to see a rust-colored twenty-year-old Cadillac burning rubber down the street, heading east. It was too far away to see the license number and too far away to shoot at. But the make, the year and the color were right.

Eddie Monk had been waiting. Carly had been abducted by Eddie Monk. He was terrified for her. If anything happened to her, he'd never forgive himself. Nick patted his pocket; he had his car keys, he would follow. He hobbled over to his parking space as fast as he could.

When he got to his car, he stopped short and stared. All four tires were flat.

Eddie Monk had planned ahead.

Carly managed to work herself into a sitting position in the back seat. Between her pounding heart, her tense shoulders, the handcuffs digging into her wrists and the taped mouth that inhibited breathing, this new position wasn't any more comfortable, but at least now she felt less vulnerable. She meant to keep track of where they drove, but this city was totally unfamiliar to her. Names blended into other names. There was a stretch on a freeway, then they were climbing, climbing, twists and curves, along a deserted dirt road, bordered by bushes and high trees. Eddie drove recklessly, like a man who had nothing to lose.

Carly had everything to lose and she knew it. She made every effort to keep a tight rein on her fears. He'd abducted her, but hadn't killed her—why, she wasn't sure. He wanted her alive, for the moment anyway. She held on to that thought for dear life.

Monk didn't speak, not once, but she met his glance in the rearview mirror a few times. His eyes were a pale, almost colorless hazel. They seemed devoid of something basic to life. They flicked on her once in a while, but she couldn't read his expression.

Finally they reached some sort of plateau in the mountains. Ahead of her was a large three-story, white stucco home, situated at the edge of what seemed to be a sheer drop. A chain-link fence encircled the dry grass and weeds that grew on all sides. The right side of the house, near the cliff edge, drooped as if unsupported. Chunks of red roof tile lay scattered around. On the chain-link fence signs were posted every few feet, warning Danger, Keep Out.

Eddie stopped the car at the fence. "Come on," he said, hauling her out of the back seat. His voice was that same hoarse whisper she'd heard at the airport—and in her dreams. He dragged her to a narrow opening in the fence, shoved her through, then followed. When they got to the rear of the house, he unlocked a small door near a wooden stairway and indicated she should go in. But it was dark inside there, and she hesitated. He shoved her, hard. She stumbled forward, falling down a step and hitting a hard concrete floor.

Amazingly enough she wasn't hurt, but the fall had knocked the wind out of her. It was a struggle to catch her breath because, as she realized with horror once again, the tape over her mouth gave her only one opening to breathe from instead of two.

Eddie Monk shoved her with his foot. "Get up and shut up," he ordered.

Carly managed to get to her knees. It was nearly pitch-black in there. The only source of light was from a high, narrow, dirt-smeared window. Her eyes adjusted and she glanced around. She was in a square, cavelike room, probably a storage cellar. Eddie pulled her by the arm, then shoved her onto the floor in a corner. There she sat, her arms pinned behind her, her knees bent to her chest, her mouth taped shut. Fear sliced through her; what did he intend to do with her now?

He took matches and lit all kinds of candles until shadows danced in the room. There was a minimum of furniture, only two wooden chairs and a few small tables, but the walls were filled—paintings, photographs, framed letters, pieces of clothing. A dried flower pinned to the wall, a scrap of ribbon. Candles were placed under a particularly large portrait.

Of Nina, Carly realized. All the pictures were of Nina. Or, as Eddie probably knew her, Amanda.

Carly was in a shrine to her late sister.

"Yeah, he was obsessed with her," the snitch told them.

Nick and Dom sat in the back of a small coffee shop in Boyle Heights. Dom had driven up to Nick's place minutes after Monk had taken off with Carly. They'd called in the sighting of Eddie's car, but so far he was still out there.

The snitch, a skinny, awkward man with red hair and bloodshot eyes, had known Eddie since they'd been kids. As he talked, his eyes darted nervously from right to left and back again. "This Amanda, he met her in Vegas, got her her first job on the line—nude dancer. Followed her to L.A., got her work in a couple of flicks. When she met Demeter, married him, Eddie went nuts. Got himself into Demeter's organization, to stay close to her. Even when he was sent back East, he still carried the torch for her. He really loved her. Went a little nuts there, if you ask me. But Eddie's always been that way."

Nick felt his gut tighten. Carly was hostage to someone who was not only a killer, but was also unbalanced. "We're looking for Monk now. Seen him?" When the snitch shook his head, Nick said, "He's not at his place—where would he be?"

"Beats me."

Leaning in, Nick grabbed him by the shirt lapels. "Think about it. Where would he go? Maybe some special place he used to talk about."

"I don't know, honest."

Nick's grip tightened. "Easy," he heard Dom say.

The snitch held up his hands. Nick let him go.

"He used to talk about a cave," the red-haired man said. "His Amanda cave, okay? But he never told me where it was. Said she used to meet him there, but you know what? I think he was lying. I don't think he ever even made it with her. It was all in his head."

Carly shivered. Monk hadn't said a word for a long time. What an eerie feeling to see Nina—a lot different from Carly's last memory of her, but Nina nevertheless—staring at her from every angle. Swallowing a sudden wave of nausea, she glanced up at Eddie. His back was to her as he gazed at one particularly glamorous studio portrait. Nina's thick blond hair framed her face, falling over one eyebrow. That same insolent smile she'd had as a child showed up now as insinuating and inviting. Her off-the-shoulder dress was cut so low, her breasts seemed on the verge of popping out of their restraints.

Eddie Monk's posture changed as he gazed at Nina. His thin shoulders relaxed, his jerky movements stilled. Then he turned around, studied Carly and frowned. "You really don't look anything like her, do you? I was hoping—" Instead of completing the sentence, his whole body seemed to sag with disappointment. "Oh, well."

He'd been in love with her sister, Carly realized. Obviously, she thought, gazing around the room once more, to the point of obsession. Again, she struggled to speak and muffled sounds came out.

"You want the tape off, huh?" Reaching into his waistband, he drew out his gun. He glanced at it, then at her. "You want to talk? Maybe scream a little? Nah, I don't think so. Not that it would do you any good. I could take that gag off and you could scream your head off, but it wouldn't make no difference. No one would hear." He was bragging, like a clever little boy who was sure no one could ever have a mind as quick as his.

After another glance at his gun, he returned it to his waistband. "I don't want you to talk, I want to pretend for just a while longer."

He grabbed her elbows and pulled her up to a standing position. Then he placed her next to yet another framed photograph of Nina's face. Holding a candle, first to the picture, then to Carly's face—so close the flame licked her skin and she cringed—he tilted his head and assessed her. With a sudden movement, he plucked her glasses off and threw them across the room.

"Better." Then he fluffed out her hair and unbuttoned several buttons of her sweater, so the top lace of her bra peaked out. She tensed, half expecting him to grab her. But he looked over at the picture again and his eyes got a faraway look.

"Amanda," he said dreamily. Suddenly, he turned and faced Carly, a look of pure venom on his face. "You're not Amanda."

She flinched, waiting for a blow, but then Eddie's forehead wrinkled as he went off on another tangent. "Oh, yeah, that's right, you knew her as Nina. Stupid name. Her hair was so beautiful, so long." With another lightning-quick temperament change, he came back to the present, peering at Carly with a look of speculation in his eyes. "I changed my mind. You do look a lot like her, except she was prettier. We did a good job on you though. When old Pete took a look at you—" he smiled slyly "—he didn't know what hit him."

The smile stayed on his face, but his eyes glazed over as he seemed to turn inward. Again, Carly perceived that edge of violence in him.

And madness.

She felt closed in, trapped. Her heart thumped loudly in her chest.

No, she told herself. You may not panic. You *must* keep your wits about you.

"She was much more an Amanda than a Nina," Eddie said, leaning in until his face was an inch from hers. "Am I right?"

Bile rose in her throat. Swallowing hard, she nodded. She tried to swallow again, but wound up coughing. The sound of choking got Eddie's attention. With one swift movement, he ripped the tape off. She muffled a scream of pain. After a moment the stinging sensation was bearable and she whispered, "Thank you."

He stared hard at her, his mouth open slightly. "Just then, you sounded like her, like Amanda."

That's it, Carly thought. That's how she would keep herself alive. "We were sisters," she said quickly, careful to keep her voice pitched low. "We were a lot alike. Now, tell me more." Her hands were still imprisoned behind her back, her neck and shoulders hurt. But maybe, just maybe, she'd found some kind of handle. "Tell me all about your Amanda."

"Where the hell is he?" Nick said.

"They'll get him," Dom replied, roaring onto the Santa Monica Freeway. "It's only a matter of time."

Dom might have been trying to calm him down, but he drove like a man possessed, so Nick knew he felt more personally involved than he usually allowed himself to. To Dom's credit, not once since they'd left the snitch and begun to cruise the streets had he said, "Told you so." And he could have, with ease.

If Nick hadn't given Carly her twenty-four-hour reprieve. If he'd been more tuned into her this morning, cut her some slack instead of blowing up at her. If his knee hadn't given out. If the APB had turned up Monk's car before he snatched Carly. If, if, if...

He'd told Carly to trust him, that he would take care of her. But he'd failed to do that, and the sense of helplessness—and guilt—was overwhelming. What if they didn't find her? They had not one single clue to where he might have taken her. Not the yacht, not his place. The snitch had referred to a cave. What cave? Where could Nick even begin to look for her?

Carly was being held by a killer. Maybe she was dead already. Dear God, he thought. Please no. Keeping an eye on every passing car, he said, "You're sure you guys found nothing at Monk's apartment?"

"I told you already, Nick. We broke in, the place was

cleaned out. We thought he'd gone to Boston, remember, so it made sense.''

Knowing he had to do something before he exploded, he faced Dom. "I want to see for myself. I want to go to Monk's place.''

"I already told you—''

"I know,'' he interrupted abruptly, "and I'm probably nuts. But I'm asking.''

His face set with his own tension, Dom glanced over at Nick. Then he shrugged. "Okay, we go to Monk's place.''

With the plain unit's portable red light flashing and occasional use of the siren, he covered the fifteen miles to West Hollywood in ten minutes.

Nick and Dom walked around the one-bedroom place. Beds lay stripped, drawers hung open, old milk stank up the refrigerator; all the signs were there of a tenant moving out. A large plastic garbage bag stood in a corner of the bedroom. Nick knew it had already been searched, but he poked around in there anyway. Torn-up papers, socks with holes. Something sharp—a rectangle of metal.

He withdrew it and stared at a framed photo of a large, Spanish-style house with mountains in the background. In the corner of the picture someone had tacked up an embossed invitation to a party given several years earlier by Mr. and Mrs. Peter Demeter.

As Nick stared at the invitation, he flashed on the information Bobbie Kim had supplied. This would be the Silver Lake mansion that had been destroyed by an earthquake. Which meant, if it hadn't already been torn down, it was, at the least, condemned. Which meant it was deserted.

A perfect place to take a kidnap victim.

It was a long shot, but what did he have to lose? "Let's go," he told Dom, heading for the front door.

"He killed her," Eddie said. "Demeter. He was driving the car. He got out with a couple of scratches, but she was smashed all to pieces.''

Carly was still standing next to the photograph of Nina, her knees quivering with the effort to keep her voice friendly and interested. She nodded understandingly. ''So, he had to be punished.''

He rewarded her with a smirk both arrogant and sneaky at the same time, like a child who'd set a cherry bomb but wouldn't say where. ''Yeah. But not just taken out, that would be way too easy. He had to suffer.'' As the smile left his face, anger distorted his features. ''It had to be agonizing.''

''So you came up with a plan,'' she said soothingly. ''Will you tell me about it? May I sit down?'' She eased her way over toward a chair.

As she lowered herself onto the seat, Eddie watched her carefully. ''You're doing a number on me, aren't you? Stalling for time.''

Had she gone too far? ''No, I promise. I was just thinking that I understood why Amanda cared about you and, well—'' she shrugged shyly ''—I feel the same.''

He seemed to wage an inner battle between doubting her and preening at her attentions. His ego won out, and he smiled smugly. ''Sure, why not.''

Alternating between pacing restlessly around the small room and stopping to worship at various pictures of Amanda, he told her all about it. About how Pete had been in rough shape since Amanda's death, tormented by memories of her, until he imagined her ghost had come back to haunt him. Eddie remembered Amanda had told him about her kid sister, and how much they looked alike. He traced Carly, watched her as she left her office one day. More digging turned up Richard's gambling habit, and Eddie bought up his markers. Now all the elements were in place for his plan...

Carly, made up as Amanda, would be found sitting on Pete's yacht, in the living area, when he got up on Saturday morning. Pete would think his dead wife had actually come back to life. Eddie would stay hidden and watch them.

Pete would begin to make love to his "wife." Eddie would wait till consummation was near, then would interrupt, tie Pete up and force him to watch while Eddie took over with "Amanda." Then Eddie would kill him. The last picture Pete would see would be his wife and Eddie Monk making it.

Payback.

Eddie had even been prepared in case Carly wasn't willing. "There's this drug 'cocktail' they use in some Asian countries," he told her proudly, "when they're taking those little farm girls off to the city, you know, where they promise them good-paying jobs then sell them to the slavers. Works great. It's a combination of Chinese herbs, roofies and Ecstasy. You heard of that? Where you have great sex?" The drug combination would induce a complete memory blackout for hours, and would also make sure Carly was sexually voracious. "It all woulda worked perfectly, except for your stupid Richard."

Monk glared at Carly accusingly. "Once we got to the yacht, he was supposed to get lost till it was over. Instead, he was breathing down my neck the whole time. 'Don't hurt her,' he kept saying. 'That's not part of the deal. Only Demeter, you promised.'" Eddie sneered. "Give me a break."

"How did I get here? To L.A.?"

It was the first time Carly had spoken since Monk had begun his story and he seemed startled to hear her voice, as though, again, he'd completely forgotten she was there. She held her breath, hoping she hadn't made another tactical error.

Then he offered his sly, half-lidded, I've-got-a-secret smile again. "Demeter's private jet. Nice touch, huh? On the plane, we made you over, me and your punk husband, to look like Amanda. Dyed your hair, put in extensions, put on her makeup, her perfume, her dress. I know all about that stuff— I used to be in the business," he said self-importantly.

It should have worked perfectly. Pete never left the yacht, never. Except this one time. When they got there, no one was on board. Carly was given more drugs and they waited—Carly unconscious, Richard becoming more and more a nuisance.

"Finally," Eddie went on, "it's dark when Pete comes up the gangplank with his two bodyguards—they'd decided to take a drive, can you believe it? I tell Pete I got a surprise for him down below. He heads down the stairs. Sam and Fast Frankie never take me seriously, so I have no trouble knocking them out, then making sure they stay knocked out. I sneak downstairs and I watch. You, sitting on that chair like a queen, looking just like Amanda."

He licked around his mouth, and Carly had to swallow down her revulsion again. "It was going to be perfect," Eddie said. At his sudden look of pure venom, Carly shrank back in her chair. "Except—" he spat the word at her "—you were coming out of it."

Just as Pete discovered "Amanda," Carly woke up and started to protest. Eddie was forced to kill Pete right then. Quickly, he switched to plan B, intending to place the blame on Carly, but Richard wouldn't go along. So she escaped while Eddie fought Richard for the gun.

He killed him, then took off after Carly. He followed her to the bar, then to Nick's. Trailed her all of Sunday, almost got her at the airport, but beat it when she pulled her little stunt with the maintenance vehicle. Eddie was at Nick's condo when she returned there, followed them the next day, then decided to lie low after Nick spotted him. He arranged to have it look as though he'd left for Boston, then waited outside Nick's place, hoping he'd get another chance at Carly.

A chance for what? she wondered.

As though answering her unspoken question, Eddie pulled out his gun again. Cradling it in his hand, he seemed to study it. "And so," he said almost dreamily, "here you are. Nowhere to go. End of the line."

He was going to do it. He was going to kill her. Terror gripped her, but so did the urge to live. She had to think fast. "But, Eddie—"

"Huh?" He looked up from the gun.

"I thought you were going to—" she shrugged suggestively "—you know, be with me, before you killed Pete. You never got the chance. I thought you and I...well, I thought it might happen now, with me."

It was a desperate gamble, but it was the only way she could think of to keep him from pulling the trigger and ending her life right there. Maybe if she got his mind off the gun and onto having sex with her, she might find a way to escape.

Calculation entered his expression, followed by the sly smile. Setting the gun down on the table, he pulled open a small drawer. "Yeah. I have this other little pill, been meaning to try it out on someone, and it might as well be you." He fished around in the drawer as he spoke. "If it works, it'll be a big seller, because the woman who gets it is so on fire, she can't sit still."

"Why do I need a pill?"

He didn't answer right away, then retorted, "Because all of you, all you women, you need all the help you can get."

Again, more clicked into place. Eddie needed a woman to be under the influence of some kind of drug before he was able to perform. If even then.

She had to keep him from forcing the drug on her. Her hands were useless but she still had her feet. Her glance darted around the room, looking for something she could shove at him, anything. But before she found a weapon, he had produced two small blue capsules. "Yeah, take these." A smirk. "Sorry, no water."

"I don't need anything," she purred.

"Take them, I said."

Shaking her head, Carly clamped her mouth shut. If she had to die, it would not be while at a madman's drug-induced mercy. Cursing, Eddie shoved two fingers in her mouth and tried to pry it open. She bit down, hard.

"Bitch!" he yelled, withdrawing his fingers. He slapped her across the cheek so hard she felt her brains rattle. Mad rage distorted his face. Carly was gazing on something more evil than her imagination could ever have invented.

He picked up the gun in his free hand and trained it on her. "I had a dog once," he said. "When you tried to give him medicine, he'd fight it, so you just opened his jaws, took your finger and pushed it down, way down in back, till he had to swallow it."

Shoving the barrel of the gun between her lips, he said, "Come on now. Be a good girl. Open wide and take your medicine."

Chapter 12

Be a good girl.

The gun pressed against her teeth. Cold metal tore at her lips. The mad, enraged expression on Eddie's face was now compressed with concentration—he was determined that she do as he say.

From a voice buried somewhere deep inside her came one word. Enough!

Enough death.

Enough of being terrified.

Enough of being drugged, of being used and ordered around, by everyone.

Enough of being a good girl!

Her self-defense class—had she taken it for nothing? Hadn't she learned anything this year? Of course she had. She could bite, she could scream. And she could use the classic female-confronted-with-aggressive-male maneuver. She could get him where he lived.

Eddie stood practically straddling her, so intent on giving her his pills he wasn't paying attention to anything else. Carly brought her knees together and shoved up, as hard as she could, then rolled to her side off the chair.

His howl of agony was followed by him falling backward onto the floor, then doubling over on his side, knees to chest. His hands, still holding the gun, were between his legs. It was all the time she needed. As she scrambled to her feet, a primal scream tore out of her, from somewhere in her gut. She kicked him in the head and then the ribs, again and again, until he lay still at her feet.

As she heaved deep breaths, she felt her body quivering. Had she killed him? At that moment, she didn't know and didn't care. She had to get away, *had* to get out of that cellar. She ran up the step to the door, had to turn around to grasp the knob, but she managed it. Then she was outside, running as hard as she could to the front of the house, toward the road.

As she slipped through the chain-link fence, she heard the sound of tires on gravel followed by the screech of brakes. A car was coming! Without her glasses, she couldn't make out what kind, or who was driving, but she ran toward it.

"Help!" she called out. "Help me!"

"It's her, Dom," Nick said. "It's Carly."

Carly ran toward them, her hair wild, her face bruised and dirty, no shoes, no glasses, her hands behind her back. The strongest emotion Nick had ever felt in his life surged up inside his chest. Carly was alive!

And she was the most beautiful thing he'd ever seen.

"I'll call it in, you get her," Dom said, but Nick didn't need to be told. The door was flung open and he was out of the car and running before Dom pulled to a stop.

He saw the joy on her face as she recognized him. "Nick, thank God!" she cried out as he reached her.

He pulled her to him, cradled her head against his chest. Her breaths came in quick short pants. "Tell me you're okay," he said.

He felt her nodding against his chest. "Yes," she managed to whisper.

"Where's Monk?"

"Back there, in the cellar. Oh, Nick, I kicked him and kicked him and—"

"Bitch!"

The loud, enraged cry came from the house area, but no one was visible.

Nick's cop instinct kicked in. He pushed Carly down behind him, kneeled on one knee, whipped his gun out of his holster and aimed at the sound.

Eddie Monk appeared around a corner, stumbling through the opening in the fence. Blood ran down his face. With one hand between his legs, he cradled himself; in the other hand he held a gun, pointed straight at Nick.

"Halt," Nick called out.

"I'll get you!" Eddie screamed, and kept coming.

Aiming at his head, Nick fired. Eddie recoiled, then lurched and stumbled to his left, near the edge of the cliff. He seemed to catch himself and turned to face Nick again. He stared in disbelief, his mouth open in shock. More blood poured down his face.

Then he came at them again, the gun still in his hand, still aimed toward them. Nick got off another shot, this one in the chest. Again, Eddie recoiled, again he kept coming.

A loud boom came from the vicinity of Dom's car. The shotgun blast blew Eddie backward, setting him down just at the cliff's edge. His gun flew from his hand, landing several feet away from him, out of his reach. Nick kept his gun trained on him while, for a few frantic seconds, Eddie clawed at the ground, trying to keep himself from going over. Then he seemed to sigh and give up. He slid off the side of the mountain, into the deep gorge Mother Earth had carved out for herself.

While Dom ran over to check on Monk, Nick kept watch, half expecting Eddie to rise again, like some sort of subhuman monster. But there was nothing but silence from the cliff's edge. Dom looked down, then turned around and nodded.

Eddie Monk was dead.

Nick lowered his gun. Behind him, Carly murmured in a small voice, "Is it over?"

He whipped around. She was on her knees, her manacled hands behind her, looking for all the world like a prisoner about to be executed. Returning his gun to his holster he squatted then threw his arms around her and held her close. "Yes, it's over."

"Good." She didn't cry, just seemed to need to rest against him while she caught her breath. After a while, she mumbled into his chest, "Can you get these handcuffs off me?"

"I don't have the key, and Eddie's pretty far down. It'll have to wait a few minutes, sorry."

"Don't you carry a hacksaw or something in your trunk?"

"Sorry, no."

"My glasses, they're back in that—" she shuddered "—room. I need to get them."

"We will," he soothed. "Promise." Releasing his hold on her, he took her face between his hands and planted kisses all over her skin. "Tell me again you're all right."

"I'm all right."

"Did he hurt you?"

"Not really. He was too busy crowing." She gazed at him, her dark golden eyes wide, her cheeks streaked with dirty tears. Her face was a portrait of horror revisited. "Oh, Nick, he was so sick."

But she was okay, he thought. Thank you, God, she was okay. He pulled her to him again and hugged her, too tightly, but he couldn't help himself. It was over, Nick thought, finally over, and he waited for that sweet sense of relief to hit him.

Instead, a different kind of adrenaline rush kicked in, swiftly and without warning. Without thinking, Nick grabbed Carly by the shoulders and shook her. "Why the hell did you run

out on me like that?" he said forcefully. "Do you know how
frantic I was? I imagined all kinds of things."

She stared at him, shocked. "Why are you yelling at me?"

"Because I was scared to death, dammit!"

Carly's eyes widened. Then her mouth tightened into a stubborn line. The look of fury that came over her face took him
by surprise. She jerked up her shoulders, effectively removing
herself from his grip.

"Well, tough!" she retorted, her voice rich with anger as
she scrambled awkwardly to her feet. "*You* were terrified? *I'm*
the one he drugged and transported three thousand miles to
get even with some drug lord. *I'm* the one he used and set up.
I'm the one he kidnapped and took to this godforsaken
place…and tried to force more drugs down me…and tried to
rape me. *I'm* the one who's been through hell!" Even with
her hands behind her back, she managed to stand tall and
proud. Her eyes spit fire.

Nick was stunned speechless. Carly? This was Carly? This
genuinely enraged woman spewing nails at him? If she hadn't
been handcuffed, she'd have come after him with her claws.

"So," she went on heatedly, "I refuse to stand here while
you yell at me because you were scared to death. Take your
temper out on someone else, got it? I'm sick to death of you
and all the men I've ever known trying to make me into someone they could control. I'm tired of being on trial with you.
I'm tired of being scared and playing it safe and, oh—all of
it!"

She turned on her heel and stumbled toward Dom's car.
Dom had been leaning against the hood, his shotgun propped
next to him, watching the whole thing. As Carly came toward
him, he clapped his hands slowly. "Go get him, tiger," he
said admiringly.

At first, Nick was knocked for a loop by Carly's outburst,
but then, damned if he didn't feel, well, kind of proud of her.

In fact, damned if he didn't feel a smile forming on his lips.

He wanted to laugh. In fact, he couldn't help it, he did laugh. Loudly.

That got her attention.

She whipped around and glared at him. "What is so funny?"

He walked toward her, his gut shaking with mirth, his hands held out before him in supplication. "Sorry," he mumbled through lips tight with trying to keep more hilarity from exploding out of him. When he reached her, he opened his arms, inviting her in.

She ducked out from under his attempted embrace. "What? I look cute when I'm angry? Go to hell."

That did it. Nick lost the battle for control and erupted in loud, prolonged laughter, making him hold on to his sides as he did. It was probably aftershock and relief, he realized, and it wasn't the best reaction to have, but dammit, she *did* look cute, with her face all flushed, those huge eyes of hers indignant with temper.

"I suggest you put a lid on it, Nick," Dom said. "Carly's pretty steamed."

He tried to stop, but couldn't seem to. "Yeah, I know, but—"

Sirens interrupted his reply. In moments, several L.A.P.D. police cars came screeching along the road, red lights flashing. Their arrival acted like cold water on Nick's laughter, and he stopped abruptly.

Carly looked from Nick to the police cars and then glared again at Nick. "Maybe one of them can get me out of these damned handcuffs."

The next several hours went by in a blur, but Carly got through them. After the handcuffs were removed, she was checked out for wounds, pronounced fit and hustled off to a large building near downtown Los Angeles where she was interviewed, her story tape-recorded. Then came the questions, which she answered over and over again until she was on the point of babbling incoherently. Nick wasn't allowed in the interview room; if she longed for his presence at all, she was only dimly aware of it.

She'd been through a horrific ordeal and knew it. But she was so deeply exhausted, nothing much registered. All she was able to concentrate on were the questions and the answers.

When she emerged from the final interview, Nick was there, waiting for her across the corridor, leaning against a wall. His face was creased in lines of fatigue and concern. When he saw her, he straightened and stared at her. In his eyes, she read wariness and concern, but even those emotions scarcely registered.

"They said I can go," she told him. She could barely get the words out, barely keep her eyes open. She was so very tired, it felt as though she might even be sleepwalking. "I told them everything I know and they said I can go."

"Where do you want to go?"

"Home."

His jaw tensed up. "Home to Hull? Or home with me?"

Interesting question, she thought with a brain that felt as fuzzy as a crocheted afghan. Back to Hull, she supposed. That was home. But not right now.

She swiped a lock of hair back off her face. Even that much movement wore her out. "I'm dead on my feet, Nick. I need a bath and then I need to sleep."

He seemed relieved, probably because she hadn't asked him to buy her a plane ticket. Nodding, he took her arm.

They went back to his place where he ran a bath for her, carried her into the tub, bathed her gently, dressed her in a long, clean T-shirt and tucked her into bed. Most of his actions felt like part of a dream. By the time he murmured good-night, she was already asleep.

Her sleep was restless at first. Images swirled through her dreams—Eddie Monk's glassy-eyed stare, Demeter's bloody head. Guns, trees, cliffs, being closed in. Nina smirking, pos-

ing, laughing. Richard's dead body. Handcuffs. Pictures of little girls in pink dresses.

She awoke several times in panic, but each time Nick was
there; he held her, soothed her, whispered words of comfort
in her ear. Toward morning, she fell into a deep, dreamless
sleep.

Wednesday afternoon

Consciousness returned slowly, but it returned. With it came
the rich odor of fresh coffee and the drone of a faraway air-
plane. Light gleamed brightly—too brightly—behind her
closed eyes, so she kept them shut for a while longer. She
wanted to take stock before greeting the day.

The nightmare was over. Carly was safe, the bad guy was
dead. She was rested, clean. Healed...to some degree, at least.
It seemed to her that this must be how survivors of a major
disaster must feel after the danger had passed—relief and gratitude, and just a small niggling sense of worry that it might
start up all over again.

But, no, she assured herself. Eddie Monk was dead. Never
again would she have to feel endangered by him and his sick,
warped obsession for her sister.

Others were dead also. A fresh wave of sadness for Nina
and Richard washed over her. But it was a clean sadness, not
all murked up with guilt or fear or self-doubt. She would, as
soon as she got back home, arrange for some sort of memorial
for both of them, although just what kind she wasn't...

As soon as she got back home. The phrase repeated itself,
then reverberated in her head. Was that what she wanted to
do? Go back home to Hull? Was that her next move? And if
so, why was she suddenly gripped with an unbearable sense
of loss and desolation?

"Good morning."

Her eyes popped open to a room filled with bright California sunlight. Nick stood over her, staring down at her, the planes of his face tense with watchfulness.

Nick, she thought, and the sense of loss evaporated as quickly as it had arisen. Nick.

Nick was where she wanted to be.

Stretching her arms out to the side, she yawned luxuriously. "What time is it?"

"Two."

"In the afternoon?"

"Yes. There's coffee on the table. Want to sit up?"

Without waiting for her reply, he fluffed up the pillows and helped her into a sitting position. Wordlessly, he handed her the coffee then remained standing, studying her with his deep green gaze.

She seemed okay, Nick thought, rested, clear-eyed. But she might still be angry at him. Or worse. There had been indifference in her eyes when she'd come out of the interrogation room yesterday. Had it cemented, so that she was about to bounce up, thank him for the bed and board and hop on a plane back to Massachusetts?

No. Not acceptable, this he knew. This was one woman who was not walking out on him. She was too damned important to him. If she wanted to walk, he wouldn't let her. She might put up a fight, but she'd lose.

As he felt his hands fisting at his side, Nick realized he was working himself into battle readiness and Carly was barely awake. Calm down, he told himself. Take it slow.

Easier said than done. He'd been watching her all morning while she slept, wondering what he'd say to her, wondering how she'd take whatever he did say to her. By now he felt ready to jump out of his skin.

Carly emitted a long, loud sigh. "You know what, Nick? I feel spoiled. All you've done is take care of me."

"You needed taking care of."

She nodded her agreement. "Yes, I did." She sipped her

coffee, set it down on the night table, then smiled sleepy thanks at him.

He was brimming over with emotion. "I love you."

It came out, just like that. He'd meant to lead up to it, dress it up, make it smoother, more confident-sounding, less desperate. But he'd blown it.

Carly's reaction to his pronouncement was to go very still. Then she raised an eyebrow. "Well, now, isn't that interest—"

Nick plowed ahead, determined to shoot down any arguments she might come up with before she even thought of them. "Look, I know it's too soon—three days, right? I know it doesn't happen this way, that forever feeling, so quickly, but—" he shrugged "—there it is. I...think we should get married."

The smile left her face as her mouth dropped open. "Uh, Nick? Hold it just a minute—"

No way. He was too wound up, so he paced next to the bed. "Yeah, I'm going too fast, I know it. I'm willing to wait. We can—" he raked restless fingers through his hair "—I don't know, go out on dates if you'd like. Although that feels a little backward, given the way we started. But, hey, I'm willing."

"Nick, slow down—"

"Let me finish this. If I don't get it out, I don't know what will happen. Look, I know you hate cops, so you wouldn't want to marry one, but I'm not going to be a cop." He reached the foot of the bed, gripped the brass footboard tightly. "I've made my decision, Carly. I'm going to teach. Regular hours, no more danger, no more midnight raids, no more all-night stakeouts."

"But you love your work. You love being a cop." She seemed indignant for him, and it gave him hope.

"And I was a good one. But my body is telling me what my mind won't let me hear. Between my hip and my knee—"

He frowned, disgusted with himself. "I sound like some kind of cripple."

"Trust me." She bit her bottom lip, as though trying to hold back laughter. "You're not a cripple."

Her amusement barely registered because Nick was on a roll, desperate to get all of it out, to answer any and all objections she might have. "Anyhow—" He resumed pacing. "I like teaching, I'm good at it. And you know what? That adrenaline rush I used to get from the chase, from going after the bad guys? Now it's more about the puzzle, about figuring it out in my head. And I think I can get the same rush from teaching, working with kids, you know?"

He looked over at her and she nodded. He went on. "I like that. Talking to the kid, Miguel, it was good for me. Made me see. Anyhow, there comes a time when you have to move on. And that's now. I move on, I teach. I leave the old life and I make a new one—" he swallowed and looked right at her "—with you, I hope. And that's it."

Carly hardly knew what to say, what to do. Nick was acting in a way she hadn't seen before. Talking and pacing and talking some more. It was as though—could it be?—he felt insecure. About her.

Her hand flew to her chest. She was moved, unbearably moved. "You take my breath away," she said softly.

"Good."

He came around to sit down next to her on the bed. His hands gripped her arms, tight. His eyes burned with green fire. "When that son of a bitch took you, when I thought you might be dead, I wanted to die." The intensity of his voice matched his expression. "I knew then that I would sacrifice my life if it meant you lived. And that's gotta be love. Yeah." He nodded. "I'm in love, Carly, probably for the first time in my life."

Suddenly, he released his grip on her and she fell back against the pillows. He raked his fingers through his hair, then muttered a curse. "I've never made a speech this long. Ever."

Carly felt her eyes fill with tears; her heart filled, too, with love and compassion. The man was a wreck. Nick Holmes, strong, tough, man-of-few-words Nick was a complete and total, dithering wreck. And all because of her.

She could only shake her head in wonder. "It's so strange. Most of the time—just yesterday, in fact—if you'd said this to me, I'd have said, me? How could I arouse so much emotion? Why would you want to marry me? I'm not interesting or sexy or even very brave."

"Bull. You're interesting and sexy and very very brave." His jaw clenched with determination. "Do you love me?" he barked.

"Yes."

His face filled with a mixture of happiness and relief, he reached for her. "Carly, I—"

She held up her hand for him to wait. "But I'm still a little terrified of your temper."

He seemed surprised. "Really? You let loose pretty good yourself yesterday."

She thought about that, then smiled, pleased with herself. "I did, didn't I?"

It had been a sudden flare-up that had seemed to come out of nowhere, burned brightly for a short while, then extinguished itself. And it had felt absolutely wonderful.

"I guess I'd just been through so much, I suppose I snapped." She remembered the next part, though, and felt irritated with him all over again. "Then you laughed at me," she said accusingly.

Leaning one hand on the pillow next to her head, he tried to bite back a smile. Apparently, the memory made him want to laugh all over again. Already she sensed the change in him—now that he knew she returned his feelings, he was no longer ripped by insecurity. And she no longer felt as powerful.

Carly smiled, at herself now, at the direction of her

thoughts. As if she could ever have power over Nick. As if he would let her. As if she would even want to.

She chuckled. Nick's face lost all remaining traces of tension and he joined her. She held out her arms and he lay down next to her on the bed and they laughed together, cleansing, healing laughter. Afterward, they lay there in silence for a time. So much had been said, Carly thought. So much decided.

Nick emitted a satisfied sigh and rolled over onto his side so he faced her. "I know I have this temper, Carly," he said. "I can work on it as much as possible, but it's there. It's how I blow off steam. But nothing happens after that. I don't hit people, or lock little girls up in jails overnight. It's just my way of getting rid of tension. If you wait around for about ten seconds, it's gone."

She played with the edge of the blanket. "I think I finally understand that."

"Actually, I think we might get into some pretty interesting fights. Not all the time, but married people do fight, then they have a great time making up." He smiled suggestively, then his gaze wandered lovingly over her face. There was so much tenderness in his eyes, she felt her heart shudder with emotion.

"You've thought all this through, haven't you?" she said quietly.

"Uh-uh," he denied. "I'm going on instruments here."

"You're doing great."

"Thank you." He kissed her then, a sweet, loving kiss. When he pulled away, she gazed at him through tear-filled eyes.

"You are like someone I dreamed up," she said.

"Is that good?"

"Very."

"Well, I don't know that I've ever dreamed about someone like you, but if I didn't, I'm a fool. I've watched you change, Carly. The little scared rabbit who came into the kitchen wearing my robe and asking the name of the ocean outside my window—I don't see anything left of that Carly."

"She's still there, trust me."

"But you can never go back, not all the way. Not really."

Carly wondered if what Nick said was right, because it felt right. She felt…liberated. She'd gone through some pretty rough times these past few days, then she'd stood up for herself, and nothing awful had happened. In standing up for herself, she'd escaped from a madman. In standing up for herself, something pretty special had happened. Nick.

It was her turn to explore his face. He had the sexiest green eyes, she thought. A mouth that knew all there was to know about pleasing a woman. She loved the way she could tell his mood from his jaw, its tension or lack of it. She'd known him such a short time, but gazing at him now, it felt as though they'd known each other forever. He was her soul mate and she was his. A feeling of total and complete well-being poured through her bloodstream like warm milk.

This was the man she loved, she knew it with a certainty that left no unanswered questions. It felt wonderful to love Nick. Totally wonderful.

Stroking his cheek with the back of her hand, she gave her own version of a suggestive smile. "Did anyone ever tell you that you talk too much?"

One side of his mouth quirked up. "I'm done. Except for this. I love you. Tell me you love me."

Her heart brimmed with more emotion than she knew what to do with. "Oh, Nick, how could I help loving you?"

"Say the words."

"I love you. I love you. I love—"

He stopped her with his mouth, and she let him.

For the rest of their lives together, she thought, he would probably want to call most of the shots and she'd have to fight to get what she wanted. Sometimes she'd have to fight pretty hard, she imagined. At other times, less so.

And then there would be times—moments like these, for

instance—when he was kissing her senseless, making her blood heat and her bones melt. At moments like these, she was pretty sure, she probably wouldn't feel like fighting at all.

* * * * *

In **July 1998** comes

THE MACKENZIE FAMILY

by *New York Times* bestselling author

LINDA HOWARD

The dynasty continues with:

Mackenzie's Pleasure: Rescuing a pampered ambassador's daughter from her terrorist kidnappers was a piece of cake for navy SEAL Zane Mackenzie. It was only afterward, when they were alone together, that the real danger began....

Mackenzie's Magic: Talented trainer Maris Mackenzie was wanted for horse theft, but with no memory, she had little chance of proving her innocence or eluding the real villains. Her only hope for salvation? The stranger in her bed.

Available this July for the first time ever in a two-in-one trade-size edition. Fall in love with the Mackenzies for the first time—or all over again!

Available at your favorite retail outlet.

*Silhouette Books*

PSMACFMLY

Take 2 bestselling love stories FREE

Plus get a FREE surprise gift!

Special Limited-Time Offer

Mail to Silhouette Reader Service™

3010 Walden Avenue
P.O. Box 1867
Buffalo, N.Y. 14240-1867

YES! Please send me 2 free Silhouette Intimate Moments® novels and my free surprise gift. Then send me 6 brand-new novels every month, which I will receive months before they appear in bookstores. Bill me at the low price of $3.57 each plus 25¢ delivery and applicable sales tax, if any.* That's the complete price, and a saving of over 10% off the cover prices—quite a bargain! I understand that accepting the books and gift places me under no obligation ever to buy any books. I can always return a shipment and cancel at any time. Even if I never buy another book from Silhouette, the 2 free books and the surprise gift are mine to keep forever.

245 SEN CH7Y

Name	(PLEASE PRINT)	
Address	Apt. No.	
City	State	Zip

This offer is limited to one order per household and not valid to present Silhouette Intimate Moments® subscribers. *Terms and prices are subject to change without notice.
Sales tax applicable in N.Y.

UIM-98   ©1990 Harlequin Enterprises Limited

SILHOUETTE·INTIMATE·MOMENTS®
commemorates its

15th Anniversary

15 years of rugged, irresistible heroes!

15 years of warm, wonderful heroines!

15 years of exciting, emotion-filled romance!

In May, June and July 1998 join the celebration as Intimate Moments brings you new stories from some of your favorite authors—authors like:

Marie Ferrarella
Maggie Shayne
Sharon Sala
Beverly Barton
Rachel Lee
Merline Lovelace
and many more!

Don't miss this special event! Look for our distinctive anniversary covers during all three celebration months. Only from Silhouette Intimate Moments, committed to bringing you the best in romance fiction, today, tomorrow—always.

Available at your favorite retail outlet.